Praise for
THE ENEMY WITHIN

"A dark, yet fascinating tale, *The Enemy Within* gives readers an intriguing look at what could have happened in 1964 New York."
—*RT Book Reviews*

"Rusch weaves a convincing alternate history tale of 'what ifs' that interlaces with our own history of those troubled times. … non-stop political intrigue!"
—Dave Dickinson, *Astroguyz*

"*[Enemy Within]* is a blend of mystery, political thriller, and alternate history. It was a compelling read I had trouble putting down. … This is one fans of political thrillers won't want to miss."
—Keith West, *Adventures Fantastic*

Praise for
"G-MEN"

"Rusch brings out the mad opportunism and bleak acquiescence of her characters very deftly."
—Nick Gevers, *Locus* [recommended story]

"If you liked E.L. Doctorow's *Ragtime* or the writing of Caleb Carr (*The Alienist*), you'll enjoy this tale."
—*New York Times* bestselling author Jeffrey Deaver

Praise for
SNIPERS

"Told in roughly alternating chapters set in 1913 and 2005, [Snipers] is a deft mixture of SF and mystery with some very sharp plotting, some nice twists, and a trio of compelling characters."

—*Booklist,* starred review

"Chilling murders, mind-blowing suspense, a touch of time travel and a bit of romance combine to a thought-provoking, entertaining vacation from reality."

—*RT Book Reviews*

"*Snipers* is an excellent amalgamation of history, thriller, mystery & science fiction. Rusch lays out the period in meticulous detail, as only she can."

—Dave Dickinson, *Astroguyz*

"This is a fast-moving thriller, and the ending implies that a sequel is in the works. I'll be reading it."

—*Bill Crider's Pop Culture Magazine*

"Rusch explores the mind-bending possibilities of time travel and alternate realities with relish, but never allows the novel to stray too far from its gritty, procedural straight-and-narrow; keeping the story taut and suspenseful, the author spins one of her trademark stories that brims with intelligence and surprise."

—*The Edge Philadephia*

THE
ENEMY
WITHIN

KRISTINE KATHRYN RUSCH

*wmg*PUBLISHING

The Enemy Within

Copyright © 2014 by Kristine Kathryn Rusch

All rights reserved

Published 2014 by WMG Publishing
www.wmgpublishing.com
Cover and Layout copyright © 2014 by WMG Publishing
Cover design by Allyson Longueira/WMG Publishing
Cover art copyright © Liz Van Steenburgh/Dreamstime
ISBN-13: 978-0-615-92985-9
ISBN-10: 0-615-92985-0

THE
ENEMY
WITHIN

The Crime

There's something addicting about a secret.

—J. Edgar Hoover

1

THE SQUALID LITTLE ALLEY smelled of piss despite the February cold. Detective Seamus O'Reilly tugged his overcoat closed and wished he'd worn boots. He could feel the chill of his metal flashlight through the worn glove on his right hand.

He had been working swing shift since Kennedy's assassination almost three months before. He'd volunteered. He wanted the night murders—the muggings gone bad, the 3 a.m. domestic tragedies, the knifings after last call—because he knew day shifts would get protection duty and the political cases. New York got its share of dignitaries, and after Dallas, all of them were afraid they'd be next.

He wanted straightforward crime, not babysitting so-called famous people. The kids were grown, and with Nola working nights at the hospital, swing seemed best for him as well.

Except at moments like this, when he stood next to a coroner's van outside a dirty little alley, and that feeling in his gut, the one he'd learned to trust at Anzio twenty years ago, flared so badly that he wanted to turn around and go home.

Instead, he glanced over his shoulder to make sure his new partner was behind him.

Joseph McKinnon was ten years younger, twenty pounds lighter, and six inches taller. He had the thick neck and broad shoulders of a former

3

quarterback, and an all-American handsomeness that should have kept him out of undercover work. But it hadn't; he'd been one of the best vice cops in the city, and as a promotion, he'd asked for homicide.

McKinnon was just beginning to learn that homicide wasn't really a step up. O'Reilly was just beginning to learn that having a new partner didn't mean he had a better partner.

McKinnon was looking at the surrounding buildings, his flashlight pointed down. The street was dark and empty. Which was not a surprise. Police presence made anyone who lived on this block vanish.

This neighborhood teetered between swank and corrupt. It was far enough from Central Park for degenerates and muggers to use the alleys as corridors and, conversely, close enough for new money to want to live with a peek of the city's most famous expanse of green.

So far, the new money hadn't overtaken the old ways—at least, not on this block. O'Reilly had handled four murders here since he transferred, but all of them were on the street itself, the bodies found by cops or delivery men. Someone in the alley might not get found for days.

On this block, most people looked the other way. One block north, they started watching out their windows. On the block across from the park, they might actually call the cops if they saw something going down.

But in this alley, it was amazing anyone had found the bodies at all.

Unlike the street, the alley wasn't dark. It looked like daylight in the small rectangular space. The coroner had set up his trademark battery-operated lights on garbage can lids placed on top of the dirty ice, one at the head of the bodies, the other near the feet.

O'Reilly wasn't going to look at the bodies—not yet. He liked to absorb the scene first. Sometimes, these few moments yielded the most important information. Impressions, feelings, seemingly small details often led him to the heart of any case he was working on.

Which was why he had one of the highest closure rates in the department, and why his bosses had fought his transfer to nights so hard.

The lights created crisp shadows on the brick walls. The two beat cops who had discovered the bodies were standing near the front of the alley, their shadows elongated and thick. The coroner's assistant stood behind one of the lights, next to the gurney he'd brought, so his shadow looked like someone had painted him in black. It was an eerie tableau, made eerier by the fact that the coroner—in the middle of the lights—had no shadow at all.

Thomas Brunner, the coroner, bent over the bodies. O'Reilly liked working with Brunner. They were the same age and had the same attitude toward work: get it done, do the best job possible, and move on. Most everyone else in the department disliked Brunner. He was blunt, bigoted, and hard-nosed.

But he never messed with O'Reilly. They'd had a run-in the very first time they'd worked together—1946 or '47—right after both of them had come back from the war. O'Reilly's temper—hot, sudden, and violent— had won the encounter, but his willingness to forgive and forget had made the two of them if not friends, then at least amicable colleagues.

O'Reilly stepped into the alley proper. His dress shoes slipped on the ice, and he had to catch himself so that he wouldn't fall. Most of the sidewalks in the city were clear—a week of unusual warmth before this had guaranteed that the snow and ice would melt—but apparently the sun never got to this corner of the city.

And somehow that didn't surprise him.

The bodies, male and well dressed, sprawled side by side. They rested on their stomachs, heads facing north, arms bent as if they tried to catch themselves. One leg on each body was straight, the other bent at the knee, like the old white chalk images of dead bodies in black-and-white movies.

The entire thing looked like a movie set—like this neighborhood had looked not five years before when some Hollywood types filmed the exteriors for *West Side Story*. That had been one of the few times he hadn't minded doing protection—until he realized just how dull film-making could be.

He squatted beside Brunner. The dead men were white and fleshy, with manicured fingers and expensive wool coats. Too well dressed for this neighborhood. Maybe they'd walked down the wrong block.

Although that didn't explain how they got into the alley.

Their faces were mashed into the ice, their features distorted from the force of the impact. He wouldn't know what they really looked like until Brunner turned them over.

Clearly Brunner wasn't ready to do that. He was using his gloved hands to press lightly on the back of the corpse closest to him.

"What've we got?" O'Reilly asked.

"Dunno yet." The pressure from Brunner's hand caused blood to well out of a hole on the body's left side. The shot was perfect. It would have gone directly through a rib and into the heart.

"Looks like a good shot," O'Reilly said.

"Good shot, yeah," Brunner said. "Single shot. Matches the one on his friend here. They both died instantly."

"You sound unhappy about that."

Brunner kept his hand on the corpse's back, but looked at O'Reilly. Brunner was balding, his face whitish gray in the strong light.

"You see as many bodies as I do, you realize how rare it is for anybody to receive a perfectly made kill shot, let alone have two anybodies right next to each other get the exact same shot."

O'Reilly leaned forward. He didn't touch the bodies—he didn't have to—but he could see the blood soaking the other corpse, and the hole in the exact same spot as the one Brunner had just found.

"Christ," O'Reilly said. "You think these guys were targeted."

"I'm hoping." Brunner looked at him sideways, expression tight.

O'Reilly wasn't sure he'd heard Brunner right. "You're *hoping* they were targeted?"

"Damn straight. Otherwise we got a problem."

O'Reilly frowned, not quite following Brunner's point. At that moment, McKinnon came into the alley. He shined his flashlight on the darkened windows of the southern building's upper story.

Sometimes O'Reilly didn't understand his partner. Any more than he was understanding Brunner at the moment.

"What kind of problem?" O'Reilly asked.

"This ain't the only call I've had around here tonight."

"Really?" O'Reilly asked. "What else we got?"

"Some colored limosine driver shot a block from here." Brunner pressed on the back again. The blood stopped seeping. This corpse had to have a heck of an exit wound. "And two white guys pulled out of their cars and shot about two blocks from that."

O'Reilly felt a shiver run through him that had nothing to do with the cold. A limosine driver? Two white men pulled out of cars? Brunner was right; if these killings were random, then O'Reilly had a hell of a problem.

He asked, "You think the shootings are related?"

"Dunno," Brunner said. "But I think it's odd, don't you? Five dead in the space of an hour, all in a six-block radius."

O'Reilly closed his eyes for a moment. Two white guys pulled out of their cars, one Negro driver of a limosine, and now two white guys in an alley. Maybe they were related, maybe they weren't.

He opened his eyes, then wished he hadn't. Brunner had his finger inside a bullet hole, his favorite in-the-field way to judge caliber.

"Same type of bullet," Brunner said.

"You handled the other shootings?"

"I was on scene with the driver when some fag called this one in."

O'Reilly looked at Brunner. Eighteen years, and he still wasn't used to the man's casual bigotry.

"How did you know the guy was homosexual?" O'Reilly asked. "You talk to him?"

"Didn't have to." Brunner nodded toward the building in front of them. "Weekly party for degenerates in the penthouse apartment every Thursday night. Thought you knew."

O'Reilly looked up. Now he understood why McKinnon had been shining his flashlight at the upper story windows. Everyone in vice would have known about a party like that.

But homicide didn't.

"No, I didn't know," O'Reilly said. "No reason I should either."

"I thought everyone knew," Brunner said.

"Why would you think that?" O'Reilly asked.

McKinnon was the one who answered. "Because of the standing orders."

"I'm not playing twenty questions," O'Reilly said. "I don't know about a party in this building and I don't know about standing orders."

"The standing orders are," McKinnon said as if he were an elementary school teacher, "not to bust it, no matter what kind of lead you got. You see someone go in, you forget about it. You see someone come out, you avert your eyes. You complain, you get moved to a different shift, maybe a different precinct."

"Jesus." O'Reilly was too far below to see if there was any movement against the glass in the penthouse suite. But whoever lived there—whoever partied there—had learned to shut off the lights before the cops arrived.

"It's gonna take forever for the scene-of-the-crime guys to arrive." Brunner looked at his assistant. "I need pictures. Then we're rolling these guys over."

The assistant, a young man that O'Reilly didn't recognize, winced. He left the gurney in the alley and went back to the coroner's van.

Pictures would help, but they wouldn't give a real sense of this scene. The alley was small. With five men in it, as there had been a moment ago, it felt crowded.

The victims would have seen their shooter. Unless he hid. And the victims were lying lengthwise across the alley, head and feet pointing toward the walls. If the victims been trying to leave the alley, they would have been lying in the alley's narrow width. And if they'd been shot in the back while leaving, their heads would have pointed toward the street.

O'Reilly rocked back on his heels. The alley didn't have much. Two metal garbage cans—now without lids thanks to Brunner—and a pile of unmelted snow against a wire mesh fence marked the back end. The

8

north building was all brick. On this level, there weren't even windows. The windows started about six feet up and continued on all six stories.

He squinted at the south building. A door, carefully painted to mimic the brick around it, was barely visible, and there was no stoop. Whoever stepped out of that door would drop nearly a foot to the ground.

Footprints had formed in the ice from repeated use, and the footprints faced into the alley. This was an exit, not an entrance, a fact confirmed by the lack of a doorknob or handle on this side.

This building rose eight stories, and the glass windows here actually looked clean. He had a sense that people were watching from above, but that might simply have been because of Brunner's talk of the private party.

The victims had come out of that door. They had dropped to the alley floor, taken a few steps, and then gotten shot.

O'Reilly rose and walked past the lights. He crouched near the wall. The ice here was smooth. He rapped it with his gloved knuckles. It was still hard too. Someone standing here wouldn't have broken through the ice's surface.

There were no cigarette butts, no gum wrappers, no crumpled coffee cups. No sign of waiting. There weren't beer bottles either, which he found odd on this block, and no empty needles.

There were also no shell casings. He still wasn't sure of the murder weapon's caliber, so he wasn't sure if the lack of shell casings was important or not.

The assistant had come back. He was using one of those Polaroid cameras to take pictures of the bodies. The flash glared.

"Don't you have a good camera?" O'Reilly asked Brunner.

"It's not my job to take pictures of the crime scene. I'm just doing it with the equipment we got so we don't spend all night in this alley."

The assistant walked around, taking photos, waiting for the sound of the film to be ejected, and then taking the next shot. O'Reilly made him take pictures of the ice behind the lights, although the assistant clearly thought he was crazy.

"Check the photos," he said to McKinnon. If they weren't clear, he wanted a reshoot before Brunner rolled the bodies.

McKinnon nodded.

O'Reilly went back to the door. Someone had deliberately hidden it. And if this wasn't a mugging gone wrong (and, judging by the perfection of those shots, it wasn't), then whoever had stood here had known that these victims or someone like them would come out of that door tonight.

O'Reilly stood and hovered near the brick. If he stood on the east side of the door, whoever came out would see him. But if he went to the west, the door—which opened outward—would hide him.

He could shoot—twice—before the second victim had a chance to turn around.

The shiver came back. He was convinced this crime wasn't random. He was convinced that the killer had been waiting for victims to come out of that door.

Which didn't surprise him. So-called degenerates who frequented famous spots in the city were vulnerable to all kinds of crime. If victims were mugged outside one of the men-only bars in the Village, they wouldn't call it in because they'd have to admit where they'd been.

He suspected this place was the same. If he wanted to mug some well-known men, this was the place to do it.

But to murder them? Was the killer practicing his accuracy or was he actually targeting someone?

"Photos are good enough," McKinnon said.

O'Reilly frowned. That was the other problem with a well-known party scene like this. *Good enough* became the watch-phrase. No one cared about solving the crime because the crimes were expected.

But O'Reilly didn't care who the victims were. They deserved the best he could give.

"Lemme check," he said and extended his hand. McKinnon carefully handed him each photograph, reminding him not to place one on top of the other. The emulsifier hadn't set yet, and the photos would stick together if they were placed on top of each other.

The photos showed the bodies from different angles, but didn't get a lot of detail. He wasn't sure the Polaroid was capable of the kind of detail he wanted.

At least the pictures would remind him of the scene.

That had to be good enough.

He handed the photos back to the assistant.

"All right then," O'Reilly said to Brunner. "Roll away."

Brunner grabbed an arm and shoulder on the nearest body and pulled it to him. The man's coat was buttoned, hiding the damage from the exit wound, although the ice below was stained black.

He was older—maybe sixty, sixty-five—with a receding hairline. His dark eyes were open. He'd been handsome when he was young; his high cheekbones and well-defined forehead remained. His nose had become bulbous with age and drink but his large chin balanced it.

He wasn't anyone O'Reilly knew.

So much for the celebrity guests at the party upstairs.

"Recognize him?" O'Reilly asked.

The men around him shook their heads.

"Still got his wallet?" O'Reilly asked.

"I didn't even check. I figured it was a mugging," Brunner said, "and forgot once I found that shot."

O'Reilly nodded. "Let's see if he has one now."

Brunner reached into the back pants pocket of the corpse and clearly found nothing. So he grabbed the front of the overcoat and reached inside.

He removed a long, thin wallet—old fashioned, the kind made for the larger bills of forty years before. Hand-tailored, beautifully made— or it had been, before it was covered in blood.

Brunner wiped the wallet on the end of the long overcoat, then handed the wallet to O'Reilly. O'Reilly opened it. And stopped when he saw the badge inside. His mouth went dry.

"We got a feebee," he said, his voice sounding strangled.

"What?" McKinnon asked.

"FBI," Brunner said dryly. Vice rarely had to deal with FBI. Homicide did only on sensational cases. McKinnon had probably never worked with an FBI agent in his life. He didn't know what pains they could be.

O'Reilly hated having them on scene, with their little notebooks and their sly questions. He had no idea what they'd be like with the death of one of their own.

He poked deeper into the wallet. "Not just any feebee either. The Associate Director, Clyde A. Tolson."

The driver's license listed a District of Columbia address. This man wasn't just an important FBI agent, he was here from out of town.

O'Reilly wondered how many people knew Tolson was in New York. And how many more would know he had come here.

McKinnon whistled. "Who's the other guy?"

O'Reilly handled this one. He gave the wallet to McKinnon, then grabbed the shoulder of the other corpse. He pulled it over, his eyes watering at the sudden stench of blood-contaminated perfume. Around him the others gasped, and for a moment, he thought it was because of the overwhelming smell.

Then he blinked the water from his eyes and looked at the corpse's face.

It was familiar. He'd seen it on countless posters, on *Time Magazine*'s cover not too long ago, on the front page of *The New York Times* damn near every week.

Corpuscular and jowly with the rheumy eyes of a man heading into old age. Hair slicked back and clearly darkened with some kind of gel. He didn't look formidable anymore.

He looked old.

"Son of bitch," Brunner said. "It's J. Edgar Hoover."

"Hoover?" McKinnon asked. He sounded scared. "The Director of the FBI? That guy?"

O'Reilly nodded. He peered down at the familiar face. So much for the quiet swing shift. So much for anonymous crimes.

This was the Director of the Federal Bureau of Investigation, one of the most powerful men in the entire world. Killed by a single bullet—a well-placed bullet—in a back alley in New York three months after the President of the United States, the leader of the Free World, had been assassinated in Dallas.

This case wasn't just political. It was as political as a case could be.

In a few hours, this case would be the focus of an entire nation. Maybe the entire world.

And O'Reilly would be at the center of it all.

2

FRANCIS XAVIER BRYCE—Frank to his friends, what few of them he had left—sat at the counter in his spacious kitchen and stared at the chipped cup in front of him. The cup was Wedgwood and had been a wedding present, as Mary had screeched at him the day he dropped it. He wasn't sure how she had kept track of everything in their too-large apartment—the wedding presents, her possessions, his possessions, and the antiques his family had collected since before he was born—but she had.

And she had taken only her possessions when she left. Apparently, when a woman asked the Church and her lawyer to annul a marriage, she also annulled the wedding presents.

A yellow oil rested on top of the milk froth inside the cup. He couldn't even see the honey he'd just poured into the mess. He stirred it, frowning at the odor. Hot milk, butter, and honey didn't smell as soothing as it had when he was a child.

His mother always swore by it, although she never made it. She'd left that to the housekeeper or the current nanny or the butler if no one else would help.

He picked up the cup, careful to avoid the chip, and sipped, then wished he hadn't. The honey didn't mask the sour taste of boiled milk. It added to it.

Maybe this wasn't a remedy for upset stomach after all. Maybe it was for sore throat. That first sip certainly coated his.

He set the cup on its (unchipped) saucer, and stared at the Jim Beam bottle near the sink. The bottle was nearly hidden by the dirty plates and the open containers of takeout that he somehow couldn't bring himself to toss away. Cleaning the apartment was an admission that he now lived alone and was responsible for every single task.

He wasn't sure he was ready to do that.

But he was ready to open that Jim Beam bottle, and he knew better. Drinking alone was a trouble sign, the kind that could get him officially demoted at work instead of shuffled off to other, less desirable jobs.

Ever since he'd started opening his mouth—and when had that been? Last year?—he'd moved from high-level investigations to trailing suspected Communists to monitoring wire-taps to this new low he found himself at, digging dirt on other agents.

Bryce stood and walked to the sink. He stared at that bottle, then grabbed a dirty glass, rinsed it out, and filled it with tap water. The water here had a mineral taste to it, but anything would be better than the taste of sour milk.

He made himself walk away from the bottle and out of the spacious kitchen. Once the kitchen had been his favorite room in this ten-room apartment—back when he was a child, and he could sit here with the servants, who seemed much more interesting to him than his parents ever were. When his parents were out for the evening, he got to eat in the kitchen which, in those days, smelled of warm bread and coffee instead of rotting Chinese food and untended garbage.

He hadn't touched the formal dining room since Mary left, except to walk through it and trail his fingers along the dust. He went back to the den—his space which was, he knew, well-named. He had used it as a den, the hidden home of a wild animal, which Mary claimed he was.

She had wanted him to quit the FBI and go into the family business. But he couldn't imagine himself as a broker, not even a high-level one, which he would be if he stepped into Bryce, Westlake, and

Clark. His brother would help him make the transition—he'd made that abundantly clear over the years—and for once, Bryce would have the prestige everyone expected him to have.

The prestige that went with this apartment. Mary had thought she married a Bryce when she married him. He had the apartment and the antiques and a stipend. His older brother got the house in the Hamptons and the business—no stipend needed. Everyone knew that William Jay McGuire Bryce the Third was the brains in the family. He'd inherited the talent for numbers and a gift for predicting market trends, the gift that had made their grandfather a millionaire, and allowed their father to add the word "multi" to his million-dollar fortune.

William—who never for a moment, not even as a cherubic child, had been Will or Bill or (God forbid) Willy or Billy—was supposed to take care of his baby brother in perpetuity. And he tried. When the small plane their parents were on went down over the Atlantic six years ago, William had offered Bryce a job everyone else in his set would have killed for, with an outrageous salary and nothing that he really had to do except show up once a week.

Bryce had turned him down, shocking everyone, including Mary.

They all thought he had become an FBI agent as a rebellion against his stuffy, snotty, social-climbing parents, and maybe, back when he joined, he had been rebelling.

But he loved the work, and he had a talent for it. Investigation had become a passion for him, and he worked hard.

If only he could have kept his opinions to himself.

The den was in better shape than the kitchen. He had bought the furniture in here—a cloth sofa that fit his six-foot frame, an overstuffed chair that he could sink into, excellent reading lights, and a coffee table that was so ugly no one would notice the stains. A large color television sat in front of the mahogany bookshelves his father had had custom built.

The television had been his boon companion since the last few months of his marriage. In fact, the room hadn't changed much since then. A few more glasses had accumulated on the coffee table—Mary had stopped sneaking in to remove them—but the heavy quilt he favored and an oversized pillow were squeezed on one end of the couch in case he fell asleep here, which he often did.

He did his best thinking here. Even though he now lived alone, he still felt like the den was the only room in the place that was completely his.

The radio was playing some Sinatra, lonely boozy songs for a lonely sober night. Bryce still thought about that bottle of Jim Beam in the kitchen. It would be so easy to open it, to pour some nice amber liquid into a glass, and to get lost.

It was the second best thing to sleeping.

And he knew he wasn't sleeping tonight.

Every time he closed his eyes, he saw Essie Seward's face, ghost-pale and literally bloodless. The blood filled her bathtub and spilled, with the water she had run, onto the floor of her apartment.

He'd seen suicides before, but he had never felt responsible for them. He felt responsible for Essie.

She hadn't been pretty. That was the first thing he'd noticed about her. With her history, she should have been. Maybe she didn't photograph well. Maybe when her face was animated, she had a charm that otherwise went undetected.

He would never know.

All he knew was that she had turned her life around. Not too many years ago, she'd been a highly paid escort who had gotten pregnant. She'd gone to a back-alley butcher to get rid of the baby, and nearly died.

She'd managed to make it to a nearby church, and the priest there had gotten her to the hospital, saving her life. He'd saved it in other ways as well. He made sure she never went back to her old job. He gave her a place to stay, a job at the church, and gradually, she became someone else.

Someone an FBI agent could fall in love with.

On the radio, Sinatra gave way to Peggy Lee. Her bluesy voice made Bryce even more uncomfortable. He got up and flicked the radio off, then stood beside the door, hands in his pockets.

He hadn't been the one to fall in love with Essie. That had been Walter Cain, an up-and-comer, the kind of man who didn't call his bosses narrow-minded idiots when they made a questionable decision. If anything, Cain was too intense, too into the job. The best driver in the New York regional office, the best marksman, the best interrogator.

Everyone agreed that Cain was on his way up, and he wouldn't be in New York for long.

Or they had until tonight.

"Dumb ass." Bryce rubbed his face with his hands. It wasn't Essie he was going to have trouble forgetting. It was that look in Cain's eyes when Bryce told him that his fiancée had killed herself.

His ex-fiancée.

The Bureau had told Cain to call off the wedding or lose his job. J. Edgar Hoover had rules of conduct for his agents. They covered everything from what a man wore to whom he married. Each potential spouse went through a vetting process.

Bryce—as punishment for his loud mouth—had handled Essie's, and he'd gone about it wrong. He went after it to prove to the entire department that he was still the best investigator in New York. His report was detailed, thorough, and devastating.

He'd never investigated a fellow agent or a member of the agent's family before. He treated Essie Seward like a suspect, found and pulled her arrest record, and even interviewed that butcher who'd almost killed her.

Then he presented the report to the Special Agent in Charge of the New York Regional Office, Eugene Hart. Hart was new, ambitious, and ruthless. He didn't call Cain. He called Essie and told her that in order to protect her beloved's career, she had to call off the wedding.

And then he told her why.

It was in the middle of that phone call that Bryce realized what he'd done.

He should have gone to Cain. He should have quietly presented the report, and he should have let Cain make the decision.

Or, if Bryce were really humane—humane in the ways he wanted his bosses to be—he should have buried the information, forgotten that he'd learned it. How many KGB agents blackmailed FBI agents because of a spouse's history? How many criminals forced an agent to give up a case because his wife had once been a high-class hooker?

Even though Hoover believed such things were possible—and they probably were—they were extremely unlikely. For the past five years, Essie Seward had been an upstanding citizen.

And like the upstanding citizen she was, she broke her engagement with Walter Cain. She sacrificed everything for him.

That might have ended it. But Hart, who thought Cain was the best man in the regional office, went one step farther. Hart told Essie that the best thing to do was never to contact Cain again.

She agreed.

Then she hung up, ran some hot water in her bathtub, and slit her wrists.

Bryce had gone to the scene that afternoon. He'd been called in because someone had found the Regional Office phone number on a pad beside the phone.

He saw her, and knew what he had to do.

He had to tell Cain.

And he had.

He balled his hand into a fist, and rested it on the door. Then he sighed.

"Screw it," he said, and started for the kitchen.

Halfway there, the phone rang.

He froze. No one called at two a.m. Not since his de facto demotion. He wasn't important enough.

Maybe it was Mary having a change of heart. Or his brother with some kind of emergency.

Although if William had an emergency, he wouldn't call Bryce first. He probably wouldn't call Bryce at all.

Still, Bryce went back into the den. He had to flop on the couch to reach the phone he'd placed on the floor months ago.

"Yeah?" he said, expecting the voice on the other side to be Mary. It wouldn't do to sound too eager to hear from her.

Not that he was eager. He didn't really miss her, just the fact of having someone else in the apartment.

"Frank Bryce?" The male voice on the other end was official. It took Bryce a moment to place it. Then his back straightened.

Eugene Hart, SAC of the New York Regional Office. The man who'd made that God-awful phone call and encouraged a fragile woman to sacrifice everything.

Eugene Hart.

Maybe he was having the two a.m. doldrums as well.

"Yes, sir. This is Frank."

"Good," Hart said. "I need you at a crime scene ASAP."

Bryce blinked. He had expected Hart to mention Essie Seward, and maybe devolve into a drunken commiseration. He hadn't expected an order—especially an order involving an active crime scene.

"A crime scene, sir?"

"We need boots on the ground," Hart said. "We have a situation."

"What kind of situation?"

"One I can't discuss on the phone. Tell me how far you are from this address." Hart rattled off an address five blocks and several income levels down.

"Ten minutes, sir," Bryce said.

"Good. Get over there and secure the scene. I'll be sending backup, but it'll take some time to get there."

"Is the NYPD there, sir?"

"It was the NYPD who contacted me," Hart said.

Bryce rubbed his forehead with the heel of his hand. He was glad he hadn't had that drink. This conversation was confusing enough without it.

"The NYPD, sir? They're inviting us to a crime scene?"

"Hell, no," Hart said. "I've got a man on the street there. He let me know what's going on. I want you to take over the scene."

"We don't have jurisdiction, sir," Bryce said, then bit his lower lip. Hart had to know that. The FBI assisted with investigations. It didn't conduct them.

And the NYPD hated it when the FBI got involved in open cases. In fact, NYPD policy discouraged FBI involvement in anything except suspected Communist infiltration in the workplace or cold cases that still had a bit of public interest.

"Pretend we do," Hart said.

Bryce was beginning to think he'd fallen asleep on the couch and was dreaming this conversation.

"What?"

"Pretend we have jurisdiction," Hart said. "Bully, bluster, cajole those assholes. But make sure we own every part of that crime scene. You'll understand when you get there."

Bryce's indigestion grew worse. It was almost like Hart had a direct pipeline to his stomach.

"Who is your man inside, sir?" Bryce figured he needed all the help he could get.

"He's a patrolman. He won't be able to help you. The detectives and coroner are already on scene, which is why I need you there ASAP. I'll get some men over there as soon as I can, but this is sensitive, and it might take some time. Do your best."

Then Hart hung up. Bryce held onto the receiver for a long moment, listening to that faint hum on the other end which indicated a dead line. He was half waiting for Hart to pick up again, which would reestablish the connection.

But Hart didn't. Not in the thirty seconds that Bryce waited.

Slowly he set the receiver in its cradle and stood up. A crime scene in the middle of the night. Stealing jurisdiction from the NYPD. Blustering and cajoling and blundering his way into a "sensitive" case.

This was career suicide. If he went, he'd be the fall guy for any mistakes that happened on the ground. If he stayed, he'd be fired.

They weren't sending him because he lived nearby—although he doubted any other agents lived this close—they were sending him because his career was already on the skids.

They needed deniability. They needed a fall guy.

And they lucked out.

Bryce lived only a few blocks away.

The natural fall guy, who'd already screwed up one case today. Whose marriage was gone, whose life was in tatters, whose reputation was shot.

And who, a few years and a lot of intemperate behavior ago, had been the best investigator in the New York Regional Office.

The only way to get himself down there was to pretend they needed his investigation skills, not his screwup skills.

He had to delude himself.

And he had to start now.

3

THE SCENE WASN'T HARD TO FIND; a coroner's van blocked the entrance to the alley. Bryce walked quickly, his heartburn worse than it had been when he hung up the phone. He wore his regulation wool overcoat and for once he was happy to have the hated hat on his head because the night had turned cold.

Sirens sounded in the distance, probably more squads showing up to work the crime scene, whatever it was. Someone was dead and that someone had the Bureau's attention.

But he had no idea how he would take control.

The law simply didn't allow for that. Hoover had made certain that the Federal Bureau of Investigation was about *investigation*, not about resolving crimes—unless those crimes were sensational, like kidnapping or the Public Enemy Number One cases from the 1930s.

While there was still a Public Enemy Number One, not even Bryce, a relatively well-informed agent, could name him. The hype wasn't what it used to be. The Bureau focused mostly on finding Communists in every pumpkin patch or providing analysis for other departments.

It didn't handle fresh cases, not even when those cases were dramatic and filled with national importance—like the assassination of a president.

That had been one of the times Bryce had opened his stupid mouth. He figured a single sniper, no matter how good he was (and the evidence was coming in that Oswald wasn't good at all), could kill the President of the United States.

The fact that a goon like Jack Ruby could infiltrate the Dallas P.D.'s transfer site a few days later and assassinate the assassin proved to Bryce that Oswald hadn't worked alone.

Everyone in the New York office—or at least everyone who'd been in the New York office for the last ten years—recognized Ruby's name. He was one of those small-time hoods that the mob liked to use to carry money or guns, to run special missions to Cuba, or to infiltrate a local business and find out where its weaknesses were.

Ruby had shown up in New York City more than once, and the younger agents would often tail him. The younger agents thought the Communist threat overrated, at least in the five boroughs, and figured New York—and by extension, the entire country—had more to fear from organized crime.

Bryce had said that on November 29th to Hart, when the orders had come in ordering them to give up their files on Oswald—not that they had any. They had files on Ruby, and Bryce had said that. He also said they had volumes of files on Ruby's known associates.

But Hart had shut Bryce down. *We follow orders around here, cowboy,* he had said. *Orders are about Oswald, not Ruby. As far as we're concerned, Ruby did his patriotic duty. He got a Bad Guy off the street.*

And buried any knowledge we'll ever have of what happened. Bryce had raised his voice. *This is how the mob works. You know it and so do I. How many murders we got that were done by a patsy only to have the patsy murdered once he got into custody?*

We're dealing with it, Hart had said tightly. *It's not your business.*

Like hell, Bryce had said. *He was my president.*

Hart had stared at him. *You gonna be trouble on this, Bryce?*

And Bryce had stared back, not sure how to answer. *I'm your best fucking investigator. Put me on this.*

You've got attitude problems, Hart had said. *You're not working on anything important 'til your crap at home gets settled.*

And then he had kicked Bryce out of his office, before Bryce even had a chance to say that his "crap" had been settled the day before the patsy supposedly shot the president.

From that moment on, Bryce had found himself assigned to cold cases that had no hope of resolution or transcribing wiretaps so old they dated from the Eisenhower Administration. When he'd gotten the assignment to investigate Essie Seward, he had seen it as an investigation, a way back, instead of what it was—a farther step down, a perfunctory examination of the fiancée of an agent to satisfy the bozos in Washington.

Bryce wiped his gloved hand over his ice-cold face. The very thought of Essie Seward made his stomach ache.

This case, whatever it was, was another step down. It couldn't be anything else.

But he would do his best. He could see no other choice.

As he walked down the last block toward the scene, he made himself concentrate on the area around him.

The neighborhood was in transition. A project the mayor was euphemistically calling "urban renewal" had knocked down some wonderful but dilapidated turn-of-the-century buildings. But so far, the buildings that had replaced them were the worst kind of modern—all planes and angles and white with few windows.

In the buildings closest to the park, the lights worked and the streets looked safe. But here, on a side street not far from the construction, the city's shady side showed. The dirty snow was piled against the curb, the streets were dark, and nothing seemed inhabited except that alley with the coroner's van blocking the entrance.

The coroner's van and at least one unmarked car. No press, which surprised him. Anything that caught the Bureau's attention usually had the press's first. It was probably just another sign of the many things that could go wrong. And why he was sent here.

The distant sirens faded. Obviously they weren't coming to this scene, either. He had the impression of isolation, of secrecy, of a crime scene not even the police wanted anyone to know about.

He wasn't sure if he was overreacting or responding to some subtle stimuli. He wasn't sure of anything anymore.

He shoved his gloved hands in the pockets of his overcoat even though it was against FBI dress code, and slipped between the van and the wall of a grimy brick building.

The alley was brighter than he expected. Two battery-operated lights lit up everything from the ground to three feet up. After that, the light faded until it disappeared into darkness at about six feet.

Which meant he could see the faces of the two beat cops who put out their hands to stop him, but he couldn't see the face on the bruiser in plain clothes toward the back.

Two older men crouched near the bodies, and a younger man clutched a Polaroid camera as if it were about to bite him.

Bryce pulled out his identification wallet and opened it for the beat cops. "I'm expected," he said.

He supposed that was a lie. Only the patrolman who called the regional office knew he was coming—and he had no way of knowing if either of these two men were the one who called.

He didn't really care. He needed to bulldoze his way in and take this over, even though he was greatly outnumbered and he didn't know what he was facing.

Still, the beat cops looked at his identification and parted. They didn't give him any crap at all.

Maybe he *was* expected.

As he stepped into the alley, he sank into slush. He looked over at those battery-operated lights.

Some genius had put them on metal garbage can covers on top of the ice. The heat was radiating through the metal and melting the crime scene.

"I hope to hell you got pictures of this before you decided to ruin it," he snapped, then suppressed a grimace. That was the kind of comment which was always getting him in trouble. He should have wormed his way into this scene politely, respectfully, but with force.

Instead, he just insulted everyone on the ground.

The two older men stood and one of them flushed. The second looked at the garbage can lids and swore.

"Move those things," he said to the kid with the camera.

"Too late now," Bryce said. "You have to leave them. They've contaminated the scene and we need to know how."

All six men stared at him.

"So," he said, "no one has answered my question. Did you get photographs before you decided to melt all the trace away?"

"I…I, um, took some shots," the kid with the Polaroid said.

But the older man, the one who flushed, waved a hand at him, an obvious order to shut up.

"Who the hell are you?" he said to Bryce.

"Special Agent Frank Bryce. I've been sent to take over this scene. This is an FBI investigation now." He hadn't even practiced the words, but they felt natural to him.

"Like hell," said the other man. "Homicides are a local crime. There's no federal jurisdiction."

"Seamus," the bruiser in the back said. He stepped closer to the light. He had one of those square jaws and jutting foreheads that some folks thought made for all-American handsomeness. The kind of guy who played quarterback in college, dated the head cheerleader, and beat up brilliant little rich kids like Bryce for practice before each game. "Maybe he has a point."

It took Bryce a minute to realize that the bruiser was actually defending him. How come an NYPD detective was so willing to give up his turf?

"No, he doesn't. He has no point at all." The older man crossed his arms. "You go tell the Special Agent *in Charge* that if he wants to help on this investigation, he goes through channels."

Effective. The older man had just told Bryce that he'd worked with the FBI before, that he knew Bryce wasn't the head of the New York office, and that he had no jurisdiction at all.

"I talked to him not five minutes ago," Bryce said. "He's sending a team. He told me that this scene is unusual and important and I'm supposed to secure it. So he seems to believe we do have jurisdiction. He'll be here within the hour. You can argue with him. Until then, nothing'll get removed, we'll repair what we can—"

He looked pointedly at the melting ice as he said that.

"—and we'll pretend we're colleagues as we investigate this crime. You'll make sure no one else from the NYPD comes on scene, and no civilians wander in as well. Then when the Special Agent in Charge gets here, you can argue jurisdiction all you want. It will no longer be my concern."

He wasn't quite sure why it was now. He took one step closer and froze as his gaze found the bodies.

For a moment, he didn't believe what he saw. Hoover's jowly face had never been that particular shade of gray. His cheeks were abnormally red, and it took Bryce a moment to realize the old man was wearing a light dusting of rouge. There was a smear on the left side of his face—he'd clearly been rolled over—and his eyes were open. Sunken into his head, they didn't seem as large as they had before.

Or as frightening.

Bryce blinked, then frowned, forcing his gaze to the other corpse. And that was when he became convinced he really was looking at Hoover. Because Hoover went clubbing every time he came to New York with the Associate Director, Clyde Tolson.

Tolson was the closest thing to a wife that Hoover ever had.

Bryce had done HooverWatch off and on for years—which meant that he had been part of the security team tailing Hoover—and he'd watched the two old men hold hands as they slipped inside some of the most exclusive gentlemen's clubs in New York.

Bryce frowned, then looked up. Was this the building that had the late-night parties, the ones that were so notorious for the number of notable New York men who attended? He would bet half a year's pay that it was.

He said, "You guys are really going to keep the FBI from investigating the death of the Director of the FBI? The most famous crime-fighting unit in the entire federal government, and you're going to keep us out of it?"

The police detectives were frowning at him.

Bryce made himself sound tougher than he felt. "Go right ahead. And when you screw this up as badly as Dallas screwed the Kennedy assassination, then you can answer all those questions about why you shut the FBI out of the investigation."

"Homicides," the older man named Seamus said, "are local."

"Seamus," the bruiser said again. "You said you didn't want political cases. You said—"

"I said I'd take whatever came on this shift," the older man said, "and if you can't shut up, then you're going back to the car with a whole string of complaints in your jacket."

The bruiser visibly clamped his mouth shut.

"If we're going to fight jurisdiction," Bryce said, "I'd like to know who I'm fighting with."

"I'm Seamus O'Reilly," the older man said. "Lead detective on this case."

"Well, Mr. Lead Detective," Bryce said. "Where are the other bodies?"

The two older men started. His question surprised them, but not in the way he expected. He had thought they would look at him like he was crazy, not like they had a guilty secret.

"What do you mean, 'other bodies'?" the bruiser asked. His tone also suggested that he was withholding information.

"The Director never went anyone without his driver or his bodyguards." Bryce didn't want to tell these guys that the driver would have had orders to park a block away and the so-called bodyguards of HooverWatch would be even farther away. Hoover liked to protect the anonymity of his friends, so he made sure the agents tailing him could only see that people went in and out of these parties and clubs, not who the people actually were.

"As you can tell," the bruiser said, "there are no other bodies in this alley, and no evidence of any."

"I can't tell a damn thing," Bryce said. "You've melted my fucking evidence."

The other older man, the one who hadn't introduced himself, clenched his hands into fists. Bryce had a hunch this was the guy who had ordered the lights be placed on the ice in the first place.

"Besides," Bryce said. "The other bodies wouldn't be in the alley. One would be parked a block away. He would be a black man in a bulletproof limosine. Has anyone talked to him?"

The bruiser looked at O'Reilly. O'Reilly hadn't changed his posture.

"And the bodyguards would be about a block or so away from the limosine. Anyone want to tell me why they haven't approached this scene?"

O'Reilly studied him for a moment. A cold wind suddenly whipped through the alley, toying with Bryce's hat, then letting it remain on his head. He didn't move, though. He'd rather lose the hat than stop staring back at O'Reilly.

"This is a goddamn fuck-up," O'Reilly said. "I'm not conceding this investigation to you."

"I can tell," Bryce said.

"But it seems you know a few things that we haven't yet figured out although—" and now O'Reilly looked at the older man and the bruiser "—I'm not exactly sure why. Apparently we do have three other bodies. We thought they were separate crime scenes, and we were going to see if they were related, but we hadn't gotten to it yet. As you can probably figure out, we were a bit surprised to find Director Hoover and Assistant Director Tolson here. This isn't the best of neighborhoods."

It wasn't a surprise to anyone who worked in the New York Regional Office, particularly anyone who worked HooverWatch. The old man was known for his predilections, not because he foisted them on anyone—he seemed to be relatively monogamous—but because he took the moral high ground on everything else.

Everything from the precision of the dress code (too many violations and you could get demoted) to making certain his agents did not drink coffee on the job (Hoover didn't want anyone to think the FBI needed help remaining awake) to investigating potential agents and approving existing agents' future wives. Every day, someone grumbled about Hoover and his double standards.

The hell of it was if you discounted the fact that Hoover and Tolson were the same gender, he didn't violate his own standards. The old men were monogamous and, except for their questionable sexual interests, they lived clean lives.

But you couldn't discount that relationship. Hoover had destroyed half a dozen agents that Bryce knew of because they shared the same urges. Hoover had always said that the Communists, particularly the KGB, would use secrets like a man's homosexuality to compromise him and to get him to act as a double agent.

Which, if Bryce was actually thinking this through, was precisely why Hart had sent him here.

They didn't want Bryce to handle the investigation. They wanted him to suppress it. They wanted him to find a way to cover it up.

It was too damn ironic that the nation's chief law enforcement officer died of a mugging in an alley on his way out of an illegal sex party.

Imagine if the news got ahold of that. It would be the worst scandal in the nation's history.

It might call everything Hoover had done—hell, everything the government had done, since everyone who was anyone knew about him—it would call all of that into question.

Bryce had been right all along. He was here to take over the scene, sure. But if that was impossible, then the screwups would be blamed on him.

O'Reilly was still staring at him, and Bryce realized that he was taking too long to answer the implied question.

"People tend to get killed in neighborhoods that aren't the best," Bryce said. "That's one of the reasons the neighborhood has such a rotten reputation."

"This one has a reputation for something else," the bruiser said, and looked up at the building that Bryce had been looking at.

"If you're referring to the party, I've heard of it. Everyone in the New York Bureau has. Seems there are a lot of rumors of Communist spies infiltrating some of these kinds of places. We've been investigating for awhile."

It was the best he could do on short notice. In fact, there were rumors of Communist spies at these places and more than one agent had been sent to check the parties out. Bryce often wondered if the agents weren't just inadvertently clearing the way for Hoover and Tolson to spend an evening with like-minded people, but it wasn't his job to speak up about that. And surprisingly, given his track record about speaking up on everything else, on this he had somehow managed to keep his mouth shut.

"Do you know that for a fact?" O'Reilly asked. He sounded skeptical of the explanation, and Bryce wondered whether the man knew any of the rumors about Hoover.

"I don't know anything for a fact," Bryce said. "I'm as surprised by all of this as you are."

"I'm surprised that these two men weren't carrying," the bruiser said. "Any reason they'd be without their weapons?"

Bryce wasn't here to answer questions, but he decided to answer this one. It was easier than wasting time—and contaminating more evidence—by conducting a massive search.

"They never carried weapons. That's what the bodyguards were for."

"The bodyguards who parked several blocks away," O'Reilly said.

Bryce shrugged. "I have no idea what tonight's plans were. I don't know what anyone was trying to achieve. I'm just supposed to secure the scene. Which now, apparently, extends for several blocks. How long have you known about these killings?"

"Which ones?" the older man asked.

"And you are?" Bryce asked.

"I'm the coroner," the older man said. "Thomas Brunner."

"Well, Doctor—doctor?—"

The man nodded a confirmation.

"Well, Doctor Brunner, I'm referring to all five killings. How long have you known?"

"I was called to the scene, as you call this mess, about midnight. Two men down on the street. Pulled from their cars."

"Cars?" Bryce asked. That didn't sound right.

Brunner nodded. "Then we found the limosine driver. Then we were brought over here."

"And you heard no shots?"

"None," Brunner said.

"How long have Hoover and Tolson been dead?" Bryce asked.

"Not long when I got here."

"So you should have heard shots."

"Maybe," Brunner said. "But whoever killed these two knew what he was doing. He might have known to keep the shots quiet."

A silencer. That was a rare commodity on the New York streets. Only professionals used them, and only in professional situations.

Bryce's heartburn got even worse. He would have to pick up some Bromo-Seltzer before going home.

"Since you just realized that these three cases were tied together," Bryce said, "who's handling the other two?"

"No one yet," Brunner said.

"No one?" Bryce felt his eyes widen in surprise. "Three murders and you didn't call a detective?"

"It's the neighborhood," Brunner said. "We figured we had two fags and a nigger. We'd get around to it."

Bryce blinked at the language, then made himself take a deep breath. That was normally the kind of thing that would send him flying into another agent's face, screaming. *Two fags and a nigger? You mean two adult men on personal business and one Negro who was just doing his job? Those were the people you didn't feel worth your time to call in an investigator?*

"You'd get around to it," he finally managed. His tone was flat.

"He did mention it to me," O'Reilly said. "I was going to take the cases. I figured we had a spree shooter."

A spree shooter, like Charles Starkweather in the Midwest about six years ago. Starkweather had killed seemingly randomly as he drove around the area, attracting national attention and giving the nation a new phrase for an old-fashioned kind of killer—a man who went on a "spree"; a word, until that year, Bryce had always associated with fun-filled if a bit extravagant overindulgence.

"Now you figure otherwise," Bryce said.

"Now I figure we have a targeted hit," O'Reilly said. He hadn't moved. He was still standing in front of the bodies as if he were guarding them. "Which presents a problem for both of us."

"It presents a problem for the whole damn country," Bryce said.

"You guys," O'Reilly said, "are shit at hot investigations. You need us. We have the manpower, the resources, and the wherewithal to find the shooter."

"If there's only one," Bryce said.

"All the shooters, then," O'Reilly said. "We, on the other hand, don't have a lot of pull outside this jurisdiction. So how about you handle the national angle and we'll handle the crime scenes?"

"How about you negotiate with the SAC when he gets here, like we agreed?"

O'Reilly's lips thinned. The man was itching to get to work, and Bryce had to admire that. But he wasn't going to make any deals with a lowly detective of the NYPD.

"Tell you what," Bryce said to O'Reilly. "You and me, let's figure out the parameters of the crime scene."

O'Reilly frowned.

Bryce didn't give him a chance to disagree. "You two," he said to the beat cops, "make sure no one else gets into this area at least not until the SAC arrives. You—"

And now he was looking at the bruiser.

"You make sure that no one leaves the nearby buildings, not without getting ID'd and fingerprinted. Hold them if you can."

"I'll need more manpower for that," the bruiser said.

"Call for some backup. I'm pretty sure my men'll be here soon, but they're probably not going to want to guard a bunch of folks who just want to go to work."

Besides, Bryce wasn't sure the FBI would be there soon. He wasn't sure how long he was going to be left alone at this crime scene, how much time he would actually be given to screw up so that the real truths about this crime (and Hoover) would never come out.

"And you two," he said to Brunner and the Polaroid guy, "see if you can figure out how to recover the important evidence from this scene before it all washes down the storm drain. I want a series of candid shots. And where the hell are your scene-of-the-crime guys?"

"Fag kill," Brunner said. "They'll get here when they get here."

Now Bryce had had enough. He leaned into Brunner's face, pressing his nose as close to the older man's as he possibly could.

"If I hear the word 'fag' one more time and if I ever hear you say 'nigger' again, I will make your life a living hell, you got that?"

Brunner just glared at him. But Bryce wasn't done.

"Whether or not these were FBI agents doesn't really matter, now does it? You judge them on how they look or where they were killed. Well, I'm a lot more interested in *how* they were killed and by whom. So you better get yourself off your bigoted ass and make sure the rest of this goddamn scene is done right. If I understand NYPD protocol, you're the guy in charge until the SOCO people arrive, and you've fucked that up royally so far. This is probably the most important case of your life, and you melted it. So I don't want to hear any more excuses or judgments. I just want you to do your goddamn job. Is that clear?"

Brunner continued to glare at him. O'Reilly nudged the man with his elbow.

"Yes," Brunner said sullenly. "It's clear."

"Then get to it," Bryce said. He looked at all of them and felt the anger that had been building ever since he saw Essie Seward's body into his voice. "Let's try not to make this any worse."

4

Jake Haskell removed his overcoat, then pulled the rubbers off his shoes like he did every morning when he arrived at FBI Headquarters. Only most mornings, he arrived promptly at 8 a.m. He'd never been called into Headquarters at 2:30 a.m.

Fortunately, the roads had been empty. He'd driven like a madman, fishtailing on a dusting of new snow as if it were a sheet of ice. When he'd arrived at FBI parking, he'd noticed half a dozen other cars belonging to agents.

Now, as he left his coat, hat, and gloves in the cloakroom, he could hear the hesitant sound of conversation filtering through the door. This place should have been empty except for the usual guards. No one should have been here—not unless there was some kind of national emergency.

And usually the kinds of national emergencies that kept people up late did not keep them up late at the FBI. The national headquarters followed what one newly promoted agent called *banker's hours.*

A few dozen agents—lower ranking all—working the evening, and only a handful worked overnight, usually on some project that they'd gotten behind on.

Haskell couldn't remember the last time he'd been called in like this—and he'd been working at the national headquarters since the late

1950s through the loss of Cuba, the Bay of Pigs, the Cuban Missile Crisis, and the President's assassination.

Whatever had happened tonight, it had to be big.

He adjusted the same suit coat he had worn earlier that day. He'd brushed it off when he got home and hung it on a cedar hanger in his closet, just like FBI instructions stated. Only it didn't feel clean like it usually did. He didn't feel sharp either. He was sleep-mussed and muzzy-headed, not the crisp to-the-point agent he tried to be whenever he walked through these doors.

He stepped into the main corridor and saw other agents—all of them senior ranking—milling outside the Director's suite. One agent actually leaned on the wooden standalone sign that read

Director
Federal Bureau of Investigation

in fancy 1940s script. The lack of discipline struck Haskell as odd. Odder still considering the breathlessness and fear Assistant Director Ross had had in his voice when he'd called Haskell.

"What's going on?" Haskell asked.

No one heard him at first. They were still talking, all of them looking tired, a few with their hair sticking straight up as if they'd forgotten to comb it when they'd gotten out of bed.

"What's happening?" he asked even louder.

"That's the sixty-four thousand dollar question," said Lewis Small. Small was one of Ross's right-hand men. If anyone knew what was happening in the office, Small did.

"Where's the Director?" Haskell asked. Last he'd heard, the Director had gone to New York to finish some business with the New York office.

Small was the only person in the main room who looked like he had just stepped out of an ad for the perfect FBI agent. His clothes were pressed, his hair—what there was of it—was neatly combed, and he smelled faintly of aftershave.

"Dunno that either," Small said. "All we know is that we have to be ready to launch a full-scale investigation. We're going to coordinate when we get the go-ahead."

"Investigation of what?" Haskell asked.

"We've all been asking that," said Hale Pearson, one of the other agents. Pearson looked like Haskell felt—bleary-eyed and a little nervous. His clothes were askew as well, not like they'd come off a hanger, but like they'd been pulled off a hotel room floor. "No one's got an answer."

"No one except Assistant Director Ross," said Small, "and he's not talking. Not yet."

"How many people has he called in?" Haskell asked. While he spoke, part of his brain tried to figure out what could cause this level of emergency. Another part began to record information because he might have to pass it along. And the remaining part focused on trying to wake up.

"Senior staff," Small said. "I think it'll be up to our discretion who we call after that."

"Anything on the news?" Haskell asked, even though he knew it wasn't. He spent half his driving time here spinning the a.m. dial trying to find a signal—any signal—that might give him the news of the hour. He did pick up a station in Florida, but it was Cuban music and couldn't help him.

"Nothing. Maybe we'll hear at dawn when the TV stations come back on," someone said from the back.

They'd all thought of the same things he had. They were all trained just the same way he was.

"We could call the other agents and tell them to come in. He doesn't have to," Haskell said. "You want me to tell him that? He can worry about the other coordination."

"I don't think he's talking to the other agents." Small had lowered his voice. "I think he's talking to Miss Gandy."

Helen Gandy was the Director's private secretary. She knew more about the man than anyone else alive, and that included the Associate Director (and Hoover's Number One Man) Clyde Tolson.

At the mention of Gandy's name, Haskell froze. "Why is Ross calling Miss Gandy?"

"I assume she knows the Director's schedule," Small said without a trace of guile. "She probably knows where he's staying and how to reach him. I'm pretty certain that's why the Assistant Director is talking with her."

Haskell nodded, then gave an uncertain smile, and thanked Small. Haskell pushed his way into the throng of agents, breathing deeply to slow his racing heart.

Most of the agents here, even the ones at senior rank like he was, didn't know the procedures past their own level. Haskell had made it a point to know. And over time, that knowledge had been very useful.

He had a hunch it was useful right now. The Director's schedule, including where he was going to stay, should have been on the calendar in his office. It also should have been on the desk of each Assistant Director as well as those of their assistants.

J. Edgar Hoover was nothing if not thorough. After all, despite his press, he was nothing more than a glorified file clerk, a man who made himself useful only because he knew how to organize information.

Small wasn't an assistant to anyone. He may not have known what Hoover did with his schedule before he left on a trip. Unlike Haskell, Small had no interests in the workings of the department.

He probably didn't know that his assumptions about the Assistant Director were wrong.

There was only one reason an Assistant Director of the FBI would call Helen Gandy in the middle of the night.

He was activating Hoover's personal emergency protocol, the protocol that only went into effect if the Director was incapacitated or dead.

No one—not the Attorney General, not the President, not the lowly bureaucrats of the FBI called out of their beds in the middle of the night—was going to know what had happened to Hoover, not until Miss Gandy got here.

It was her job—hers and Clyde Tolson's, really—to protect the Director's Personal and Confidential files. On this point, Haskell wasn't entirely clear—he had a hunch the orders Miss Gandy was to follow were verbal—but he suspected she was supposed to remove or destroy those files if the Director was dead.

That would require her to get her elderly fanny into the office in the middle of the night.

That would require an Assistant Director to call her before almost anyone else, although Ross had been smart—he'd brought in a small army to protect her before he called her.

Haskell felt a shiver run down his back.

J. Edgar Hoover had run the FBI like his personal kingdom for more than forty years.

With the man gone, everything would change.

With the man gone, the fight for control would be ugly.

And Jake Haskell knew who he wanted to be in charge.

He slipped into a side office, pulled an emergency phone number from his pocket, and started to dial.

5

THE SECONDARY DEATH SCENE was only a block away. Two beat cops protected it as well. Their patrol car was parked behind the limousine.

No one had put up crime scene tape.

"Your coroner handle this scene already?" Bryce asked O'Reilly. The older cop was walking at least one step ahead of him, as if it were his idea to investigate this, not Bryce's.

"He said he'd been here, but I'm not sure if he did much more than look." O'Reilly walked quicker, clearly determined to get to the beat cops before Bryce. "He's a good man."

"Doesn't sound like it," Bryce said. "From what I've seen so far, he's a screwup, and that's the last thing we need on this case."

"He's the best in the department," O'Reilly said.

"You're not adding to my confidence level." Bryce wasn't sure how to handle that lack of confidence, however. Examination and disposal of bodies belonged solely to the local precinct. The FBI had consultants, but they were often medical examiners from the area. Brunner himself could take an occasional check from the FBI.

"Look," O'Reilly said, "until the two bodies turned up in the alley, this was just some muggings gone wrong. Stuff in this neighborhood—"

"Gets ignored, I know." Bryce frowned at the limosine, looming out of the dim light like a shadowy outline of a moving car. He recognized the shape.

It was thicker than most limosines and rode lower to the ground because it was encased in an extra frame, making it bulletproof. Supposedly, the glass would all be bulletproof as well.

"You said the driver was shot inside the limosine?" Bryce asked.

"That's what they tell me," O'Reilly said.

"You haven't been here either." Bryce was surprised. He'd thought this cop at least was somewhat competent, just from his demeanor.

"I got called in about fifteen minutes before you did—and it wasn't until we were deep in the alley investigation that Brunner told me about the other bodies. I hadn't had a chance to get out here, but I dispatched the beat cops."

"Great," Bryce said. "How long do you think this poor bastard sat here while the NYPD tried to figure out if his death was worth investigating?"

O'Reilly put a hand on Bryce's chest, stopping both of them. "Look, I know we made some mistakes back there—"

Bryce was impressed. Most cops would have foisted the mistakes on the man they probably belonged to, that inept coroner.

"—but if you want any chance at cooperation between our departments, you better start acting like a colleague, not an asshole. Are we clear?"

Bryce paused for a moment. Then he decided to tell the truth. "I am treating you like a colleague."

"Fuck, it's amazing you still have a job."

Bryce silently concurred. But instead of saying anything, he looked down at O'Reilly's hand which remained on his chest. "What is it that you don't want me to see at this crime scene?"

"Jesus." O'Reilly let his hand drop. "We're looking at it together, and it's mine, remember."

"We didn't agree on that, *remember*?" Bryce said. "In fact, I should send you back to that alley to wait for the SAC."

"I'm sure it'll take him a while to get here," O'Reilly said. "I'm sure he's got a lot of people to consult before he even sets foot on this crime scene."

In spite of himself, Bryce glanced at O'Reilly. The bastard was smart; Bryce had to give him that much. Not even Bryce had figured that Hart couldn't come here immediately. But of course he couldn't. The Director was dead and it was, as the coroner so ineptly put it, obviously a fag kill because it had occurred in one of the most notorious neighborhoods in New York.

The FBI had to control the information about this crime from the outset. Any mistakes meant that there'd be holes—and stories, just like there were about Kennedy. Rumors led to discontent, and discontent could mean trouble.

Especially with two of the most important national figures murdered in the last three months.

Bryce nodded and walked to the limosine. O'Reilly trained his flashlight on the driver's side.

The window wasn't broken like Bryce had expected. It had been rolled down.

"You got here one James Crawford," said one of the beat cops. "He got identification says he's a feebee, but I ain't never heard of no colored feebee."

"There're only five," Bryce said dryly. And they all worked for Hoover as his personal servants. "Can I see that identification?"

The beat cop handed him a wallet that matched the ones on Tolson and Hoover. Inside was a badge and identification for James Crawford as well as family photographs. Neither Tolson nor Hoover had had any photographs in their wallets.

Bryce studied Crawford's identification photo for a moment. It showed a pleasant-faced man in late middle age, with just a bit of silver touching his dark curls. Bryce recognized him. He'd often come into the regional office, trailing Hoover and Tolson, hands folded in front of him as if he were afraid to touch anything.

Bryce sighed. He hated investigating cases when he'd known the victim. Hoover was in a class by himself. But Crawford had always been polite and soft-spoken, someone who took the time to say hello when someone said hello to him.

In a job as cutthroat as the one Bryce had, even the littlest gestures meant a lot.

And in a murder investigation, those little gestures, that feeling of amiability, could often cloud an investigator's open mind.

Bryce took a deep breath, reminding himself he'd never exchanged more than a comment about the weather with Crawford. They weren't friends. They barely counted as colleagues.

Bryce motioned O'Reilly to move his flashlight a little closer to the body. The head was tilted toward the window. The right side of the skull was gone, the hair glistening with drying blood. With one gloved finger, Bryce pushed the head upright. A single entrance wound above the left ear had caused the damage.

The coroner had been here then, because the head had been moved. The force of the shot would have pushed the head away from the window. Not even the blowback from the exit wound would have caused the head to tilt toward the side window.

"Let me have your light," Bryce said.

O'Reilly glared at him, and for a moment, Bryce thought he'd tell him to get his own. Then he handed the flashlight over. It was heavy and metal, sturdier than FBI standard issue.

Bryce trained the light inside the front seat. The built-in ashtray was open and half full. It looked like a cigarette had burned itself out in one of the slots.

Otherwise the interior was clean. There were no papers, no food wrappers, no extra coat. Nothing except a blood-covered log sheet which he recognized as the one provided by the regional motor pool.

"Brunner says the shots are the same caliber," O'Reilly said.

"Brunner also said that these cases weren't worth investigating," Bryce said. "We'll handle caliber."

"He's good at it," O'Reilly said. "He measures on scene—"

"I don't care," Bryce said.

"I do," O'Reilly said. "I've worked with him for eighteen years and he hasn't been wrong about caliber. Whoever shot the two men in the alley shot this guy."

Bryce was glad that O'Reilly hadn't named the men in the alley. He wasn't sure how much the beat cops knew, and he didn't want them calling wives and girlfriends the moment they got off duty, telling them what kind of case they were witnessing. He was going to have to make certain everyone was told to keep his mouth shut before he left the scene. In fact, he—or someone from the Bureau—was going to have to give these men incentives to keep their mouths shut.

He wasn't quite sure how to do that.

Maybe that was one of the many things Hart was working on, preventing the man and his assistants from getting their asses down here already.

"I'm not willing to make that judgment," Bryce said. "All we know was that these men were shot. Even if the guns were the same caliber, it might just mean that our shooters used the same type of weapon. It doesn't mean that the same shooter killed all five men. It's those kinds of assumptions that lead to mistakes in investigations."

And it was those kinds of statements that caused his colleagues to hate him. It was just that lately he hadn't been able to censor them.

The comment seemed to roll off O'Reilly however. "You're thinking this was a hit."

"I'm thinking this was planned," Bryce said. "But I'm still willing to entertain the idea that all five deaths were random, that some idiot with a gun decided to shoot everyone on the street and happened to get our guys."

"You don't really believe that," O'Reilly said.

"I think it's not very likely," Bryce said. "But for this reason. Trained agents on bodyguard duty don't stay in their car when they hear gunshots. They're out and moving up the street. No matter what order these shootings occurred in, Agent Crawford here shouldn't be sitting calmly in the seat of his limosine with the window rolled down. He should be out of the car, investigating. Or at the very least, that window should be up."

"He was smoking," the nearest beat cop said.

Bryce looked up at the man. He was young, with a wide brash face and the clear eyes of a rookie.

"Yes," Bryce said. "He was smoking and using the ashtray, not flicking the ash outside the window. It's cold. And even if it weren't, he would've been damn careless to have the window rolled down while he was having his cigarette—particularly if there were gunshots."

"The windows are bulletproof?" O'Reilly asked.

"The whole damn car is bulletproof," Bryce said. "See how low it rides? The Director demanded years ago to have the entire body encased. These fuckers are twice as heavy as a regular limosine and probably five times safer."

"So if he heard shots and had been ordered to stay with the limosine, he would've had the engine running and the windows rolled up."

"He probably would have had the doors locked too, until he saw or got a signal from our friends in the alley." Bryce stared at the lolling head. "That window bothers me. The shot couldn't have gone through it—"

"Are you sure? We haven't rolled it up to see," O'Reilly said.

Which on any other car would be a good point. But on this car, it didn't matter.

"The glass would've spidered," Bryce said. "It would have taken two or three shots to penetrate. By then he would have started the car and driven away."

O'Reilly was frowning.

"Besides," Bryce said, "there's no glass fragments in either the scalp or on the seat. The window was down."

"Which begs the question," O'Reilly said. "Why would you roll a window down on a cold February night?"

"I told you," the beat cop said. "He was smoking. I don't care if he used the ashtray. If he was sitting here awhile, he'd want some fresh air to get the smoke out of the car."

"Possibly," Bryce said.

"But you don't think that's it," O'Reilly said.

"I don't know." Bryce aimed his flashlight at the curb. "When the scene-of-the-crime boys get here, have them pick up every cigarette butt and piece of trash from that area. Maybe we'll catch a break."

O'Reilly took the flashlight back. "And have them dust the exterior of the limosine, including that window."

"Beg pardon, detective," the beat cop said, "but if it was rolled down—"

"You never knocked on a window to get a buddy's attention?" O'Reilly asked.

Bryce looked at him sideways. That was exactly what Bryce had been thinking—that someone Crawford knew knocked on the window, got him to roll it down, then shot him in the head. But he hadn't expressed that.

Maybe O'Reilly was the investigator Bryce had thought he was.

"Yeah, I done that a few times," the beat cop said, "but who would this guy know in this neighborhood?"

Bryce rolled his eyes. "Just because Crawford's a Negro doesn't mean—"

"Don't start," O'Reilly said. "Officer Vaden here has a point. Who rolls down his window for anyone in this neighborhood? Hell, even if I knew someone who lived here I might not do it."

Bryce paused. Crawford was Hoover's D.C. driver. Which made it even less likely that he knew anyone in New York.

"Your advice was good the first time," Bryce said. "Have them dust the exterior, including the window. You two could be onto something. This sure as hell isn't a normal crime scene. The more information we get, the better."

He looked down the street. He couldn't see the HooverWatch car. It was lost in the darkness.

"We're gonna need more people. We've got an entire neighborhood to scour." Bryce sighed. He looked at the beat cop. "Call it in. Ask for more bodies on site. And tell them that Detective O'Reilly needs the scene-of-the-crime guys here immediately."

The beat cop went to the squad to radio in Bryce's orders. O'Reilly stared at him.

"I thought we weren't cooperating."

"We have a huge crime scene, and nothing is straightforward," Bryce said. "We have to protect a lot of ground, and the minute the sun comes up, people are gonna start moving through it. I'd like to block off the roads around here, but I can't do it all by my own self. And as you said, the SAC probably won't be here for a while. He ordered me to secure the scene, and that's what I'm doing."

"By using us."

Bryce shrugged. "If you don't like it, I'll get on the horn with Hart, see what the holdup is."

"No," O'Reilly said. "The more we do, the more it becomes an NYPD scene. I'm fine with that."

And for the moment, Bryce was, too.

6

ATTORNEY GENERAL ROBERT F. KENNEDY sat in his favorite chair near the fire in his library. His dog, Brumus, a large black Newfoundland, snored beside him. Hickory Hill, the house he had bought from his brother Jack seven years before, was quiet even though Ethel and their eight children were asleep upstairs. Outside, the rolling landscape was covered in a light dusting of snow—rare for McLean, Virginia, even at this time of year.

He held a book in his left hand, his finger marking the spot. The Greeks had comforted him in the few months since Jack died, but lately Kennedy had discovered Camus.

On this night, Kennedy had been rereading *The Notebooks* again, copying favorite quotes into his commonplace book. He certainly couldn't sleep. Sleep had left him on November 22, 1963, and it visited only rarely since.

He was rather glad it had left. When he slept, he dreamed about his brother's murder. Only he'd been the one holding the rifle. He'd been the one leaning out the window in that goddamn Texas Book Depository, looking down on Dealey Plaza in the bright sunshine, watching his brother's thick thatch of chestnut hair blow in the wind.

Because they thought he was safe. Because they thought no one would shoot the President, not on a beautiful sunny day, not with his pretty wife beside him, not with all those adoring people waving from the sidelines.

Even though three previous presidents had been shot, they'd been shot generations ago—a century ago in one case. No one would be fool enough to do it now.

At least that's how the television anchormen and the pundits in the newspapers were reading this whole mess, even now. They didn't know about the warnings or the cancelled trips. They didn't know that the FBI had word of an attack planned for November 18 in Tampa, a plan that so frightened Kennedy he talked his brother into canceling the trip.

The outline for that plan was an outline for what eventually happened in Dallas.

And even though there were threats concerning Dallas, Kennedy couldn't talk Jack out of that trip. Jack said it was important for the re-election. He needed Texas, especially if they dumped Lyndon Johnson from the ticket.

Goddamn Jack for believing in his own immortality. Goddamn the Secret Service for letting him ride without the bulletproof bubble top on the car.

Goddamn himself for not realizing that every goddamn thing he'd done since becoming Attorney General had doomed his brother, maybe even the entire family.

Kennedy bent the corner of the page he'd been reading and closed the book. Then he leaned his head back and shut his eyes.

Jackie told him that he was full of Catholic guilt. That he couldn't have done anything. That he wasn't the one in that plaza with a gun. Jackie—not Ethel—had told him to go to church and beg for absolution.

Ethel probably figured he had already done it.

But he hadn't. He had been to church since...he'd had to. How many memorial services had he attended? And he had to pretend to get back to normal for the kids. Kathleen was twelve now, old enough to know when her parents were distraught.

So he'd gone to church, and knelt and prayed and taken the sacraments, even though he probably shouldn't have, given the state of his soul. He couldn't bring himself to go to confession. How many Hail Marys would it take to absolve him of complicity in his brother's murder? How many times would he have to press those rosary beads against his fingers to obtain forgiveness for pursuing and lying to the very men who'd ordered his brother's execution?

Some things not even God could forgive.

Which was why Kennedy found comfort in the ancient Greeks. Euripides, Sophocles, they knew that often a man had to live with himself after he'd ruined not just his own life, but the lives of others around him. Those old Greeks even wrote about men who, in ruining their own lives, had ruined the lives of a nation.

The long days store up many things nearer to grief than joy.

He'd been quoting that for weeks now, muttering the line from *Oedipus at Colonus* as if it, not the Hail Marys, could give him absolution. Ethel had barked at him about it a few days ago.

Stop reciting that line, she'd snapped. *We're all grieving, and we're all going to get over it.*

Maybe they would. His family had the Church and each other. They had the same naïve belief that the rest of the country had—that Oswald acted alone. Oswald was too damn dumb to act alone. And he wasn't a marksman. That was a marksman's shot.

If the killing shot had even come from the Book Depository.

Kennedy shook his head, wishing the thoughts would leave him. He was torturing himself, and he was afraid to stop. If he stopped, if he figured out how to enjoy living again, wouldn't that be a betrayal of Jack?

Jackie kept reminding him that Jack had been all about enjoying life. He loved everything about it—sometimes more than she even knew.

But Kennedy had never loved life like his brother had. Life was serious business, run by serious men. Because he'd known that, he'd been able to step in for Jack when Jack had needed him.

Except at the end. At the end, Kennedy should have argued for the bubble top. He should have prevented the trip.

He should have known what was coming.

He stood up, looking down so that he wouldn't see the copies of his own book on organized crime, *The Enemy Within*, covering the shelves above the mantel. He went over to the banking fire to warm himself. That was the other thing: He couldn't get warm. Ethel said it was because he'd lost so much weight. He needed to eat.

He'd been eating—at least, he thought he had. And he'd tried not to drink, although he had a glass of bourbon sitting by his chair even now. The glass was untouched. It was more of a symbol than anything else.

A symbol of times gone.

The phone rang, the sound so shrill that it startled him. It startled Brumus too. The dog looked up, then looked at Kennedy as if demanding an explanation.

He glanced at his watch. Nearly three in the morning. Who called that late, except someone with an emergency?

He was tired of emergencies. Let another member of the family handle it. Let Teddy deal with all the crises that made up the Kennedy clan for once. Baby Teddy for whom life was easy, who had never dealt with anything difficult in his entire charmed existence.

The phone rang again, and this time, Kennedy realized it was the direct line from the Justice Department. It wasn't Kennedy family business. It was United States business—and it was something important. The minor things in the middle of the night went to a dozen deputy A.G.s or to Nick Katzenbach, his valued Assistant Attorney General. Nick had handled a lot of things these last three months, probably more than he'd signed on for.

But if the phone from Justice was ringing here, now, that meant that there was something Nick felt he couldn't tackle on his own, something that only Kennedy could deal with.

He signed and picked up the receiver. "What?"

"Attorney General Kennedy, sir?" The voice on the other end sounded urgent. The voice sounded familiar to him even though he couldn't place it.

"Yes?"

"This is Special Agent John Haskell. You asked me to contact you, sir, if I heard anything important about Director Hoover, no matter what the time."

Kennedy leaned against the desk. He had made that request back when his brother had been president, back when Kennedy had been the first attorney general since the 1920s who actually demanded accountability from Hoover.

Since Lyndon Johnson had taken over the Presidency, accountability had gone by the wayside. These days Hoover rarely returned Kennedy's phone calls.

"Yes, I did tell you that," Kennedy said, resisting the urge to add, but *I don't care about that old man any longer.*

"Sir, I have reason to believe that the Director died tonight."

"Reason to believe?" Kennedy didn't like the phrasing of that.

"I can't get confirmation, sir, but one of the Assistant Directors is calling Helen Gandy while I call you, sir."

Kennedy frowned. "I'm supposed to see significance in that?"

"Sir, I have been at the National Headquarters of the Bureau for more than ten years. Never before, not in any national crisis of any kind, have the senior agents been called in during the middle of the night. But we were, just a half an hour ago. We have no instructions yet, except that we're going to do some investigative work."

"All right." Kennedy still wasn't sure what to make of this.

"And sir, I've made it my business to know some things since you asked me to keep an eye on the Director for you. There are protocols that are need-to-know for Assistant Directors and above only. One of them is this: If the Director dies or is permanently incapacitated, the Assistant Director must call Clyde Tolson and Helen Gandy *first*, before they contact you, sir, or the President himself."

"Before?"

"Yessir. They're to come in and secure the Director's personal and confidential files."

"The files." Kennedy let the word sink in. "Hoover's blackmail files?"

"I assume so, yessir."

Kennedy sank into the chair behind the desk. Hoover's confidential files were one of the reasons the old bastard still had his job. He had everything on everyone. And the material he'd had on Jack....Kennedy shook his head. The material Hoover had on Jack would ruin Jack's legacy—hell, it would ruin the Kennedy family in politics forever.

"So," Kennedy said as he processed this information. "This Assistant Director is calling Miss Gandy now."

"Yessir."

Kennedy wasn't sure where Helen Gandy lived, but he had a hunch she could arrive at the Justice Building a lot faster than he could.

"And there's no way to know what's happened to Hoover," Kennedy said.

"Not until Miss Gandy is already here, sir."

"But there is a possibility that he's fine."

"Yessir. But I don't think so. Beg pardon, sir, but no one has ever acted like this before. Not even when the President died, sir."

Kennedy's stomach tightened. It wasn't proof, but it sounded like he wouldn't have proof, not until it was too late. He would have to play this smart. And if Hoover was still alive, so be it. They already hated each other.

"Has anyone contacted Associate Director Tolson?"

"Both he and the Director are in New York."

Kennedy let out a breath. So whatever happened had happened in New York. Then Miss Gandy would be the logical choice to handle the files here.

"Okay," Kennedy said. "Do you know where those files are?"

"Yessir. I made it my business to know."

God, he'd picked the right man. He'd been looking for someone competent and disgruntled and high-ranking on Hoover's staff, and he'd found Haskell to be all three. But Haskell had actually taken pride in his work, found a way to discover things that only a handful of others knew, and—the greatest miracle of all—knew the right moment to call Kennedy.

"All right," Kennedy said. "Here's what I want you to do. I want you to secure those files."

"Sir?"

"I want you to do whatever it takes. I want you to take some trusted men and I want you to have those men guard the files until I figure out what to do with them. No one, and I repeat no one, can get near them without my express permission. That includes Miss Gandy."

"Yessir."

"And I want someone to secure Hoover's house too. I'm acting on the orders of the President. If anyone tells you that they are doing the same, they're mistaken. The President made his wishes clear on this point. He often said if anything happens to that old queer—" And here Kennedy deliberately used LBJ's favorite phrase for Hoover "—then we need those files before they can get into the wrong hands."

"I'm on it, sir."

"I can't stress to you the importance of this," Kennedy said. In fact, he couldn't talk about the importance at all. Those files could ruin his brother's legacy. The secrets in there could bring down Kennedy too, and his entire family.

"And if I'm wrong about the Director, sir?"

"That's my worry," Kennedy said. "Just remember. You're working for the President, just like the Director of the FBI does. Is that clear?"

"Yes, sir."

"Thank you, Agent Haskell. I'll be there as quickly as I can." And then Bobby Kennedy hung up.

He sat for a moment, stunned at what he had just done. If Hoover was still alive, Kennedy had just committed career suicide. Hoover and Lyndon Johnson were close. In any battle, Johnson would back Hoover over Kennedy.

Particularly when Johnson learned what Kennedy had done. Because the president upon whose orders Kennedy acted wasn't the current one. Kennedy was following the orders of the only man he believed should be president.

His brother, Jack.

7

BRYCE WALKED SLOWLY to the remaining part of the crime scene. Technically, the sidewalk he was walking on might actually be part of the whole scene. There was no way to tell, not in the deep shadows along this street.

Most of the streetlights were out. Only a few porch lights, yellow with dirt, cast any kind of illumination on the sidewalk. It was ice-covered and slick—no one had bothered to shovel here since winter began.

O'Reilly continued to dog him. Bryce was beginning to regret his suggestion that they investigate the outer parts of the scene together. He thought he could keep an eye on O'Reilly, but he had a very real sense that O'Reilly was keeping an eye on him.

No one guarded the empty sidewalk and street between the murder sites. He would wager that no one had canvassed the buildings either. The amount of work it would take to do a proper investigation of this crime scene was overwhelming. The number of man-hours was impossible for a detective and his partner. It would take a task force or some dedicated beat cops to talk to everyone in these buildings—and that was if the people had stayed.

He had a hunch a lot of the residents had seen the squad cars and bolted. Or would bolt the moment the squads disappeared.

Only three cars were parked along the curb of the next block. Two were sedans, parked one in front of the other. The remaining car was a squad, parked messily behind the second sedan, the back end of the squad half in the road.

The squad's parking lights were on so that someone would see it, but the overhead flashing lights weren't.

He found that to be a blessing.

He stopped just before he got to the first sedan. If he squinted, he could barely make out the limosine parked more than a block away.

In no way could he see the alley entrance. Nor could he see the buildings on either side.

This was a terrible place for HooverWatch. And as a former HooverWatch member, he knew that the agents were probably stopped here as per Hoover's orders.

Bryce walked up to the first sedan and peered inside. O'Reilly stopped beside him and shined his light on the driver's side.

A spray of blood covered everything. The sedan was set up for a stakeout—a Styrofoam coffee cup sat on the interior armrest, another on the passenger-side floor. A thermos—probably soup or something a little stronger—also sat on the passenger's side, along with a bag overflowing with candy bars, jars of peanuts, and some beef jerky.

But no bodies.

"Where are the bodies?" Bryce asked the nearest beat cop.

The cop was tall and trim, with a pristine uniform despite his middle-of-the-night duty. He had freckles that ran across his nose like they'd been painted on and bright red hair to match. He could have been a double for Howdy Doody, which he'd probably heard too often in his short life.

"Coroner took them. They should be in his van."

"Christ." Bryce shoved his hands into his pockets. How the hell was he supposed to evaluate the scene if it had already been altered? "He take pictures?"

"No, sir," the beat cop said. "At the time, we had no idea what we had here. There's a bar only a few blocks down, and we all assumed—"

"Yeah, I know what you all assumed," Bryce said. "Funny how that made for sloppy police work."

O'Reilly sighed behind him. Bryce took that as a warning to go easy on the younger cop. Which was probably smart, anyway. This kid wasn't in charge of the scene and he certainly hadn't chosen whether or not photographs were taken. He was at the stage in his career where he did what he was told or start racking up the demerits.

Hell, Bryce was at that same point in his. Funny how a man could work for eleven years and find himself in the same position he'd started in.

"Were you here when the coroner arrived?" Bryce asked.

"My partner and I were the ones who found the bodies, sir," the beat cop said.

"And you are?"

"Office Ralph Voight, sir."

"Well, Officer Voight, we're going to test your powers of observation. I want you to walk me through this scene—careful not to trample any areas that might have vital evidence—and I want you to be as detailed as if you were a camera lens, photographing each minute inch of the place. Can you do that for me?"

Voight swallowed so hard that his Adam's apple bobbed, but he nodded. "I'll do my best, sir."

Bryce glanced at O'Reilly, who had crossed his arms.

"All right," Bryce said. "First, tell me what attracted you to the scene."

"Okay." Voight carefully walked them past both sedans to his squad car. He pulled out a thin flashlight.

O'Reilly was already training his on the buildings beside the scene. Broken glass littered the sidewalk—and it hadn't come from this particular crime. Rusted beer cans, half buried in the ice piles, cluttered each stoop like passed-out drunks.

"Well," Voight said, using his flashlight as a pointer, "we come up on these two cars first."

60

The two sedans were parked against the curb, one behind the other. The sedans were too nice for the neighborhood—new, black, without a dent. Bryce recognized them as FBI issue—he had access to a sedan like that himself when he needed it.

He patted his pocket, was disgusted to realize he'd left his notebook at the apartment, and turned to O'Reilly. "You got paper? I need those plates."

O'Reilly nodded. He pulled out a notebook and wrote down the plate numbers.

"The cars just looked wrong," Voight was saying. "So we stopped, figuring maybe someone needed assistance. That's when we seen the first body."

He walked them to the middle of the street. The road hadn't been plowed regularly either, and a layer of ice had built over the pavement. A large pool of blood had melted through that ice, leaving its edges reddish black and revealing the pavement below.

"The guy was face down, hands out like he'd tried to catch himself."

"Face gone?" Bryce asked, thinking maybe it was a head shot like Crawford.

"No. Turns out he was shot in the back."

Bryce glanced at O'Reilly, whose lips had thinned. Like Hoover and Tolson. Only Crawford was different. Because he was in the limosine? Or was there another reason?

"We pull our weapons, scan to see if we see anyone else, which we don't. The door's open on the first sedan, but we didn't see anyone in the dome light. And we didn't see anyone obvious on the street, but it's really dark here and the flashlights don't reach far." Voight turned his light toward the block with the parked limousine, but neither the car nor the sidewalk was visible from this distance.

"So we go to the cars, careful now, and find the other body right there."

He flashed his light on the curb beside the door to the first sedan.

"This one's on his back and the door is open. We figure he was getting out when he got plugged. Then the other guy—maybe he was outside his car trying to help this guy with I don't know what, some car trouble or something, then his buddy gets hit, so he runs for cover across the street and gets nailed. End of story."

"Did you check to see if the cars start?" O'Reilly asked. Bryce nodded that was going to be his next question as well.

"I'm not supposed to touch the scene, sir," Voight said with some resentment. "We secured the area, figured everything was okay, then called it in."

"Did you hear the other shots?"

"No," Voight said. "I know we got three more up there, and you'd think I'd've heard the shooting if something happened, but I didn't. And as you can tell, it's damn quiet around here at night."

Bryce could tell. He didn't like the silence in the middle of the city. Neighborhoods that got quiet like this so close to dawn were usually among the worst. The early morning maintenance workers and the delivery drivers stayed away whenever they could.

He peered in the sedan, then pulled the door open. The interior light went on. What he had taken for a spray of blood when he'd looked with the flashlight was in truth gobs of blood and tissue and other matter. It covered the seat and the steering wheel, as well as the Styrofoam cups and the bag of candy bars.

The keys were in the ignition. Like all Bureau issues, the car was an automatic.

Carefully, so that he wouldn't disturb anything important in the scene, he turned the key. The sedan purred to life, sounding well-tuned just like it was supposed to.

"Check to see if there are other problems," Bryce said to O'Reilly. "A flat maybe."

Although Bryce knew there wouldn't be one. He shut off the ignition.

"You didn't see the interior light when you pulled up?" he asked Voight.

"Yeah, but it was dim," Voight said. "That's why I figured there was car problems. I figured they left the lights on so they could see."

The light was dim because of the blood spatter. But Bryce nodded anyway. He understood the assumption. He backed out of the sedan, then walked around it, shining his own flashlight at the bloody hole in the ice, and then back at the first sedan.

Directly across.

He walked to the second sedan. Its interior was clean—no Styrofoam cups, no wadded-up food containers, no notebooks. Not even some tools hastily pulled to help the other drivers in need.

He let out a small sigh. He finally figured out what was bothering him.

"You find weapons on the two men?" he asked Voight.

"Yes, sir."

"Holstered?"

"The guy by the car. The other one had his in his right hand. We figured we just happened on the scene or someone would have taken the weapon."

Or not. People tended to hide for a while after shots were fired, particularly if they had nothing to do with the shootings but might get blamed anyway.

Bryce tried to open the passenger door on the second sedan, but it was locked. He walked around to the driver's door. Locked as well.

"No one looked inside this car?"

"No, sir. We figured crime scene would do it."

"But they haven't been here yet?" Bryce asked.

"No, sir. Like I said—"

"You didn't think it important."

Voight straightened. "It's not that I didn't think it was important, sir. If I'd been in charge of this scene, I'd've called for an investigative team immediately. But I wasn't. And the coroner took his own sweet time getting here. My partner didn't want to even stay, but I made sure we did. We protected the scene, sir."

"You did a good job," O'Reilly said.

Voight glared at him, obviously not liking to be patronized.

"You thought it was important, Officer," Bryce said. "Why is that?"

Voight opened his mouth, then closed it. He looked at O'Reilly, looked at Bryce, then back at O'Reilly again. Bryce could see the battle he was waging inside himself. Voight had the same tendencies Bryce did—and like Bryce at that age, knew enough not to blurt out the first thought that ran through his head.

"It's all right, Officer," Bryce said. "You can be blunt."

"Two dead men, sir. I don't care what goes on in this neighborhood. I don't even care why they were here. Sir, they were murdered, and we should treat them with the same respect we use for victims we find on Park Avenue."

Bryce let the words hang for a moment. Voight shifted from foot to foot. O'Reilly didn't move at all.

"You're right, officer," Bryce said. "We should treat everyone the same. It's clear that the NYPD does not. You should be commended for doing the right thing. In this case, you probably will. Had these two men been someone other than who they are, you probably wouldn't have. You do know that."

"I don't like it, sir."

Bryce smiled. The smile was a bitter one. How many times had he said that to a superior officer? How many times had the superior officer responded with, *You don't have to like it, agent. Just do your damn job.*

"Well," Bryce said. "It turns out that in this case you were right. These are FBI agents. You do know that, right?"

"Yes, sir. The coroner told us that when he looked in their wallets."

And he still hadn't called it in. Bryce bit back some irritation. The man assumed too much.

"Did you find car keys on either of the victims?" Bryce asked.

"No, sir," Voight said. "And I helped the coroner when he first arrived."

"Then start looking. See if they got dropped in the struggle."

Although Bryce doubted they had.

"I got something in my car to jimmy the lock," O'Reilly said.

Bryce nodded.

O'Reilly left his side for the first time since Bryce had arrived. He apparently figured he could catch up. Or maybe he assumed that Bryce wouldn't tamper with this part of the scene.

Not that there was much to tamper with.

Bryce stood back, surveying the whole thing. He didn't like how he was thinking. It was making his heartburn grow worse.

But it was the only thing that made sense.

Agents worked HooverWatch in pairs. There were two dead agents and two cars. If the second sedan was backup, there should have been four agents and two cars.

But it didn't look that way. It looked like someone had pulled up behind the HooverWatch vehicle and gotten out, carefully locking the door.

Then he went to the door of the HooverWatch car. The driver had gotten out to talk to him, and the new guy shot him.

At that point, the second HooverWatch agent was an easy target. He scrambled out of the car, grabbed his own weapon, and headed across the street—maybe shooting as he went. The shooter got him, and then casually walked up the street to the limosine, which he had to know was there because it was barely visible in the shadowy light.

As the shooter approached the limosine, the limosine driver lowered his window. He would have recognized the approaching man, and thought he was going to report on the danger.

Instead, the man shot him, then went to lie in wait for Hoover and Tolson.

Bryce shivered. It would have happened very fast, and long before the beat cops showed up.

The guy in the street had time to bleed out. The limosine driver couldn't warn his boss. And the beat cops hadn't heard the shots in the alley, which they would have on such a quiet night.

O'Reilly brought the jimmy, shoved it into the space between the window and the lock, and flipped the lock up with a single movement. Then he opened the door.

No keys in the ignition.

Bryce flipped open the glove box. Nothing inside but the vehicle registration. Which, as he expected, identified it as an FBI vehicle.

The shooter had planned to come back. He'd planned to drive away in this car. But he got delayed. And by the time he got here, the two beat cops were on scene. He couldn't get his car.

So he had to improvise. He probably walked away or took the subway, hoping the cops would think the extra car belonged to one of the victims.

And that was his mistake.

"How come you guys were here in the middle of the night?" Bryce asked Voight.

Voight swallowed. It was the first sign of nervousness he'd shown. "This is part of our beat."

"But?" Bryce asked.

Voight looked away. "We're supposed to go up Central Park West."

"And you don't."

"Yeah, we do. Just not every time."

"Because?"

"Because I figure, you know, when the bars let out, we could, you know, let our presence be known."

"Prevent a lifestyle kill."

"Yes, sir."

"And you care about this because…?"

"Everyone should," Voight snapped. "Serve and protect, right, sir?"

Voight was touchy. He thought Bryce was accusing him of protecting the lifestyle because he lived it.

"Does your partner like this drive?" Bryce asked.

"He complains, sir, but he lets me do it."

"Have you stopped any crimes?"

"Broken up a few fights," Voight said.

"But not something like this."

"No, sir."

"You don't patrol every night, do you, Voight?"

"No, sir. We get different regions different nights."

"Do you think our killer would have thought that this street was unprotected?"

"It usually is, sir."

O'Reilly was frowning, but not at Voight. At Bryce. "You think the killer knew all this?" O'Reilly asked.

Bryce didn't answer. This was a Bureau matter, and he wasn't sure how the Bureau would handle it.

But he did think the killing was planned. He had a hunch it would be easy to solve because of the abandoned sedan.

And that abandoned sedan bothered him more than he wanted to admit. Because the presence of that sedan meant only one thing: The person who had shot all five FBI agents was—almost without a doubt—an FBI agent himself.

8

OF THE TWENTY AGENTS GATHERED at FBI headquarters that night, Haskell only trusted four. He tapped them, brought them into the corridor outside the Attorney General's office, and explained to them that they had special orders from the President.

Difficult orders, pertaining to the files.

Everyone knew what he meant by *the files*, and he suspected at least two of the agents—Barrett Keyes and Jasper Livingston—knew why the President was giving such an order. All four men looked serious and a little frightened.

Coming on the heels of the Kennedy assassination, anything odd in the middle of the night was going to unnerve the most hardened FBI agent.

Now Haskell was tapping them for an assignment that, if handled incorrectly, could cost them their careers. Hoover (if he was indeed still alive) wouldn't take kindly to the argument that the men were just following orders.

Haskell led them across the hall to the Director's sanctum. It was composed of several rooms. Through the double wood doors, the agents entered Helen Gandy's office, which doubled as reception.

Then there was the waiting area—filled with souvenirs from the Director's career, including a plaster of Paris death mask made of John Dillinger—and the Director's private office suite.

The five men stopped inside Helen Gandy's office. Her large desk sat squarely in front of two more large double doors. Above them was the seal of the Federal Government; on either side of them, two American flags—one an original Colonial flag and the other a modern flag with its brand new fifty stars.

"We guard this," Haskell said. "No one gets in or out. No one touches any file or any file folder on any desk. This order came directly from the President, but I don't have to tell you that some in this Bureau will fight it. I'm trusting you to serve your President."

He didn't add the rest of the sentence because they all probably heard it anyway: *I'm trusting you to serve your President, not the Director of the FBI.*

The men nodded, and he helped them map out a small strategy.

Then he took the most difficult post, the one in the corridor. He stood in front of the doors leading into Miss Gandy's office, after he made sure the doors were locked.

He hadn't been there fifteen minutes when the voices in the nearby corridor grew slowly silent. He felt his cheeks grow warm. He wondered if the Assistant Director had come out into the group to let them know Hoover was dead.

And then he saw the cause of the silence. She swept into the corridor like a tiny dynamo.

Helen Gandy had to be in her late sixties, but she struggled not to show it. Her permed hair was dyed an even, reddish-brown color that no longer suited her pale skin. She had put on some weight in her forty-plus years as Hoover's secretary and that weight made her look solid.

It had also given her a bit of a double chin. She jutted that chin forward now, and her dark eyes flashed.

"You may move," she said to Haskell. "I'm here now."

He crossed his arms. "I'm sorry, ma'am, but no one is allowed inside."

She raised her penciled eyebrows. Her makeup was as perfect as it had been that morning, her lipstick fresh and her rouge well-blended into her powder-covered skin. She smelled faintly of lilac water.

She wore a black business dress with padded shoulders which, unlike his suit, was not the same outfit she'd worn earlier in the day. A pearl and diamond brooch glittered on one large lapel.

She looked like a woman prepared for a new day.

She looked like a woman prepared for battle.

"As you know, Agent Haskell," she said, "such orders never include me."

"I'm sorry, ma'am. Tonight they do."

He kept his voice low. He didn't want anyone in the outer area to hear.

Miss Gandy gave him a withering stare, the one that had nearly destroyed him when he'd been brought to this suite of offices as a brand new agent, after getting his "Meet the Boss" training before his introduction to the Director. She had frightened him more than Hoover had.

"On whose authority?" she asked in a chillingly cold voice.

"The President of the United States, ma'am."

"Surely, President Johnson did not mean me."

"Ma'am, my instructions are explicit. No one, not even you, is allowed inside."

She straightened. For a moment, he thought she was going to hit him with her purse. But she didn't.

Instead, she said with a precision that reminded him of his first-grade teacher, "In cases like this, the Director has express orders that require me to remove his personal items from his office."

So there it was. Oblique confirmation that something had happened to the Director, something awful.

Haskell's shoulders relaxed, although he kept his stern posture. He wasn't going to lose his job. He had already tied himself to the new regime, whatever that was going to be.

"I'm sorry, ma'am," he said gently. "Because of tonight's events, the Director's orders no longer stand."

She poked him in the chest with one bony finger. "It is precisely because of tonight's events, Agent Haskell, that I need to get in there."

He didn't move.

After a moment, she realized he wasn't going to. She let her hand fall, then clutched her purse against her stomach. Her lower lip trembled.

He found this display more disturbing than her anger had been.

"I have a few personal items that I'd like to get, if you don't mind. And the Director instructed me that in the case of..." and for the first time, she paused. Her voice didn't break nor did she clear her throat. But she seemed to need a moment to gather herself. "In case of emergency, I was to remove some of his personal items as well."

"If you could tell me what they are, ma'am, I'll get them."

Her eyes narrowed. "The Director doesn't like others to touch his possessions."

"I'm sorry, ma'am," he said, gambling that Hoover was really and truly dead. "But I don't think that matters any longer."

She stared at Haskell for a long moment. He watched as she slowly realized that her status had changed in the space of a few hours. Anguish showed in her eyes.

That anguish was the best confirmation he could have. Hoover wasn't just incapacitated. He was dead.

Any other woman would have broken down. But Helen Gandy wasn't any woman. Haskell watched her mood change from anguish to realization to something akin to panic.

"It still matters," she said. "Now if you'll excuse me..."

She tried to wriggle past him. She was wiry and stronger than he expected. He had to put out an arm to block her.

"Ma'am," he said in the gentlest tone he could summon, "the President's orders supersede the Director's."

How often had he wanted to say that over the years? How often had he wanted to remind everyone in the Bureau that the President led the Free World, not J. Edgar Hoover.

"In this instance," she snapped, "they do not."

"Ma'am, I'd hate to have some agents restrain you." But he'd only hate it because it would call attention to what he was doing. Otherwise, he might enjoy watching the rude and unyielding Helen Gandy get pulled away by some of his agents.

"You wouldn't dare," she said.

"Ma'am," he replied in that same gentle voice he'd been using all along. "You're distraught."

"I am not." She clipped each word.

"You are because I say you are, ma'am."

She raised her chin. For a moment, he thought she hadn't understood. But she finally did.

The balance of power had shifted completely. It was now on his side.

"Do I have to call the President then to get my personal effects?" she asked.

But they both knew she wasn't talking about her personal things. And the President was smart enough to know that as well. As hungry to get those files as the Attorney General had seemed despite his Eastern reserve, the President would be utterly ravenous. He wouldn't let some old skirt, as he'd been known to call Miss Gandy, get in his way.

"Go ahead," Haskell said. "Feel free to use the phone in the office across the hall."

She glared at him, then turned on one foot and marched down the corridor. But she didn't head toward a phone—at least not one he could see.

He wondered who she would call. The President wouldn't listen. The Attorney General had issued the order in the President's name. Maybe she would talk to one of Hoover's Assistant Directors, the four or five men that Hoover had in his pocket.

Haskell had been waiting for them. But they still hadn't figured out what he was doing. They were probably in their offices, following the Director's secret protocols, just like Helen Gandy was supposed to be doing.

Someone would be here soon. Someone other than Helen Gandy. She was just the first volley. Others would make the same attempt to get at these files.

Haskell shifted slightly. Sometimes he wished he hadn't let the A.G. know how he felt about the Director. Sometimes he wished he were still a humble assistant, the man who had joined the FBI because he wanted to be a top cop like his hero J. Edgar Hoover.

A so-called hero who, it turned out, never made a real arrest or fired a gun or even understood investigation.

There was a lot to admire about the Director—no matter what people said, he'd built a hell of an agency almost from scratch—but he wasn't the man his press made him out to be.

And that was the source of Haskell's disillusionment. He'd wanted to be a top cop. Instead, he snooped into homes and businesses and sometimes even investigated fairly blameless people, looking for a mistake in their past.

Since he'd been transferred to FBI HQ, he hadn't done any real investigating at all. His arrests had slowed, his cases dwindled.

And he'd found himself investigating his boss, trying to find out where the legend ended and the man began. Once he realized that the old man was just a bureaucrat who had learned where all the bodies were buried and had used that to make everyone bow to his bidding, Haskell was ripe for the undercover work the A.G. had asked him to do.

Only now he wasn't undercover any more. Now he was standing in the open before the Director's cache of secrets, on the President's orders, hoping that no one would call his bluff.

9

DETECTIVE SEAMUS O'REILLY stood beside the beat cops and watched Agent Bryce work. The man was a good investigator. He didn't seem to miss a detail.

O'Reilly had his notebook out and wrote down everything Bryce told him to. Then, when Bryce wasn't looking, O'Reilly flipped the pages and copied the same notes deeper into the book. That included the license plate number of the sedans—something O'Reilly found curious since the registration inside the locked sedan clearly identified it as an FBI vehicle.

Something about the sedans intrigued Bryce. After he'd looked at them closely, Bryce had stopped talking. He'd found something wrong, something outside of procedure.

So while he was examining the hole in the ice for the third time, O'Reilly peered into the cars again.

And found something that bothered him.

If the sedans belonged to Hoover's bodyguards, then either the men were very different or one had just arrived to relieve the other. Still, cops on stakeout duty worked in pairs, but it seemed like these agents were working alone.

Or someone was missing.

The first car had two Styrofoam cups, food wrappers on both sides of the front seat, and the usual mess of a stakeout. The windshield on the passenger side was smudged, probably from a hand wiping it clear as it fogged up. It was impossible to tell if the other two windshields had been smudged. Both were covered in blood.

The second car was pristine. No smudges on the windows, no Styrofoam cups, no half-smoked cigarettes. If O'Reilly had to guess, he would have thought that the second car had just been taken from the motor pool. The first had been on the street for a while.

Which begged that same question: Were these bodyguards working alone? Because if they weren't, then the third man—or the third and fourth men—were missing.

Kidnapped? Hiding? Wounded?

He felt his breath catch. Bryce might be good at evidence and investigating a scene, but FBI agents rarely did hot scenes. They worked cold scenes. And a man could take his time with a cold scene.

O'Reilly tucked the notebook into the pocket of his overcoat, then walked toward Bryce.

"I think we have a problem," he said as he approached.

Bryce didn't even look up. He was examining the edges of that hole, using the flashlight to illuminate all parts of it. Blood had pooled on the asphalt below and was probably chilling enough so that it would be sludge by the time the scene of the crime guys got here.

"Hey," O'Reilly said. "We have a problem."

This time, Bryce looked up.

"You guys work surveillance and protection in pairs, right?"

Something crossed Bryce's face—a look that, had he been a suspect, O'Reilly would have taken for guilt.

"Yeah, why?"

"Tell me if I'm wrong here, but sedan number two looks pretty untouched. So we're missing at least one guy, maybe two. The backup bodyguards? Or do you usually have two sedans on protection?"

"Depends," Bryce said.

O'Reilly was now sure that the two sedans were what had shut Bryce up. And it was Bryce's knowledge of procedure that worried him. Something had gone wrong with procedure. Something that had given Bryce some answers to this mess.

"Let's just say in this case," O'Reilly said.

Bryce shrugged. "Usually there'd be two men in one car. If it was going to be all night, we'd relieve them after twelve hours."

O'Reilly frowned. Twelve hours couldn't have gone by at that party. The timeline didn't work.

But if Hoover had been up here for another reason, then it might work.

"All I'm saying," O'Reilly said, "is that the two cars leads me to think that there should be four bodies here. Or at least three. And there were only two."

"Yeah." Bryce spoke softly. Clearly he'd already figured that out.

"So where are the other two? Have they been taken? Are they being held hostage? Are they in one of these half-empty buildings, bleeding out?"

"Jesus." Bryce stood. Obviously he hadn't thought of that. "We'll need to canvas now."

O'Reilly nodded. "Thought you'd say that. But that means calling even more squads down here, and since you feebees are supposed to be in charge of the scene, I thought maybe you'd want to call your guys."

He couldn't help the needling. It'd been at least an hour since Bryce showed up. It didn't take anyone an hour to get across Manhattan at this time of night. The FBI should have been swarming this place, and they weren't.

"Just do it." Bryce shook his head. "I can be so thick at times."

O'Reilly suddenly felt petty. Bryce was clearly upset. There might be two dying agents somewhere in this neighborhood, and neither man had thought to look for them until now.

"Shit happens," O'Reilly said. "You're not used to working hot."

"I'm used to working alone, too," Bryce said. "If I'd told you what I suspected we could've started that search twenty minutes ago."

"I'll go to the radio car," O'Reilly said. "We'll start now."

"If they're dead when we find them—" Bryce started.

"Then it's the shooter's fault." O'Reilly put a hand on Bryce's arm and led him out of the street. "C'mon. Let's start the canvas."

"I gotta make a call first, see where my men are."

"You do that." O'Reilly let him go when they approached the squad. O'Reilly leaned in, gave his badge number, and requested more men on the scene.

The FBI wouldn't like that. The more men on scene, the more leaks to the press.

But the FBI had sent one guy to button this whole thing up and they weren't giving him any support. They could complain all they wanted, but this mess was their fault.

As O'Reilly answered the dispatch's questions, his gaze wandered back to the sedans. The locked doors still bothered him. Who locked their door in the middle of a crisis?

Had he read the scene wrong? Was Bryce protecting everything because he thought someone in an FBI sedan had been the shooter?

O'Reilly squeezed the handheld mike a little too tight, making the dispatch complain about the feedback. He apologized, but didn't stop looking at the car.

Someone posing as an FBI agent helped the scene make sense. That's why one man had stepped out of the first car, why the other had to flee after his partner was shot.

It would explain why Crawford's window was down. If the man heard shots, then had someone knock on his window and press an FBI badge against it, Crawford would've had no qualms about rolling that window down.

O'Reilly finished with his radio call, then sat in the front seat of the squad. This scenario made more sense than some kind of shootout down here.

But he'd been to maybe a thousand crime scenes in his career and a good half of them never made sense.

He'd learned long ago not to assume.

No matter how tempting it was.

10

THE PAYPHONE WAS HALF A BLOCK AWAY, shrouded in darkness. It smelled of sweat and urine. Bryce did not close the door because the smell was so strong.

He wiped off the handset with his gloves, then put the thing against his ear. It was ice cold. He dialed Headquarters and asked for the motor pool. The late-night operator sounded surprised.

Apparently no one called for a car at three a.m.

It took several rings before someone answered. Gus, the mechanic whom Bryce had always asked for back when he'd had a regularly assigned car, was the one who growled into the phone.

"Hey, Gus, you there alone?" Bryce asked after identifying himself.

"Some new hire's manning the phones, but he dozed half an hour ago. What can I do you for, Agent Bryce?"

"I have some license plates I want you to verify against our records. I think the cars were signed out tonight. Can you tell me who has them?"

"Sure thing."

Bryce could hear paper shuffling, then Gus coughed. In the background, a radio played some dance music that sounded horribly out of place.

"Okay. Read me them numbers," Gus said.

Bryce read off the numbers on both plates. Then he waited some more as Gus looked through the paperwork.

"Got your first one," Gus said. "Signed out by Wade Stockton. You know him?"

Bryce did know him. He knew almost everyone in the office, at least by name. "When?"

"About five. Doesn't say who was with him, if anybody."

"Thanks," Bryce said. "And the other?"

"Still looking. This crap isn't in order. You'd think with all the god-damn regulations and D.C. on our backs all the time to fill this stuff out proper, that it'd be right from the get-go. I tell you, my paperwork is always right. I fill out each section on each car, no matter what a pain in the patootie it all is."

Bryce would have interrupted the monologue, except that he heard more rustling paper. He'd also worked with Gus on several occasions and knew that the man talked almost continually, yet somehow managed to get the job done.

"Here it is. Ah, shit. It's that poor kid."

Bryce's breath caught. There were very few agents in the regional office who could be called a poor kid. He was almost afraid to ask for clarification, but he did anyway.

"Who's that?"

"You know, the one what lost his fiancée yesterday. Walt Cain. Hell, I'd've thought twice about giving him a brand new sedan, but he probably had family stuff to take care of. Poor kid. What a thing. Sometimes I hate this place with all its goddamn rules. If he'd been a security guard, him and that pretty girl'd be married now. I tell you..."

Bryce tuned him out. He leaned against the cold glass of the booth, trying to catch his breath. Walter Cain.

Walter Cain was on bereavement leave. Bryce had signed him up for it before going over to tell him about Essie's suicide.

And when he had told Cain about the leave, Cain had glared at him. Bryce wasn't even sure Cain had understood what Bryce had told him, so Bryce left the paperwork.

He had also planned on following up the next day.

Today, actually.

In just a few hours.

Amazing how plans changed.

"You sure?" Bryce said, interrupting Gus. "You sure you're not looking at last week's log or something?"

"Yeah," Gus said. "Strangest goddamn thing. But sometimes the Bureau does right. That kid's been going through enough, and that girl dying like that, anyone'd be messed up. Sure hope he can drive upset. Some folks can't, you know."

"I know." Bryce turned inside the booth, squinted that half block up the road, but could only faintly make out the cars. O'Reilly was moving his flashlight, telling the beat cops to begin the canvas.

Had Cain just gone back to the job, trying to forget what happened? Was he one of the missing agents? Could he be lying, bleeding out in one of these buildings?

Bryce wasn't sure he could take the irony.

"Hey, Gus," he said, interrupting again. "Does it say on the slip what he took the car for or how long he planned to have it?"

"Nope."

"When did he sign it out?"

"Ahhhh." Gus elongated the sound as he thumbed through the paperwork again. "Signed out at 10:15."

"P.M.?"

"Yep. Say, Bryce, what're you asking for? The kid didn't crack up the car, did he?"

"No," Bryce said, relieved he didn't have to lie about that. "The kid didn't crack up the car."

"Thank the Lord for small favors. People're more likely to have accidents when they're upset and tired, you know."

"I do," Bryce said.

"And I suppose you can't tell me why the inquiry, right?"

"I'm not supposed to," Bryce lied. Technically, he didn't have to keep this secret. No one had asked him to—not yet. "Gus, can you transfer me upstairs?"

"Sure, but I doubt anyone's up there. I'm usually alone around these parts in the wee small hours."

"You work them often?"

"I'm the only competent mechanic you assholes got. I'm working twelve, eighteen hours to keep those fancy cars in speeding shape. Yeah. I'm here while you're at your desk and while you're sleeping in your fancy apartment."

Gus had dropped him off at the apartment once, and hadn't gotten over it. Bryce smiled at the normality of the dig.

"Thanks, Gus. Transfer me, okay?"

After a few clicks, Gus managed to put him on hold. There were a few more clicks before the operator picked up.

Bryce asked for Hart. She connected him, but the phone in Hart's office just rang and rang. When the operator picked up again, Bryce asked for the floor phone.

No one answered that, either.

He glanced at his watch. He'd been on scene more than an hour and no one had come to relieve him.

No one was down here trying to find out what happened or if there were missing agents. The idiots in his office were trying to prevent leaks and were probably calling Washington just to protect their own butts.

He hung up the phone, keeping a hand on the receiver for just a moment. His head ached from the smell and the cold.

Cain. Why would Cain ask for a car and why would it end up here? Did he know Stockton? Was Cain supposed to be on HooverWatch and had blown it off?

Bryce took a deep breath, then stepped out of the booth. To hell with regulation. To hell with his orders. He was going to let the NYPD run this scene.

Someone had to. And the FBI wasn't following through. If he got fired over this, so be it.

It wasn't like they wanted to keep him on the job anyway.

Better that he went out doing something right than trying to follow orders that made no sense.

He walked up the half block. He would get a flashlight from one of the beat cops and join the canvas.

It was the least he could do.

11

KENNEDY TOOK THE ELEVATOR to the fifth floor of the Justice Department. His drive in from McLean had been a combination of daring and distraction. He'd managed not to slide on the light coating of snow covering the roads, but he might have gone through two—maybe three—red lights.

Fortunately no one was on the roads to pick him up. In fact, there had been no lights anywhere until he'd reached the heart of D.C. The monuments were lit, as they always were, and so was the White House, looking like a photograph in the darkness.

Justice itself, which should have been dark, had lights on throughout. Any reporter driving by would know that something was happening just by the number of office lights illuminated.

As Kennedy stepped off the elevator, he was surprised to see two high-ranking FBI agents standing by the doors. Both men looked nervous until they recognized him.

He realized they had been watching the elevator come up, waiting to see who emerged, so that they would know who was in the building.

"Attorney General Kennedy, sir," said the nearest man, whose name Kennedy couldn't remember. "You've heard then."

So the word was spreading—whatever the word was. "Not the details," he said.

"Would you like someone to brief you, sir?" asked the other agent.

"I believe it's protocol to brief me first," Kennedy said, "but to hell with that tonight. Why don't you guys tell me what you know."

"Not a lot," said the first. "Just that the Director is dead."

"And the Associate Director, too," said the other.

Kennedy hadn't expected anything to happen to Tolson. He crossed his arms. "A car accident then?"

"They're not releasing cause of death yet."

"I understand both men were in New York," Kennedy said.

"That's right, sir. We don't know much else."

Kennedy nodded. "I'm going to check on a few things and then I'll be in my office. Send someone to me for an official briefing in about—" he glanced at his watch "—fifteen minutes. Has anyone notified the President?"

"I don't know, sir," the first agent said.

"Well, technically that's my responsibility," Kennedy said, and he wanted to retain control of that responsibility. He wasn't sure when he'd get around to telling Johnson. Probably as soon as he knew that the files were secure.

"Yes, sir," said the first agent. "We'll let Assistant Director Ross know."

Kennedy nodded and headed down the corridor. His office was just across the hall from Hoover's—something Kennedy had set up the moment he'd become Attorney General, much to Hoover's disgust.

So the old man was dead. Kennedy wasn't sorry. He hoped he'd shown the appropriate amount of concern back there by the elevators, but deep down he didn't care.

He might have cared ten years ago, but since the day that Jack died, Kennedy and Hoover were more than two men who fought over control of the Justice Department. They'd become enemies, whether Hoover knew it or not.

For a moment, Kennedy flashed back to that unseasonably warm afternoon in November. He'd been sitting by the pool at Hickory Hill with the Federal Attorney for New York City, Robert Morganthau, and the chief of Morganthau's criminal division, Silvio Mollo. They were planning the upcoming prosecutions of various organized crime figures, including Kennedy's nemesis, the head of the Teamsters Union, James Hoffa.

Kennedy could still remember the glint of the sunlight on the clear water, the taste of the tuna fish sandwich Ethel had brought him, the way the men—despite their topic—had seemed lighthearted.

Then the phone rang, and J. Edgar Hoover was on the line. Kennedy almost didn't take the call, but he eventually did and Hoover's cold voice said without preamble, *I have news for you. The President's been shot.*

Nothing else. Just *The President's been shot.* No condolences, no sympathetic tone. If anything, he might have had a thread of glee in his voice.

Hoover had warned Kennedy that his brother's recklessness would get him killed one day. And that phone call felt not so much like a notification as an "I-told-you-so."

The fat bastard hadn't even changed his plans that night. He'd gone to the track with Tolson to play the ponies, just like they'd planned.

Kennedy clenched a fist at the memory. He had to keep control of his emotions to get through the next few hours. He couldn't think about Hoover and he couldn't think about the implications of the shooting.

Kennedy had to complete his mission, and then he'd worry about what was going to happen next.

Throughout the corridor, men sat in their offices, their doors open. A few agents were on the phone. Others sat with their head in their hands or stared out a nearby window.

It took Kennedy a moment to realize these underlings were actually mourning Hoover. Somehow that man had commanded not just loyalty but some kind of odd affection.

Kennedy couldn't understand it. Hoover was cold and superior. He wiped his palms with a tissue after he shook someone's hand. He rarely smiled.

Kennedy had always figured that the loyalty the old man inspired came from fear. It startled him to think it might also have come from some kind of genuine feeling.

He shook off the thought and headed not to his office, but to Hoover's. As he passed one final door, he saw Helen Gandy inside, clutching her purse like it was a shield. She was talking to an agent Kennedy didn't recognize.

She looked like she had just come from the beauty salon. He had never seen her look anything less than completely put together, but he was surprised by her perfect appearance on this night, after the news that her long-time boss was dead.

Kennedy tugged at the overcoat he'd put on over his favorite sweater. He hadn't taken the time to change or even comb his hair. He probably looked as tousled as he had in the days after Jack died.

Although, for the first time in three months, Kennedy felt like he had a purpose. He didn't know how long this feeling would last, or how long he wanted it to. But this death had given him an odd kind of hope that control was coming back into his world.

Haskell stood in front of the Director's office suite, arms crossed. The man was taller than Kennedy remembered, and thinner. His suit coat bulged over his shoulder holster.

He looked tired—and prepared to take on anyone.

When he saw Kennedy, Haskell's shoulders visibly relaxed.

"Was that the dragon lady I just saw?" Kennedy asked.

"She wanted to get some personal effects from her office," Haskell said.

"Did you let her?"

"No." And the tension in Haskell's voice told Kennedy how difficult that refusal had been. "You said the orders were to secure it, so I have."

"Excellent." Kennedy glanced in both directions and saw no one in the corridor. "Make sure your staff continues to protect the doors. I'm going inside."

"Sir?" Haskell raised his eyebrows.

"I'm going to make sure the files are here," Kennedy said. "I'm worried that he moved everything to his house."

The lie came easily. Kennedy would have heard if Hoover had moved files to his own home. But Haskell didn't know that.

Haskell unlocked the doors and moved away. Two more agents stood inside, guarding the interior doors.

"Give me a minute, please, gentlemen," Kennedy said.

The men nodded and went outside.

Kennedy stopped and took a deep breath. He had been in Miss Gandy's office countless times, but he had never really looked at it. He'd always been staring at the door to Hoover's inner sanctum, waiting for it to open and the old man to come out.

That office was interesting. In the antechamber, Hoover had memorabilia and photographs from his major cases. He even had the plaster-of-Paris death mask of John Dillinger on display. It was a ghastly thing, which made Kennedy think of the way that English kings used to keep severed heads on the entrance to London Bridge to warn traitors of their potential fate.

But this office had always looked like a waiting room to him. Nothing very special. The woman behind the desk was the focal point. Jack had been the one who nicknamed her the Dragon Lady and had even called her that to her face once, only with his trademark grin, so infectious that she hadn't made a sound or a grimace in protest.

Of course, she hadn't smiled back either.

Her desk was clear except for a blotter, a telephone, and a jar of pens. A typewriter sat on a credenza with paper stacked beside it.

But it wasn't the desk that interested him the most. It was the floor-to-ceiling filing cabinets and storage bins. He walked to them. Instead of the typical system—marked by letters of the alphabet—this one had numbers that were clearly part of a code.

He pulled open the nearest drawer and found row after row of accordion files, each with its own number, and manila folders with the first number set followed by another. He cursed softly under his breath.

Of course the old dog wouldn't file his confidentials by name. He'd use a secret code. The old man liked nothing more than his secrets.

Still, Kennedy opened half a dozen drawers just to see if the system continued throughout. And it wasn't until he got to a bin near the corner of the desk that he found a file labeled "Obscene."

His hand shook as he pulled it out. Jack, for all his brilliance, had been sexually insatiable. Back when their brother Joe was still alive and no one ever thought Jack would be running for president, Jack had had an affair with a Danish émigré named Inga Arvad. Inga Binga, as Jack used to call her, was married to a man with ties to Hitler. She'd even met and liked Der Führer, and had said so in print.

She'd been the target of FBI surveillance as a possible spy, and during that surveillance who should turn up in her bed but a young naval lieutenant whose father had once been Ambassador to England. The Ambassador, as he preferred to be called even by his sons, found out about the affair and told Jack in no uncertain terms to end it. Then the Ambassador guaranteed the affair ended by assigning Jack to a PT boat in the Pacific, as far from Inga Binga as possible.

Kennedy had always suspected that Hoover had leaked the information to the Ambassador, but he hadn't known for certain until Jack became President.

The day after the inauguration, Hoover had asked for and had received an audience with the President and his brother. They'd met in the Oval Office. Hoover had brought just one piece of paper with him, but on it were several names and even more dates.

One of the names was Inga Arvad. There were others, details that Kennedy didn't know and didn't want to know, and there would be more over the years as Jack's behavior continued unabated, maybe even exacerbated by Jack's aides, Kenny O'Donnell and Dave Powers, and the heady feeling of being the President of the United States.

Not that it mattered then. What mattered was that smarmy look on Hoover's face and the flat look on Jack's, confirming everything.

Hoover didn't make any threats; he didn't have to. Jack's expression was enough for both of them.

But Kennedy was furious. He hated being blackmailed, and he must have shown it, because Hoover turned to him, and said with an extension of that smarmy smile, *Ever since the war, I have been surveilling you and your siblings. I've done so at your father's request. He knew what kind of trouble you all could get into. I made sure that certain activities got reported to him, and then he curtailed them.*

Jack was still staring at the paper. Kennedy felt the blood rush to his face. He wanted nothing more than to deck the old man.

Or he forced you to curtail them. Hoover smiled at Jack. *Shame about Miss Arvad. I have a hunch she would have been a much more interesting companion than the not-nearly-as-experienced Miss Bouvier.*

That was when Jack whirled on the old man, and Kennedy had had to catch his arms. Jack might have treated Jackie like crap, but he did love her in his own way, and he never tolerated anyone saying anything bad about her.

Hoover had put his fat hands up like a man who wasn't surprised at being threatened. *I'm just saying…*

We understand what you're saying, Kennedy snapped. *You can leave now.*

Somehow he hadn't added, *you fat fuck,* like he wanted to.

Hoover had nodded and left. And that was when Kennedy reminded Jack that Hoover would hit mandatory retirement age at the beginning of their second term.

If I can't drive him out before then, Kennedy had said, *I'll make sure he goes the day the law says he has to.*

Jack had seemed reassured. Kennedy wasn't, and he'd kept an eye on the old man ever since. He had always wanted a way to get to those files.

And now he had them.

Or so he thought.

Kennedy opened the file, and was shocked to see Richard Nixon's name on the pink sheets inside. Kennedy thumbed through quickly. There wasn't anything in this file of a sexual nature at all. It was about taxes and men with strange names. It seemed to be written in some kind of shorthand.

Kennedy would look at these later. Nixon, despite what he'd told the press after losing the California Governor's race a few years ago, was still around, making pronouncements and testing the waters for a presidential bid later in the year.

Kennedy doubted such a bid would be successful—the entire country saw Nixon as a failure. Yet Hoover had kept files on Nixon just to be safe.

That old bastard really and truly had known where all the bodies were buried. And it wouldn't be easy to find them.

Kennedy took a deep breath. He stood, shoved his hands in his pockets, and surveyed the walls of files. It would take days to search each folder. He didn't have days. He probably didn't have hours.

But he was Hoover's immediate supervisor, whether the old man had recognized it or not. Hoover answered to him. Which meant that the files belonged to the Justice Department, of which the FBI was only one small part.

Kennedy glanced at his watch. No one had pounded on the door. If he didn't call Johnson like he'd offered to, he probably had until dawn before someone tried to stop him. If he was really lucky, no one would think of the files until mid-morning.

He went to the door and beckoned Haskell inside.

"We're taking the files to my office," he said.

"All of them, sir?"

"All of them. These first, then whatever is in Hoover's office, and then any other confidential files you can find."

Haskell looked up the wall as if he couldn't believe the command. "That'll take some time, sir."

"Not if you get a lot of people to help."

"Sir, I thought you wanted to keep this secret."

He did. But it wouldn't remain secret for long. So he had to control when the information got out—just like he had to control the information itself.

"Get this done as quickly as possible," Kennedy said.

Haskell nodded and turned the doorknob, but Kennedy stopped him before he went out.

"These are filed by code," he said. "Do you know where the key is?"

"I was told that Miss Gandy had the keys to everything from codes to offices," Haskell said.

Kennedy felt a shiver run through him. Knowing Hoover, he would have made sure he had the key to the Attorney General's office as well.

"Do you have any idea where she might have kept the code keys?" Kennedy asked.

"No," Haskell said. "I wasn't part of the need-to-know group. I already knew too much."

Kennedy nodded. He appreciated how much Haskell had learned over the years. It had gotten him this far.

"On your way out," Kennedy said, "call building maintenance and have them change all the locks in my office."

"Yes, sir." Haskell kept his hand on the doorknob. "Are you sure you want to do this, sir? Couldn't you just change the locks here? Wouldn't that secure everything for the President?"

"Everyone in Washington wants these files," Kennedy said. "They're going to come to this office suite. They won't think of mine."

"Until they heard that you moved everything."

Kennedy nodded. "And then they'll know how futile their quest really is."

12

Six units canvassing the neighborhood, looking in alleys, rousting bums, knocking on doors, and finding nothing. Twelve cops that Bryce counted, plus himself, O'Reilly, and O'Reilly's partner McKinnon weren't turning up the missing FBI agents.

If there were missing FBI agents. Bryce wasn't so sure.

He pulled himself out of the canvas after going through three full buildings (and seeing such squalid conditions in one that he couldn't believe the family that lived there allowed their children to play in the hallway) and walked back to the phone booth.

This time, he pulled the door closed despite the smell. He wanted the light. He picked up the phone book. Most of the pages were gone, but he still managed to find Cain's listing.

Maybe this was all a false alarm. Maybe someone else had signed out the car for Cain or maybe the new secretary in the motor pool had written down the name wrong.

Or maybe Gus had been looking on the wrong day.

Bryce dialed Cain's number and prayed that he would answer. Of course, part of Bryce didn't want him to answer—explaining why he was calling in the middle of the night wouldn't be easy, particularly after their last encounter—but he'd rather do that than find an injured or possibly dead man.

Or worse.

Bryce held the cold receiver to his ear and listened to the distant ring.

"Come on," he whispered. "Pick up. Pick up."

No one did. He let it ring twenty times.

His stomach knotted so tightly he wondered if he'd ever get food down there again.

He didn't like what he was thinking. He was thinking maybe Cain *had* been down here—Cain, who in good times had professed a dislike for Hoover; Cain, who when he was reminded that his fiancée had to get vetted, snapped *How come no one vetted Tolson?*; Cain, who was the best shooter in the entire regional office.

Bryce depressed the disconnect. Then he hit it a few more times, until he rousted an operator. This time, he had her look up the number and dial it.

She did, and the damn thing just rang and rang and rang.

Finally, Bryce hung up. He pushed the door open, letting in cold fresh air which, somehow, did not dispel the stench of urine.

Then he stepped out. The cops were still looking. The coroner's van remained in the alley.

And Bryce's backup hadn't arrived yet.

If Cain was the shooter—if he had snapped and done this (and oh, it made some kind of strange sense; the agents in the first sedan would have trusted him until he fired that first shot)—then Bryce was somehow responsible.

Bryce, who told him about Essie's death.

Bryce, who had investigated Essie.

Bryce, who had given the full, damning report to Hart just a few days ago.

He couldn't quite let himself out of the booth. He picked up the phone again, and this time dialed the Regional office. When the operator answered, he asked for Hart.

Only to be told that Hart wasn't in the office. No one was.

Bryce hung up.

He was trapped here, with the NYPD and the biggest case of the year. Maybe even the biggest case of the century.

Someone had to back him up.

Someone had to find Cain.

Someone had to find evidence of a different shooter.

Because right now, Bryce didn't like the way this night was going.

And he somehow suspected it was going to get worse before—if—it was ever going to get better.

13

KENNEDY USED A SHARP METAL LETTER OPENER to break the lock on the bottom drawer of Helen Gandy's desk. He felt like a thief, even though he had to keep reminding himself he wasn't.

Everything in this building belonged to the Federal Government. And technically, everything in this building was under his jurisdiction as Attorney General. Even though Hoover hadn't really believed it.

Hardly anyone had believed it after Jack's death. Everyone knew that Hoover couldn't be tamed.

And now he was dead.

Kennedy pried the door open, wincing slightly at the overpowering scent of that lilac water Helen Gandy had sprayed on herself every morning since 1919.

The drawer held the index files he was looking for—the keys to the files that Haskell's trusted FBI agents were, even now, moving to Kennedy's office. Kennedy thumbed through the cards just to make sure.

He was beginning to recognize the numbering system. The key to the code was on the alphabetical dividers. Using that key, he looked up Jack's name, and winced again when he saw how many entries there were.

Kennedy made himself close the box. Then he set it beside his foot and pulled the drawer open farther. He found two more boxes of index cards and, in the very back, reel-to-reel tapes.

The small kind.

The kind he and Jack used to use in the Oval Office.

The ones Kennedy had gone in and confiscated the night Jack was murdered.

Hell, Kennedy hadn't just confiscated the tapes. He'd had one of his most trusted allies—the man who'd installed the system—dismantle it.

The tapes and the national security files and Jack's private files were in an office building not too far from here, under lock and key, with only Kennedy and Jackie having access. At some point the two of them would have to remove all those files, decide what to do with them, decide whether or not to destroy them, but for now, they waited.

Kennedy pulled out one of the tapes Hoover had stored. It was labeled by day and by hour. There had to be a secret taping system in Hoover's office as well.

Kennedy needed the tapes from that. He wouldn't need to dismantle it—the secret recorders were Hoover's problem, not Kennedy's—but he wanted all the material from it and he wanted it now.

He took the index files to his own office. The office was huge, and it took him a few minutes to walk across it. His office was as long as a football field, with stunning windows along the walls. The watercolors painted by his children had been covered by the cabinets. His furniture was pushed aside to make room for the bins, and file folders that were starting to trickle in. Even with the size of the office, this place would be overwhelmed soon enough.

He couldn't think about that. He needed to deal with the index cards and the tapes. He opened the safe behind his desk, and put the index card holders inside. Then he flipped the combination lock closed.

As he went back for the tapes, he passed two agents carrying two full file drawers each. The men were incredibly strong. He could see their muscles bulging through their suit coats.

Kennedy would have been at his limits carrying one. These men had already carried several drawers and hadn't even broken a sweat.

He dodged another agent carrying file drawers and went back to the tapes. He put them in a box and carried it across the hall.

He had just reached his office door when the phone rang.

Kennedy sighed. He'd better get used to that. It was going to be a long week, dealing with Hoover's death and all its implications, implications he hadn't wanted to think about yet, not while he was dealing with the files.

He set the tapes beside his own desk and picked up the phone. Then he turned so that he would face the door.

"Mr. Attorney General." The voice on the other end of the line sounded surprised. "Someone told me you were in the building. This is Assistant Director Curt Ross."

Kennedy decided to go on the offensive. "It's about time I heard from you, Mr. Ross. I would have thought you would have called me the moment that you heard there was a problem in New York."

Kennedy couldn't tell if the silence on the other end was because he hadn't used the man's title or because the man hadn't expected Kennedy's tone.

"I'm sorry, sir. I meant to—"

"Sorry?" Kennedy snapped. "*Sorry* doesn't cut it when you let a lowly secretary know about one of the most important events in this country before you let your boss know."

"Sir, I—"

"I'm coming to your office," Kennedy said, "and I want a complete debriefing. I want to know everything that happened, and I do mean everything."

"Yes, sir."

Kennedy hung up. Then he leaned on his desk for a long moment and made himself take a deep breath. He had just stalled again. The Assistant Director could have come here and seen the files being moved, but he hadn't.

Instead, he had called to see if Kennedy was there.

Fortunately.

Now Kennedy would go down the hall and keep the man busy for at least fifteen minutes, while Agent Haskell and his men unloaded Hoover's files into their temporary new home—the office of the Attorney General of the United States.

14

LYNDON BAINES JOHNSON, thirty-sixth President of the United States by way not of the people but of an assassin's bullet, sat on the long couch beneath the arched windows of the West Sitting Hall. He was wearing his brown robe and his pajamas, and his slippered feet were cold.

Beside him were the early morning editions of the major East Coast newspapers—all of them delivered before any of their subscribers saw a copy—and two drafts of legislation that he wanted to review before breakfast.

One of the valets had placed coffee and pastries on a tray in the hall. Johnson had poured himself a cup and taken a Danish, then reminded everyone he saw that he did not want to be disturbed.

He needed think time.

Hell, he needed rest time, but he wasn't going to get that. Last November, he'd been shoved into a limelight he'd wanted all his life, but not in the way he wanted that limelight. He wanted to be elected—by a goddamn landslide, if the truth be told—not appointed, which he essentially was.

He'd do damn near anything to bring Jack Kennedy back from the dead—if, of course, the fucking rumors that Jack was going to pull him from the 1964 ticket weren't true. Or maybe he'd bring Jack back even if they were true. Johnson would have fought to stay on that ticket.

He'd've used Hoover's files all over again, plus some of that leverage he'd gained just by observing Jack's mid-afternoon swimming parties when Jackie was out of town. He even had the strategy planned once: *Mr. President, sir,* he would have said, *I don't think you would want the press to get wind of those beautiful women that Powers escorts into the West Wing when you're supposedly getting your afternoon rest. I don't think your sophisticated habits would play well in Peoria, do you?*

Sometimes he regretted that he hadn't had the chance to make that speech. Especially on days like this one. The honeymoon—if it was fair to call what he was going through that—was over; the Congress had decided he was a traitor to his legislative roots. Initially they had figured he'd play like he had when he was a senator, but he was playing Presidential ball now, and he was playing to win.

Even if he was still using Jack Kennedy's playbook.

In those first hours on November 22, as he sat alone in the Presidential office on Air Force One, Lady Bird offering condolences in the main cabin and poor Jackie huddled in a corner still wearing her blood-stained clothes, he'd thought through what the next year or so would be like.

He was different from the Kennedys, so different, in fact, that watching him with his brash Texas style would be as much of a wake-up call as the country could handle. If he tried to run the country the way he thought it should be run, everyone would hate him—not because of what he was trying to do, Lord no. He knew more about governing than Jack Kennedy knew about women. They'd hate Johnson because he wasn't living up to the Kennedy legacy, whatever the fuck that was.

So Johnson figured it was his job to define the Kennedy legacy—because dear old horny Jack hadn't done so outside of his brilliant speeches, and Bobby was always following his own inner demons, trying to destroy the whole family while saying that he was trying to save them. Johnson had to tell the United States what their martyred president wanted—within enough reason that good ole Bobby wouldn't contradict him—and then Johnson had to provide that.

He figured he only had six months to do it, because long about May, he had to concentrate on re-election. And the Johnson who came into the White House in 1965 would be his own man, not some goddamn puppet trying to live up to a lesser man's legacy while trying to keep the country afloat.

In the middle of one of the worst crises ever.

He was still proud of himself for thinking as clearly as he had in November. He was terrified then (and if he told the truth to himself, he was terrified now) that there was a lot more to Jack Kennedy's death than a lone crazy with a mail-order rifle.

Johnson had insisted on flying Air Force One that afternoon not just because he became the president, but because part of him was convinced that Air Force Two had been sabotaged—that someone, some group of someones—was out to get the entire government, not just the President himself.

He'd been wrong about that, and it had led to good ole Bobby whining that Johnson couldn't wait to usurp the prize of the Presidency, taking over the country when Jack's body wasn't even cold.

But Bobby, as usual, was thinking about the Kennedys. Johnson was thinking about a nation that had just lost a young President in a dramatic manner. He was thinking about possible riots in the streets, the kind of chaos that young Bobby couldn't even imagine.

So Johnson took the slights, like he always had in the presence of the younger Kennedy, and stored them up for later. He'd kept Bobby on as his Attorney General—that whole legacy thing—and let Bobby believe he might be on the Vice Presidential ticket in 1964, but Johnson had plans to put Bobby in his place come the 1965 inaugural. On that day, Bobby Kennedy would learn that the Kennedys didn't run the country anymore.

"Mr. President, sir."

Johnson started. His coffee spilled onto the saucer, but he caught the cup before the entire thing toppled over. He hadn't heard his assistant approach.

The man standing hesitantly in the door of the West Sitting Hall was Bill Moyers, his youngest assistant. Johnson hadn't appointed a Chief of Staff—he didn't want that much power vested in one man—so he had a rotating team of assistants, most of whom he'd assigned various trusted jobs.

Moyers had met Johnson by way of KTBC, Johnson's television station, in Austin, Texas. Moyers was the only aide who hadn't been with Johnson in his last several Congressional campaigns, although he'd proven invaluable during the 1960 Vice Presidential campaign.

He was in his late twenties or early thirties, still blessed with the thinness men of that age always had, and his dark eyes behind his glasses were as intense as Johnson's had been when he was young.

Only they didn't look intense now. They just looked worried.

"I'm sorry to bother you, sir," Moyers said. "I knew you said you didn't want to be disturbed."

Johnson waited. His aides listened to his orders and knew better than to disturb him on routine business. So something had happened.

Something important.

"We've just gotten word from one of our agents at FBI, sir. They're saying J. Edgar Hoover is dead."

Johnson set his coffee cup down on the pending legislation. He needed a moment to gather himself. He'd known Edgar for decades. They used to live on the same street when Johnson's girls were little. In fact, they still called Edgar "Uncle Edgar," probably the only people in the entire country to use such an affectionate moniker with the old reprobate.

They'd eaten Sunday dinners together, walked their dogs around the same block, had too-strong cocktails late into the evening. Johnson had made liberal use of Hoover's official and confidential files—hell, maybe even use of the personal and confidential ones too although he'd never seen the actual documentation—and had, in turn, supplied Hoover with the gossip and innuendo that he so loved to use to his own advantage.

Johnson sat back up, now that he felt he had control of his face. "Heart attack?"

"No, sir." Moyers was twisting his hands. "They're saying he was shot."

Johnson went cold. "Shot? Like Kennedy?"

"I don't know, sir," Moyers said. "It's mostly unconfirmed. There's rumors that Associate Director Tolson was killed too."

"An assassination?" Johnson asked, feeling the fears from November rise all over again. He'd just been able to tamp them down, just been able to walk into a crowd without nearly passing out.

"No one's willing to say yet, sir," Moyers said. "Hoover and Tolson were in New York. Off-duty. In one of those questionable neighborhoods."

"You saying they were at some queer bar?" Johnson asked.

"Some private party," Moyers said. "My source says they were shot in the alley and it might be a mugging or a—well, the New York police apparently call this kind of thing a lifestyle murder."

"Someone was having target practice on queers and happened to hit the Director of the FBI?"

"It's possible, sir."

Johnson closed his eyes and leaned his head back. "I told that old queen more than once he was going to get into someone else's personal and confidential file. But who the hell could mistake J. Edgar Hoover for some random man on the street? It don't play, Bill."

"I'm just telling you what I've learned, sir."

Which was why they sent in Moyers. Moyers could keep his focus. The others might start arguing with him, letting him know that they didn't entirely agree with his interpretation.

"You keep saying *rumors* and *your source*. We haven't been officially contacted?"

"Not yet, sir."

"Well, goddammit, Bill, before you bring the President of the United States into a possible situation, you should confirm the fucking rumors."

"Yes, sir."

"Go make sure that this isn't some schoolboy story. Then get the facts and report back to me. And see why the hell Bobby didn't call. He's supposed to be Edgar's boss, and I'm supposed to be his boss. He should keep me in the loop."

"I'm sure he's trying to verify the rumors as well."

"Well, stop fucking speculating and go fucking find out!"

Johnson waited a moment, and then looked. Moyers had vanished from the hallway. Probably run like a scared jack rabbit.

Johnson rubbed a hand through his thinning hair. Moyers wasn't a dummy. He trusted his so-called source enough to come up here. And he was right to do so; the last thing they all wanted was the President to be kept out of the loop.

Which meant that J. Edgar was dead, whether it was a fucking "life-style" kill or a targeted assassination. J. Edgar was dead three months after Jack Kennedy—by a bullet.

That would cause more problems than Johnson wanted to think about: the nation's top law enforcement officer murdered either in a random street crime or by some targeted assassin.

Neither would play well with the American public.

Hell, it wasn't playing well with him.

He felt queasy. All he had in his stomach was coffee. He had to eat, because he had to keep his head clear.

Because two murdered high-ranking officials in less than three months couldn't be random. It had to be planned. Even if it was meant to look like a "lifestyle" kill.

Someone was gunning for the most important people in this country.

And if that wasn't a crisis, then nothing was.

15

BRYCE HAD JUST LEFT THE PHONE BOOTH when a phalanx of FBI sedans sped through the nearby intersection. He watched them go by with a kind of wonder—had they screwed up the directions that badly?—then realized they were going around the block to park closer to the coroner's van.

He walked up the street past the limosine. The two beat cops still stood near it, shifting from foot to foot, occasionally blowing on their gloved hands to keep warm.

"No coroner yet?" Bryce asked.

"No scene–of-the-crime guys either," one of them said.

He nodded. The NYPD might have just lost its jurisdiction over this crime scene. Even though there were no federal laws that allowed for the SAC to federalize this crime scene, he would probably try it.

And he might actually succeed.

Bryce ran the last few steps. He appeared outside the alley as the first sedans skidded to a stop by the curb.

Doors opened before all the cars had stopped, and the Special Agent in Charge of the New York Regional Office, Eugene Hart, got out of the first one. He was hatless, and Bryce wondered if that was a simple error or if the SAC was the first agent to defy Hoover's rules simply because Hoover was dead.

"Is it really him?" Hart asked as he approached Bryce.

Bryce nodded.

"Shit." Hart said the word with a preciseness that cut through the cold air. He was a tall man with a narrow face, a Roman nose, and a jutting chin. He looked like someone who took no crap from anyone, and the look matched his personality.

Hart grabbed Bryce's arm and pulled him away from the alley, all the while motioning the other agents toward the crime scene.

"Don't you want to see him?" Bryce asked.

"He's dead, right? Tolson beside him? Each with a single shot in the back. A party upstairs for rich and famous queers, a bad neighborhood, and three more FBI agents—all of whom should have been protecting him—also dead. What else am I missing?"

"The second sedan," Bryce said.

That made Hart stop. "What're you talking about?"

So Bryce told him about the two cars, one behind the other, ostensibly on HooverWatch, the canvas he'd ordered for the missing agents, and the concern he had that the canvas wasn't necessary.

"Hell, man, you made the right call," Hart said, using the street slang that he'd acquired in his undercover work nearly a decade before. "We have to find our men."

"Except I'm not sure they're missing."

Hart tilted his head. The light from the only working nearby streetlight caught his hollow cheeks and made him look like he'd been etched in shadow.

"On the basis of what?" Hart asked.

"The second car, the one that shows no evidence of occupancy and the one that was locked, that one was checked out after ten tonight by Walter Cain."

For a moment Hart didn't move. Bryce had a strange worry that Hart hadn't heard him or, if he had, hadn't understood.

"Cain," Hart said. "The one with the dead fiancée."

The fiancée you threatened. The fiancée you told to give up the love of her life and to never talk to him again. The fiancée whom you cajoled into such immediate despair that she saw no other choice than to slit her wrists.

Bryce had to wait another moment so that those words wouldn't pass through his lips. Instead, he said, "Yeah. That Cain."

"I thought you told him to go on leave."

"I did."

"You send the order through headquarters?"

"I saw him after five. I put the order into channels, but I'm sure no one's seen it yet."

"Shit," Hart said again with that odd precision. He shook his head once, then twice, as if he were trying to shake a thought out of it.

Finally he turned to Bryce. "Are you suggesting one of our own men did this?"

"The evidence points to it," Bryce said.

"As a kind of personal revenge?" Hart had raised his voice.

Bryce made a small hand gesture, telling him to lower it. "I think it's possible."

"How could it be possible?"

"Like this," Bryce said. "He's worked HooverWatch. He knows that when Hoover goes to places like this, he doesn't want the second car anywhere close. He wants his bodyguards far enough away that they can deny knowledge of what he's doing."

"Yeah," Hart said. "I've bitched about that."

"We all have," Bryce said. "But the fact is we've all done it. And I'm sure Cain did."

Hart let out a large sigh.

"He would have known that Crawford never carried a gun. He would have known that Tolson and Hoover never did either. All he had to do was take out the HooverWatch agents first, and then he had a clear run at Hoover."

"Why?" Hart asked.

Bryce couldn't tell if that was a rhetorical question.

"It doesn't make sense," Hart said, his tone almost pleading.

"But the evidence does," Bryce said. "It looks like he pulled up behind the HooverWatch sedan, got out and motioned the driver out. So the driver got out, figuring that he was going to talk to a fellow agent about something important. Instead Cain shoots him. The second agent has no shot and he's vulnerable. The driver left the door open, so Cain has a relatively clear shot. The second agent gets out the passenger side, runs and probably shoots as he goes, then gets shot and dies in the middle of the street."

"Jesus," Hart said.

"Then it looks like Cain just walked up to Crawford and knocked on the window of the limosine. Crawford would've heard the shots, but he wouldn't have seen who was involved. And because he's been with Hoover for decades, he knows all the New York HooverWatch guys, so he probably figures Cain's one of the bodyguards. He rolls down the window and Cain shoots him."

"Oh, Christ." Hart shook his head.

"After that, all Cain has to do is go to the alley, stand by the door, and wait for Hoover and Tolson to leave. Which he does, and then he shoots them, one right after the other."

Hart was still shaking his head. He finally said, "You know, if you weren't one of our best investigators, Bryce, I wouldn't even be considering this as an option."

"There are other possibilities, sir," Bryce said. "I ordered the canvas in case Cain and a partner are holed up somewhere or someone saw them get dragged off. Then there's the possibility that the guy I talked to in the motor pool was looking at the records for the wrong day."

"I hope to hell that's it," Hart said.

"Which still doesn't explain why the second sedan is here," Bryce said.

Hart glared at him. "What's the third possibility?"

"That Cain's in the coroner's wagon, one of the two dead bodies, and someone didn't follow procedure, sending two agents out in two separate cars."

"You haven't checked?" Hart asked.

"You sent me down here alone," Bryce said. "I'm dealing with one of the largest crime scenes I've ever had, some territorial New York cops, and an important crime, all by myself for more than an hour. I can crawl into the coroner's van now if you like."

"I like," Hart said. Then he put out his hand and squeezed Bryce's shoulder. "Sorry about sending you alone. I needed someone quickly and you were the closest thanks to that fancy-schmancy apartment of yours."

Bryce nodded.

"Then I got caught up. You realize this is a mess no matter how it plays."

"I do," Bryce said, "and because I was short-handed, I have half the NYPD down here doing work we should've been doing. It'll be impossible to close leaks now."

"I'm not worried about leaks," Hart said. "Unless you told them all about the party."

"A few know. The detectives who got assigned to the case, one of them is former vice."

"Shit," Hart said.

"And the coroner handled everything badly because he figures that homosexuals, no matter who they are, don't rate an investigation."

"I'll get his name," Hart said. "We might have to use that. What about the press?"

"None yet," Bryce said. "That's where our luck held. Apparently, they agree with the coroner. Any dead homosexual isn't worth the ink."

"This one will be if we don't cover it fast. Thanks, Bryce. I'd been worried about you recently, but you really came through tonight."

Hart was about to walk away, but Bryce caught his sleeve. "Sir, one more thing."

Hart nodded.

"If I'm wrong, if this isn't Cain, we have a larger problem."

Hart tilted his head. "I don't know how this can get much larger."

"Whoever did this, sir," Bryce said, "knew where the HooverWatch agents would be. Knew where Crawford would be, and knew where Hoover was. That's a leak in the department."

"Oh," Hart said.

"And the shots look professional. Now Cain, he's one of our best marksmen. But for someone else to do this, someone not FBI, then he's got to have some juice, if you know what I mean."

"You're thinking professional hit?" Hart sounded shocked.

Bryce nodded. "And given some of the stuff that's come through our office on the President's shooting, sir, some of the stuff we've been told to just file or let D.C. follow up on, I'm thinking that professional hits are in season."

"You think this could be related to President Kennedy?" Hart asked.

"I don't think we should discount it, sir."

Hart sighed again, then frowned. He stared at the coroner's van for a long moment before turning back to Bryce.

"You got some good points."

"Thank you, sir."

"But you missed one thing."

"What's that, sir?"

"They don't have to be separate."

"You think that Cain could've been doing a professional hit?"

"Maybe not Cain," Hart said. "But someone in our office. Someone bought and paid for by the kind of elements Hoover didn't believe in. The kind that Morganthau and Bobby Kennedy have been chasing for years now."

"Hoffa?"

"Or one of his friends," Hart said. "Check that van. We need to know who's inside."

"And if Cain isn't there?"

Hart shrugged. "Then we start by looking for him. But we don't end there. And we don't talk about it. Is that clear?"

"Yeah," Bryce said.

"Good. Right now, all these theories are just for you and me. No one else. Once we have a little more information, then maybe we'll talk to some folks. Got it?"

"Yeah," Bryce said again. He nodded at Hart, then headed to the coroner's van, feeling slightly discouraged. He'd thought things would get better when the FBI team arrived.

He had a very real sense, however, that things had just gotten worse.

16

"THE DIRECTOR'S DEAD."

Kennedy stood across the desk from Assistant Director Curt Ross. Ross had one hand on the phone, the other tapping nervously on the blotter covering his desk. He was a spare man with piggy little eyes. Kennedy had never liked him, but he was one of Hoover's most trusted assistants.

And, Kennedy noted, he had some file cabinets in his office that matched the ones Helen Gandy had.

"I know he's dead," Kennedy said. "That part I already heard. And not from you, by the way. Through channels. I'm your boss, Agent Ross. You should have called me immediately."

"I'm sorry, sir."

"No, you're not. Instead, you contacted Helen Gandy before you figured you had to contact me. I assume you haven't contacted the President either."

"No, sir," Ross said. "I figured you would want to do that, sir."

"You figured right." Kennedy glared at the man.

An anger that Kennedy didn't recognize nearly overwhelmed him. It took him a moment to realize he'd been suppressing this anger since his brother died. He was furious, not just at the horrible events, but at the people who treated them like another political problem.

"I would, in fact, have liked to inform him when you informed Miss Gandy, which, by my calculations, was at least an hour ago, maybe more. Don't you think the President of the United States is more important than an executive secretary, Agent Ross?"

Kennedy deliberately did not use the man's actual rank. Ross wouldn't have his job in the morning, anyway, so treating him kindly really didn't matter.

"Sir, I have my orders. I was just following them."

"Whose orders?" Kennedy asked.

Ross pulled out a yellow slip of paper and slid it to Kennedy. It was one of Hoover's ubiquitous memos, typed by Miss Gandy herself. The names along the top belonged to all of Hoover's most trusted assistants.

It said that, in the event of the Director's death or permanent incapacity (resulting in the Director being unable to make decisions for himself), the Associate Director was to contact Miss Gandy. Miss Gandy would then contact Assistant Director Ross, who would then contact his counterpart on the investigative side. Together, they were to inform the twelve assistant directors, who were to tell their divisions.

At that moment, a coded telex had to be sent to all the field offices and foreign legats.

There was no mention in the memo of the Attorney General or the President.

"Well," Kennedy said, folding the memo and placing it in the back pocket of his slacks. "It seems that the system failed from the beginning. How come you contacted Miss Gandy instead of the other way around?"

"You know why, sir. Associate Director Tolson was murdered alongside Director Hoover."

"Alongside." Kennedy let that word slide suggestively across his tongue. "I assume they were off duty."

Ross flushed. "Yes, sir."

"Then you had better tell me exactly what happened."

"I don't know what happened, sir. Except that they were shot in an alley near Central Park. It seems that several others were shot as well."

"What others?" Kennedy made his voice harsh.

"We know of Agent Crawford for certain. We've heard that there might be more."

"Heard," Kennedy said.

"Sir, it's delicate. The neighborhood that Director Hoover was found in—if we announce it, the press will understand, and then there will be a scandal."

As if that mattered to Kennedy. He really didn't care if anyone found out that Hoover was queer. When the story broke—if the story broke—Kennedy would fall on his Catholic heritage and plead naiveté. That should cover both him and Jack, but it would leave others, like Eisenhower and Johnson, exposed.

Particularly Johnson, since that man had known Hoover for decades, and had reaffirmed their friendship not one month ago.

"Sir, I'm sorry," Ross said into Kennedy's silence. "I was just following orders."

"The orders of a dead man," Kennedy said.

"Yes, sir, in the event of his death. They're his wishes."

"Wishes," Kennedy said. "By following his wishes, you put Director Hoover's personal needs above those of the United States Government."

"I didn't mean to, sir—"

"Yes, you did," Kennedy said. "Has everyone on this list been notified of the Director's death?"

"We're calling the Assistant Directors now, sir."

"Stop," Kennedy said.

"Sir?"

"I want you to stop the notifications."

"But, sir, each division deserves to know."

"And it will in due time," Kennedy said. "I trust no telex went to the field offices yet."

"No, sir. I was getting it ready when I finally reached you."

"You will not send it. In fact, no one will contact them."

"Sir, there's sensitive information at the field offices—"

"That belongs to the Justice Department, not to Director Hoover or his estate. You don't understand that, do you, Ross?"

"Sir, I'm just—"

"Following orders, I know," Kennedy said. "Well, here are a few more. I want every document in your office, including your copies of Hoover's personal and confidential files—"

"Sir, I don't—"

"Don't lie to me, Ross. I want every document in my office within the hour, even the ones you were supposed to destroy tonight. I will place a guard on you to make certain nothing goes into a burn bag or through a shredder."

"Sir, I'm an agent of the United States Government."

Kennedy stared at the man. "I'm amazed you finally remembered that."

Ross bowed his head. Kennedy could almost see the man think. He was learning that the Federal Bureau of Investigation was no longer an independent entity. Now it would answer to the Attorney General, just like every other division in the Justice Department.

Which meant that Robert F. Kennedy had just become Hoover's replacement.

He felt his own cheeks grow warm. It was the logical thing to do. Not just for the files, but for the government itself.

He pulled the memo from his pocket and shook it at Ross. "This memo is out of date. If I find anyone following this memo after this meeting, I will fire that person. Is that clear?"

Ross nodded.

"Good," Kennedy said. "Tell your cohorts that everything of importance goes into my office tonight."

"Sir, they're not going to like that."

"I don't really care," Kennedy said. "They work for me now. You all do, whether you like it or not."

17

THE INSIDE OF THE CORONER'S VAN was roomier than he expected. Bryce crawled in, his shoes clanging on the metal floor. The entire van shook as he moved.

Even though the coroner knew Bryce was in there, Bryce still felt conspicuous.

The two bodies lay side by side on the floor in the back. They were both in body bags. As he made his way toward them, he found himself wishing that Brunner had done his job.

If Brunner had just written down their personal information, then Bryce wouldn't be in here, trying to identify two bodies.

O'Reilly had just come out of a nearby building as Bryce headed toward the van, so Bryce spoke to him for a moment. So far, the canvas hadn't turned up anything.

No missing FBI agents, not even a whisper of them. The handful of people who answered their doors had uniformly not seen anything or heard anything. They seemed to be startled that the police were in the building.

O'Reilly said he believed that they were startled. To live in this neighborhood, they'd had to tune out the street noise—had to pretend that the screaming at all hours, the breaking glass, and the occasional gunshot meant nothing, maybe hadn't happened at all.

Bryce didn't understand how anyone could live like that. He was startled that people lived like that only a few blocks from his fancy-schmancy apartment.

But he supposed he shouldn't have been too surprised. Even when he was a kid, his father had ordered him not to walk through these neighborhoods, saying they were "decaying." Well, they were done decaying now. They were completely and utterly decayed.

Bryce made his way to the back of the van. The body bags looked innocuous to someone who didn't know what they were. They looked like overly full garment bags or fancy dry cleaning bags, not storage bags for human remains.

For FBI remains.

Maybe for the remains of people he knew.

Bryce took a deep breath to calm himself. The cool air went into his lungs, soothing the restlessness that still plagued his stomach.

He hated this part of the job. He'd worked cases before where he'd known the victims, and he hadn't been proud of the work he'd done. He'd been a little too zealous, taken things a bit too personally.

And that was before his so-called breakdown, before he decided that he didn't care what anyone in the Bureau thought.

Hell, if he was honest, that was before he didn't care what anyone thought.

Damn Mary and her annulment.

Damn that last year of his no-longer-existent marriage.

He had to take another deep breath. This time the air didn't feel so cool. He'd been in here long enough to warm things up by a degree or so.

He needed to gather himself and get to work.

He reached across the first bag and pulled down the zipper, then winced. No one had told him that one of the agents had been shot in the face. The gun had been far enough away to take out much of the forehead.

Bryce had to turn away to gather himself.

Then he made himself look again. He'd learned over the years that the best way to handle a shocking sight was to take the sight detail by detail.

So he looked first at the wound. It was a deep gouge that went through the skull into the brain tissue. He'd seen the results of it on the blowback covering the seat and steering wheel.

He should have figured that part out for himself.

Then he made himself look downward. The eyes were still open. Death had been some time ago. The eyes had the corpse look. They were a cloudy blue.

The nose was sharp, beaked, and suited the sharp cheekbones. Those bones were covered with bristly skin—the agent's five o'clock shadow was thick, and probably something that had bothered him in life.

It wouldn't bother him anymore.

Bryce couldn't recognize the man, not with that gouge in his forehead. Bryce wasn't able to imagine it away. Besides, sometimes people's faces in death looked nothing like their faces in life.

He reached into the bag, traced the man's side, and found his belt. Then he used that to find his wallet and removed it. He flipped it open.

The body was definitely that of Wade Stockton. They hadn't known each other very well. They'd exchanged pleasantries in passing, their longest conversation a gripe about the no-caffeine-on-the-job rule. Stockton had joined only a few years before and still seemed unbelievably young to Bryce.

Even now. Even with his five-o'clock shadow and cloudy blue eyes, he seemed young. Too young to be an FBI agent and too young to be dead.

Bryce placed the wallet on top of the body, then zipped the bag back up. Poor kid. He didn't even know if Stockton was married or who his partner was or if he'd worked other jobs before coming to the FBI.

That kid had sat in a cold sedan all night on what he'd thought was a cushy assignment. Then someone—Cain?—had pulled up behind him, gotten out, and rapped on his window, and when he'd opened the door, got shot in that overhanging forehead of his.

Bryce could almost hear the noise. The deafening echo of the gunshot at close quarters, the second agent yelling, probably "What the fuck?" and scrambling out of the car in a desperate attempt to save his own life.

He would have been reaching for his own gun at the same time. All that movement, trying to stay alive. If it had been Bryce, he would have pushed open the door, fallen out and slammed the door shut while reaching for his piece. Then he would have run—low—across the street.

But that was their training.

If the shooter (Cain?) had been FBI, then he would have had the same training.

He would have anticipated.

He would have known to shoot low.

Bryce wondered if the second agent had a secondary wound, maybe to the knee or the femur, something that hampered his passage across that street.

All the shooter had to do was crouch, shoot under the car, and he would have disabled the second agent just enough to slow his progress across that street.

To make sure the second agent died relatively quickly as well.

Bryce grabbed the zipper of the second body bag and pulled it down.

This time he knew the agent.

Knew him well.

The second man was Vance Nolan. Bryce had trained him in firearms and tested him in weapons proficiency. Nolan had been one of the few new recruits who had passed all weapons testing on the very first try.

Nolan had been a brash guy with a sharp sense of humor. He was shorter than Bryce, but stronger, with a classic handsomeness that made women turn on the street.

Bryce hadn't spoken to Vance Nolan in, what? A month? Two? Maybe not since Mary sprang the unwelcome news on him that she was going to ask for an annulment instead of a divorce. She wanted to stay in the Church, she'd said, and a divorce would make her a sinner.

The annulment would simply mean that their marriage had never happened.

Bryce had always wondered how that worked. He knew how the law worked. A judge would rule the marriage null and void. But the Church would act as if the marriage had never happened, as if the sacrament they'd taken—so important to Mary that she had insisted he go through the pre-marriage classes the priest provided—as if that sacrament hadn't taken place at all.

If God were all-seeing and all-knowing, He wouldn't be fooled by an annulment. He would know the marriage had happened, that it had been sanctioned and blessed by the Catholic Church, that it actually meant something once to all parties involved.

But Mary had told him that the Church didn't care about such details as long as there were no children involved, which there weren't. She blamed Bryce, and maybe she had a point. If thoughts could control fertility, then his had. He'd never wanted children.

He had once told her that bringing children into this world was irresponsible in the extreme.

She hadn't forgiven him for that either.

If God was all-seeing and all knowing, then He should have prevented this loss. Because Vance was one of the good guys, one of the true believers who knew how to coddle the criminal who had gone astray and frighten the one who had no soul.

Bryce stared at his friend's face. Vance's features were never so still—probably not even when he was asleep. He had been a great raconteur, an even better marksman, and one of the most cautious people Bryce had ever known.

He'd also been friends with Cain, and would have stood up for him at the wedding. Surely Cain would have seen his friend in that car. Which seemed like proof to Bryce that his assumption was wrong.

Surely Cain wouldn't have shot one of his best friends. Not twice.

Not in cold blood.

Bryce zipped up the bag. He wasn't cold anymore. He should have been, seeing these two men lying on the van's metal floor. Seeing Hoover had disturbed him, but this—this sent shocks through him so deep, he wasn't sure he knew how to handle them.

He had to gather himself. He had to be strong, like Vance.

Vance always did the tough duty.

He'd been the one who had come to see Bryce shortly before the Kennedy assassination.

I know your life isn't going the way you want, Frank, Vance had said over drinks one afternoon. *But you gotta watch your mouth. The Bureau's a conservative organization. You can't force change on it. Besides, I don't think you're trying to change the Bureau, I think you're trying to change you.*

Bryce had tipped his beer toward Vance in a mock salute. *Thank you, Dr. Freud.*

I'm serious, Frank. You're not on the fast track anymore. You're not on any track. And if you keep mouthing off, they'll find a way to let you go.

Maybe they should, Bryce had said.

Is that what you want? Vance had said. *Because I can see to it that you leave with your commendations and some good will. I know things have been bad with Mary, and they consider that extenuating circumstances….*

It's not Mary, Bryce had said, and that was true. It had been him. It had always been him.

At some point in the last few years, he realized it was no longer worth his time to run his bullshit meter. He was tired of going along with everything, tired of nodding and smiling at things he'd found objectionable.

And he found so much that was objectionable.

Like seeing one of the best men he knew inside a body bag on the cold metal floor of a coroner's van.

Bryce sat for a moment beside his old friend. For the first time in a long time, he had no words.

He had no judgments.

He just had a profound sense of regret.

He owed Vance an apology for dodging him since that conversation. For finding ways to avoid the friendly beer or excuses not to have dinner.

It wasn't that he'd thought Vance had been an asshole for telling him the truth. It was just that Vance had to tell him the truth.

That others had noticed Bryce's behavior and found it odd. He'd even found it odd.

He'd been destroying himself for no good reason. And Vance had tried to stop it. Had even asked, long about Christmas, if Bryce wanted a new partner.

Bryce, still stuck in his pride, had said no.

God, if they'd partnered up, what would have happened? There might not have been an investigation of Essie Steward. Or at least, not a damaging one.

And there certainly wouldn't have been a night of terror on Hoover-Watch. Vance wouldn't be in a bag at Bryce's feet.

Bryce shook his head.

Regrets. He couldn't live with them. They would get in the way of the job.

And this one was his. He was going to fight for it, no matter what his current reputation in the department.

He'd remind Hart every five minutes if he had to that no one had closed more cases than Francis Xavier Bryce. No one, not in the history of the New York Bureau.

And then he'd tell Hart that he was going to close this one too.

Because he had to.

As penance.

For Vance.

18

KENNEDY RETURNED TO HIS OFFICE to find it stuffed with file cabinets. Agents had found a furniture dolly and were wedging cabinets into a corner near the arched windows. The kids' watercolors were already hidden, and he could barely get to his desk.

As he stepped inside the office, he almost tripped over a man wearing a maintenance worker's uniform. He had a toolbox beside him. Wood shavings covered the carpet around him.

He had removed the doorknob, probably as a prelude to changing the lock.

Kennedy glanced at his watch. It was after four. He'd been here a little more than two hours.

Two hours in which everything had changed.

The phone rang. He couldn't even see it on the desk.

"It's been doing that all night," one of the agents said, even though his statement wasn't accurate. They hadn't been in the office all night, although it probably felt that way.

It would feel that way into the morning as well, as Kennedy brought all of the official and confidential files in here. He needed a meeting of the agents already in the office, and he needed to let them know the new reality.

Until the President appointed a new FBI director, Kennedy would run the department. What he wasn't going to say was that even after the President appointed a new director, Kennedy would run the department.

No more would there be a lone fiefdom in the corner of the Justice Department. Now every department head would answer to the Attorney General, the way it was supposed to be.

The phone stopped ringing before he reached it. Then the intercom buzzed. Kennedy had to lean around file bins, stacked precariously beside his desk, to press the intercom button.

"What?" he asked.

"Oh, good, you're here." The voice belonged to the Assistant Attorney General, Nick Katzenbach. "I've been getting a lot of panicked phone calls from the White House. You need to call the President."

"I will," Kennedy said, and let go of the intercom button. He would call the President, but not before all the files were in his office and the locks changed.

For one of the first times in his life, he was using Jack's philosophy: It was easier to ask forgiveness than it was to ask permission.

Not that LBJ would ever forgive Kennedy. They hated each other, and this would make the hatred worse. But after Jack's death, Kennedy had no leverage—and he hadn't wanted it.

Now he had leverage, and he was surprised to find how much that pleased him.

The phone rang again. He almost picked up the receiver and then stopped. The last thing he wanted was to talk to someone from the White House.

Let them track him down.

Kennedy went around his desk and pulled open the narrow top drawer. There he kept all the home numbers for everyone in the Justice Department. His personal staff's numbers were on top.

He waited until the ringing stopped, then counted to ten. Then he picked up the receiver and dialed Angie Novello. She had been his secretary since he sat on the McClellan Committee in 1957. The committee, whose true name was The Select Committee on Improper Activities in

Labor or Management, was really about the way that organized crime had infiltrated the Labor Movement.

Angie had proven indispensable then, and remained so now. She kept Kennedy organized. She had been the one to keep the office going in the weeks he'd been away.

While he had been at home reading Greek tragedies, Angie had still put in her eighteen-hour days, covering for him.

He hated waking her up in the middle of the night, but he needed her. Someone had to answer the damn phone and keep the President at bay, at least until Kennedy figured out what to do with the files.

He hadn't planned for this. Not in all his years as Attorney General. Maybe he was as bad as the glum-faced agents wandering around the hallway. He too had thought Hoover immortal.

Kennedy had planned for the old man's retirement in 1965, but not his death. The retirement was going to be a battle—Kennedy would have gone after the files then, and he probably would have lost.

But he stopped preparing for that battle when LBJ informed him in no uncertain terms that Hoover would remain with the FBI until LBJ removed him. He wasn't going to let some mandatory retirement law deprive him of an asset.

That was what he had called Hoover. An asset.

An asset that LBJ had used more than once in Kennedy's presence. He'd used information provided by that asset at the Democratic National Convention in California in the summer of 1960, sitting in a closed, badly air-conditioned room, letting Jack know why LBJ and not Stuart Symington or any of the other, more suitable candidates should be Vice President of the United States.

Kennedy hadn't been there. If he had, he would have shouted the old cornpone down, talked about Johnson's relationship with some shady Texas characters and reminded LBJ that his record with the ladies was longer and older than Jack's.

But Jack had caved. The decision had been made while Kennedy was canvassing for votes on the convention floor.

LBJ needed his asset—or at least he needed his asset's files—and Kennedy was going to do everything to make sure he didn't get them.

It took several rings, but Angie finally answered the phone, her voice husky with sleep. She promised to be in within the hour.

Kennedy asked her to arrive quicker, and was glad that he had.

Because the moment he hung up, the phone rang again. He glared at it, willing it to shut up, as two more agents came into the room, carrying file bins. A third wheeled a dolly in with another cabinet.

Kennedy's office was the size of a football field, but it was beginning to feel cramped.

The phone stopped ringing. Kennedy sighed, then ran his hand through his hair, wondering if he had enough time to move the files off premise. Not that he had any place rented off-premise. The only site he had was an office building not far from here where his brother's most confidential papers remained under guard.

There was no room there. Besides, he didn't want to tip LBJ to the location of that treasure trove. LBJ had enough blackmail material already. He didn't need any more.

And Kennedy couldn't take the files to Hickory Hill. Johnson would cry foul and the entire federal government would agree.

The entire federal government, past and present. Judging by the number of file cabinets now filling his office, everyone who had so much as touched power in the past forty years had a file.

And they all would want theirs.

Holding onto these files would be a fight. Kennedy smiled. He hadn't had a good fight in months. A fight he needed to win.

A fight he would win, no matter what the cost.

19

O'REILLY STEPPED OUT OF THE BUILDING into the cold night air. He took a deep breath. That last building had smelled of rotted food and mouse droppings. He had found one very scared young mother willing to talk to him. She had heard the gunshots—she counted six of them. She had taken her sleeping children and carried them into the bathtub, holding them there for more than an hour after the shooting ended.

She hadn't seen a thing.

No one had.

Some legitimately hadn't seen anything—like that young mother. But others supposedly hadn't even heard the gunshots. Like so many people who lived in a bad neighborhood, they simply didn't want to be involved.

He had had guards on the doors of the building with the party, so he had been saving that for last. But as he emerged from this building, half a block away, he realized that the sounds he'd heard outside while talking to that young mother were the FBI finally deciding to back up Agent Bryce.

O'Reilly steeled himself. He knew this meeting with Bryce's superior would be ugly. He also knew he had both the manpower and the law on his side.

If the FBI agent in charge didn't like what O'Reilly said, he could appeal to O'Reilly's boss.

For that matter, he could appeal all the way to the mayor, not that it would do him any good.

Still, O'Reilly wasn't looking forward to the confrontation. He walked the half block like a man getting ready for battle.

The FBI's sedans were parked around the coroner's van, blocking both the street and the alley. Agents loomed near the alley's entrance, probably destroying evidence with each step they took.

When he reached the first agent, standing at the edge of the small crowd, trying to peer around the coroner's van, he said, "Where's your boss?"

The agent pointed inside the alley.

O'Reilly stepped around him, nearly brushing his thigh on the van's bumper. Brunner had taken his lights down. Now the crime scene was illuminated by the headlights of at least two different FBI sedans.

Several agents crouched around the two corpses. Brunner stood against the wall, arms folded, his assistant nowhere in sight.

When Brunner saw O'Reilly, he pointed at the man near Hoover's skull. O'Reilly nodded once, then said, "I assume someone wants to talk to me."

The agents all stopped examining the bodies and turned toward O'Reilly. O'Reilly held up his shield.

"I'm in charge of this investigation," he said, knowing that would provoke them.

The man that Brunner had pointed to put his hands on his thighs as he stood. "Actually," the man said in a deep voice that revealed a prep school education in his background, "I'm here to relieve you of that command."

"Are you?" O'Reilly kept his tone dry. "You work for the Chief of Detectives of the NYPD?"

"No." The man walked over to him. He was ten years younger than O'Reilly and in better shape. His face was unlined, and he had a full head of dark hair. He extended his right hand. "I'm Special Agent in Charge, Eugene Hart."

O'Reilly pointedly did not take his hand. "Detective Seamus O'Reilly."

Hart let his hand drop. "We're taking jurisdiction over this case."

"Do you mean Director Hoover's case or do you mean the four other victims as well?" O'Reilly asked, just because he was feeling ornery. He'd known this was coming all night, and he was ready for it.

In fact, he was past ready for it. He didn't want these so-called experts destroying his crime scene, ruining his evidence, and lying about what had happened here. He hated cover-ups almost as much as he hated criminals, and he wasn't going to be a party to anything just because some government official might be embarrassed.

"I think the scene covers all five murders, don't you?" Hart's tone was patronizing. That was his second mistake. His first was thinking the FBI had a chance of taking on this investigation.

O'Reilly wasn't going to play Hart's games. O'Reilly was going to control this conversation, not Hart. Hart just didn't know it yet.

"On what grounds are you claiming jurisdiction?" O'Reilly asked.

"I understand that two of our agents are missing," Hart said. "We think there might be a kidnapping."

Good try. Ever since the Lindbergh baby case, the FBI could claim jurisdiction on kidnappings if it felt so inclined.

"You think," O'Reilly said. "You don't know?"

"Neither do you," said Hart.

"Actually I do," O'Reilly lied. "No one has seen these supposed agents. My men have canvassed dozens of buildings over several blocks. Even the eyewitnesses agree that the five men killed were the only people on the street—except for the shooter, of course."

"Eyewitness testimony is notoriously unreliable," Hart said.

O'Reilly knew that, but he didn't care. "Not as unreliable as a hunch."

Hart's eyes narrowed. He put a hand on O'Reilly's arm and pulled him away from the crime scene. Together they walked away from the crowd of cars.

"Detective O'Reilly," Hart said in a gentle voice. "That's our Director. The country will wonder why the FBI isn't leading this investigation."

"The country will know. Homicides belong to local jurisdictions."

"I'm sure that normally people would agree with you, but the Director is a national figure. I think that's enough to federalize the case."

"Really?" O'Reilly let his dry tone emerge again. "So the Director of the FBI is more important than the President of the Untied States?"

Hart frowned at him. "I'm not sure I understand your meaning."

"Of course you do," O'Reilly said. "The FBI made it very clear at the end of November that the Dallas Police Department would be handling the investigation into President Kennedy's assassination. I think that order probably came from Director Hoover himself. So it would seem to me that this argument is another fallacy."

Hart sighed. He put a hand on O'Reilly's shoulder. O'Reilly tried not to wince. He hated fake camaraderie. He knew this would be accompanied by that patronizing tone all over again.

"Look, Detective O'Reilly, we need to control this investigation. I'm sure you understand why."

O'Reilly moved away from Hart's grip. "No," he said. "Tell me."

Hart's lips thinned. "The neighborhood, the irregularities of the surveillance. I'm sure you've heard the rumors—"

"No," O'Reilly said. "What rumors?"

"Dammit, man, it's not a coincidence that the Director is here."

O'Reilly nodded, as if that were news to him. The confirmation was news. He'd heard rumors, just like Hart had intimated, but he hadn't really paid a lot of attention. It had sounded like sour grapes to him, and he didn't put a lot of stock in sour grapes.

"So," O'Reilly said slowly, "it's not a coincidence that the Director was murdered?"

"That's not what I'm saying," Hart said.

"It sounds like that's what you're saying."

Hart took a deep breath, as if he were trying to control his temper. "What I'm saying is that if we reveal details about this crime scene, including the location, then the Director's personal life becomes an issue."

"Really?" O'Reilly said.

"I don't like your tone, Detective."

"Good," O'Reilly said, "because I don't like yours either. You want a favor from the NYPD on this?"

"Yes, I do." Hart smiled. "Thank you for understanding, Detective."

"I'm not finished," O'Reilly said. "If you want a favor, here's what I'll grant you. I'll send you reports on each step of the investigation. If something particularly inflammatory comes to my attention, I'll let you know before we release the information throughout the department. If you like, you can attach a liaison to this case, and I will treat him with respect."

Hart stared at him. "You've got to be kidding."

"Of course I'm not kidding," O'Reilly said. "This is a homicide case. I don't care if our victim includes the Director of the FBI or the Queen of England, I will investigate this case as I have been entrusted to do by the City of New York."

"The FBI is one of the best investigative bodies in the world," Hart said.

"According to your propaganda," O'Reilly said. "But you people don't close cases. You consult on them. Now, Scotland Yard is one of the best investigative bodies in the world, and if the Queen of England were face down in that alley, I still wouldn't let them take over this investigation either. I'm being pretty magnanimous allowing a liaison."

"This case has international implications," Hart started.

O'Reilly put up a hand, stopping him. "Really? What do you know about that? What aren't you telling me? Was there a specific threat on the Director's life that he was ignoring by coming here?"

"No, but—"

"Then you're just saying that international thing to scare me, aren't you?"

"Look, Detective, we need to handle this case. Do you want me to go to your boss?"

"Yeah," O'Reilly said. "I do. He doesn't like you people any more than I do. And when he realizes that you didn't get to the scene until two hours after your first agent arrived, he'll think, just like I do, that you're more interested in covering up what happened here than you are in solving it."

"That's not true," Hart said.

"Really?"

Hart's frown turned into a glower. He obviously wasn't liking O'Reilly's dry tone.

"That's not true?" O'Reilly said. "Then why is it that the first thing you mention to me is the neighborhood? Why don't you ask what leads I have? Why don't you ask my theory of the crime? Why did you try to convince me I should give you this case based on the Director's personal life and some bad publicity instead of on your so-called superior resources?"

Hart looked away. He took several deep breaths, and when he was finished, he turned back to O'Reilly. "All right," he said. "What leads do you have?"

"I'm afraid that's on a need-to-know basis.'"

"Goddammit, man, he's our Director."

"Yes, he is. Which, as I see it, is just as complicated as if he's a member of your family. The entire Bureau should recuse itself from this case just based on your reverence for the man. You'll care more about protecting his reputation than you will about finding his killers."

Hart's eyes narrowed. "You're not going to budge on this, are you?"

"No, I'm not," O'Reilly said. "I never compromise when I'm right."

"I will talk to your boss."

"Fine," O'Reilly said. "You do that."

Because the Chief of Detectives hated the FBI more than anyone else in the department, and the Chief of Ds had juice with both the Chief of Police and with the Mayor. Hart wasn't going to get anyone to go along with this.

"And in the meantime," Hart said, poking a finger at O'Reilly's chest, "if I hear word one about this case in the news, then I'm coming after your badge."

"I'm not in charge of what the press office releases. You will hear about this in the news. It's an important murder."

"I want you to keep a lid on this information," Hart said.

"And I want you to stop poking me in the chest," O'Reilly said.

Hart stopped. "This is about a lot more than some jurisdictional pissing contest."

"Yeah, I know." O'Reilly crossed his arms, as much to protect his now-sore chest as it was to show his displeasure. "It's about whether or not this case ever gets solved."

"Excuse me?" Hart asked.

"I said it already," O'Reilly said. "I'm going to investigate. You people would just cover up. And by doing that, you'd let a stone-cold killer go free."

"We'd solve it," Hart said.

"Yeah." O'Reilly gave a small half-smile. "Like you let Jack Ruby solve the Kennedy case?"

Ruby had murdered Lee Harvey Oswald in front of television cameras. A lot of people thought that shooting cemented Oswald's guilt.

To guys like O'Reilly, on the other hand, guys who'd worked mob killings, that second murder looked familiar. It was a way of getting rid of the patsy before the patsy could blow the entire operation.

"We didn't let Ruby 'solve' the Kennedy case," Hart said.

O'Reilly snorted. "Oh, yeah. Right. You let the Dallas P.D. do that."

"See what happens when things are left in a local jurisdiction?" Hart asked. "The case gets screwed up."

"You're saying Oswald didn't do it?" O'Reilly asked.

"We're not talking about that," Hart snapped.

"Damn right we're not," O'Reilly said. "There will be no cover-up here, no leaks, and no question about jurisdiction. I'm going to do the best god-damn job I can do with the best goddamn men in the country. We'll find who murdered your Director and we'll find out why. I can promise you that."

"First rule of police work, *Detective*," Hart said. "Never make a promise you can't keep."

"I know that rule," O'Reilly said. "And you know what, Special Agent? I've kept every single promise I've ever made."

20

KENNEDY STOOD NEAR THE BACK of his office, staying out of the way as three burly agents slid file cabinets across the carpet. Folders had fallen from his desk. His office—which had been an organized mess—had just become a full-blown disaster.

The man from building maintenance was still working on the lock on the front door to Kennedy's office. Kennedy would have to have the locks on the inner door changed as well. He had decided to move some of the files into that space, although with its desk and private phone line—which he mostly used for personal calls when people were waiting in his office—there wouldn't be much room.

The phone rang incessantly. Nick Katzenbach kept peeking his head inside, reminding Kennedy that he had phone calls to make, and then looking meaningfully at the ringing line.

They had both stopped answering. It was finally clear to Katzenbach that Kennedy would not call LBJ until every last file was moved, every last lock was changed.

"This is crazy, you know that," Katzenbach had said to him at one point.

Kennedy just smiled at him. Maybe it was crazy, but probably not. The Ambassador would be proud. Kennedy's father, incapacitated by a stroke and unable to talk except for a tortured "No!," still had all his faculties. He would love this story—if Kennedy managed to pull it off.

Another agent wheeled in more files. A few of the agents were smiling as they carried bins that they had removed from some Assistant Directors' offices. Those Assistants, all favorites of Hoover's, would be gone or demoted within days.

Everyone was finally beginning to understand that changes were happening immediately, and several agents, most of them younger men who'd chafed under Hoover's goofy 1940s-era rules, were actually feeling lighter than they had when they arrived at two that morning.

Kennedy had to be careful or the party atmosphere might spread. Word would get back to the press and everyone would take a beating for enjoying themselves while Hoover was just growing cold.

Then a silence spread from the hallway into the office. First the maintenance man held up his hand for quiet. Then a few agents did. Finally Kennedy heard the noises. Rustling, murmured voices, and then Haskell saying quite loudly (and a little too guiltily):

"Good morning, Mr. President!"

Kennedy cursed under his breath. He hadn't figured the old cornpone would come here on his own, but he should have.

"Where the fuck is that bastard?" Lyndon Baines Johnson's voice echoed from the corridor. "Doesn't anyone in this building have balls enough to tell him that he works for me?"

Even though the question was rhetorical, someone tried to answer. Kennedy heard something about "your orders, sir."

"Horseshit!" Then LBJ stood in the doorway. Two Secret Service agents flanked him. He motioned with one hand at the maintenance man and the four FBI agents still setting down bins. "I suggest you get out."

The maintenance man didn't have to be told twice. He scurried away, still carrying the doorknob. The agents gave Kennedy a look, as if asking for his approval to leave.

He hoped LBJ didn't see it. The man was insecure enough without some minor FBI agents adding to it.

But LBJ was watching Kennedy. It was as if they were the only two people who mattered—and at this moment, that was probably true.

LBJ came inside alone, pushed the door closed, then grimaced as it popped back open. He grabbed a chair and set it in front of the door, then glared at Kennedy.

The glare was effective in that hangdog face, despite LBJ's attire. He wore a plaid silk pajama top stuffed into a pair of black trousers, finished with dress shoes and no socks. His hair—what remained of it—hadn't been Brylcreemed down like usual, and stood up on the sides and the back.

He slammed a hand on one of the cabinets, then started into one of his stupid monologues. Kennedy used to cut them off when Jack was alive.

Now he had to listen to every goddamn word.

"I get a phone call from some weasel underling of that Old Cocksucker," LBJ said, "informing me that he's dead, and you're raiding his tomb. I try to contact you, find out that you are indeed removing files from the Director's office, and that you won't take my calls. Now, I should've sent one of my boys over here, but I figured they're still walking on tippy-toe around you because you're in fucking mourning, and this doesn't require tippy-toe. I don't think you ever deserved tippy-toe. You're one strong-ass bastard who always knows what side his bread is buttered on. You've acted on your own interests as long as I've known you, and you're doing it now. On my orders. Like hell. This was Jack's idea, wasn't it?"

"Jack's dead," Kennedy said coldly.

LBJ had always been more than a little paranoid, but since the assassination, he'd gotten more so. He didn't trust that the office was his now. He figured everyone was plotting against him, trying to get him out of office.

Once he'd even accused Kennedy of doing that—of forcing LBJ out of the Presidency and putting himself in it. Kennedy hadn't responded then. It was only a few days after Jack's death, and it wouldn't have been appropriate.

But what he wanted to say, what he *should* have said, was that he planned to force Lyndon Baines Johnson out of the Presidency. Only he wanted to do it with a method that LBJ respected: using the votes of the people of the United States.

"I know the Holy Saint John Fitzgerald Kennedy is dead!" LBJ's voice, never soft, roared.

They probably heard him in the hallway.

For that matter, they were probably all leaning against the door, with glasses cupped against the wood, trying to make out every word.

"But you don't act on my orders," LBJ said. "You act like my orders are farts in the wind. You told someone out there that these files were coming into your office because the President ordered it. I haven't spoken to you. The chain of command has not been followed. I had to find out that the Director of the FBI was murdered from an assistant to an assistant because Moyers heard a goddamn rumor and I made him chase the fucking thing down. You know how that makes me feel?"

"Probably insecure and angry," Kennedy said.

LBJ's face flushed. "You are a tiny little rat bastard and I should break you in half."

"That'll play well on the network news," Kennedy said.

LBJ slammed his fist into the filing cabinet, sending the whole thing rocking. For a moment, Kennedy thought the cabinet was going to fall, making the entire group of cabinets topple like dominoes around the extra large room.

"You had no right to bring those files in here," LBJ shouted. "And to change the goddamn locks. What the hell were you thinking?"

Kennedy crossed his arms and raised his eyebrows, just like he used to do when he used to stand a half step behind his brother, the President, one of the few men who could talk LBJ out of a tantrum.

Now Kennedy had to do it on his own and he wasn't quite prepared. He knew he'd get a dressing down. In fact, he had expected it. But in a few hours or maybe a few days, after the crisis had passed.

"I was thinking," Kennedy said as calmly as he could, given the fury of the man in front of him, "that I am the Attorney General of the United States. Director Hoover worked for me. Now we both know he amassed some pretty important files on a whole hell of a lot of important people over decades. All of those people would be storming this office when the news broke, wanting their information. Some might even resort to stealing—"

"Like you are," LBJ said.

Kennedy wasn't going to be sidetracked. "And I wanted those files protected. Do you know what was going to happen to them? Do you know who got called first? Helen Gandy. And from what I can gather, from the bits and pieces my agents are digging up, she was supposed to remove the personal and confidential files from this building to a secret location, sort everything, and destroy most of it."

LBJ was breathing hard, but he had stopped shouting. His face was still a lively shade of puce. Kennedy made himself breathe, hoping LBJ would. LBJ had had a serious heart attack not ten years before, and he looked like a man who was about to have another.

"I got the same kind of call you did, Mr. President. One of my loyal men let me know the rumors and I had him secure the files. Helen Gandy arrived here not ten minutes later and pitched a hell of a fit. I got here as quickly as I could, but even I wasn't officially notified about Hoover's death until just a few minutes ago. If I'd waited, then those files would be gone God knows where."

LBJ was breathing hard, but the puce color was slowly fading. "You didn't have to bring them to your office."

"Where was I supposed to leave them?" Kennedy ask. "In Hoover's office, where the Dragon Lady held the keys? Damn near every man on this floor is afraid of her. I don't think I have enough men who aren't afraid of her to keep those files guarded for long. So I brought them here. They haven't left the Justice Department. They're still part of the federal government."

LBJ's eyes narrowed. The man was now holding the file cabinet like a crutch. "You don't need to read them. You just send them over to my office. We'll find a way to keep them safe."

Kennedy smiled. "Is that what you're afraid of? You're afraid I'll find the Johnson file? Must be some pretty unsavory stuff in there,

Lyndon, for the President of the United States to traipse over here on a cold February night in his pajamas."

LBJ opened his mouth, then closed it. He drew himself to his full height, which was considerably more than Kennedy's, leaned forward until his face was an inch away, and said, "I don't want you destroying files either."

Kennedy wanted to back away. He hated it when any man got close, but especially this man. "I wouldn't destroy a single file."

LBJ didn't back off. Damn the man, he seemed to know when he'd intimidated Kennedy. "But you would remove the Kennedy files, and you can't do that. We need to solve this thing."

It took Kennedy a minute to understand. "You're blaming my family for Hoover's death?"

"Not directly," LBJ said. "But we gotta think about it."

This time, Kennedy did take a step back. He hit his desk with his backside, stopping him from moving away further. "Think about what?"

"Well, there's only two things that tie J. Edgar and your brother. The first is that someone was gunning for them and succeeded. The second is that they went after the mob on your bidding. There's a lot of shit running around here that says your brother's shooting was a mob hit, and I know personally that Edgar was doing his best to make it seem like that Oswald character acted alone. But now Edgar is dead and Jack is dead and the only tie they have is the way they kowtowed to your stupid prosecution of the men that got your brother elected."

Kennedy felt lightheaded. He hadn't even thought that the deaths of his brother and J. Edgar were connected. But LBJ had a point. Maybe there was a conspiracy to kill government officials. Maybe the Syndicate was showing its power. He'd had warning.

Hell, he'd had suspicions. He hadn't let himself look at any of the evidence in his brother's assassination, not after he secured the body and prevented a disastrous autopsy in Texas. If those doctors at Parkland had done their job, they would've seen just how advanced Jack's Addison's disease was. The best kept secret of the Kennedy Administration—an administration full of secrets—was how close Jack had been to incapacitation and death.

Kennedy clutched the edge of his desk. But LBJ knew about Jack's health. LBJ knew a lot of the secrets—had even promised to keep a few of them. And he wanted the files as badly as Kennedy did.

There had to be a lot in here on LBJ too. Not just the women, which was something he had in common with Jack, but other things, from his days in Congress.

"From what I heard," Kennedy said, making certain his voice was calm even though he wasn't, "all they know is someone shot Hoover. Did you get more details than that? Something that mentions organized crime in particular?"

"I'm sure it'll come out," LBJ said.

"You've already decided that's how this is going to play, then," Kennedy said.

LBJ's face flushed that horrible puce again. "I didn't decide a goddamn thing. Someone has gunned down two of the most important people in this government. Now I've been thinking about it ever since I got word. That's too much of a coincidence. Either it's the mob or it's Castro's people because of your fucking bungled assassination attempts."

"You ever think that maybe Oswald acted alone and Hoover's death was random?"

"Don't give me that bullshit," LBJ said. "We both know Jack Ruby was connected."

"In Texas," Kennedy said. "His Syndicate connections were in Texas. Your home state."

"Now don't start that shit."

"Your home state, and Bobby Baker's home state, and goddamn if Ruby didn't used to work for Carlos Marcello, who according to one of *my* files on *my* desk, files that have been untouched since November 22, the day we were supposed to decide how the hell to toss you off the ticket in 1964 because you'd become a goddamn embarrassment, gave you money for how many campaigns? We can trace tens of thousands, Lyndon. You want to start arguing connections, I'll argue. I've always thought it mighty goddamn suspicious that my brother died in Texas, a state you fucking own."

"I warned you people not to send him down there," LBJ said. "I told all of you he wouldn't be welcome. I went along to try to grease the wheel, not to have the asshole killed. For Crissakes, you think I wanted to be President this way? I have to keep your brother's legacy alive, and you know what, Bobby? Your brother didn't have a legacy. He was the most incompetent president we've had since Herbert Hoover, maybe since Harding. You ask your daddy about them. Your daddy who used to use mob guys to protect his bootlegging operation. Your daddy, who bought your brother's election at the Cal-Neva casino in Tahoe with every major head of every major crime family in attendance."

Kennedy was shaking. He'd known his father had done shady things, especially around Jack's campaign, but he hadn't wanted to know the details.

But LBJ wasn't done. "Then you get into office, and what do you do? You break every promise your old man made. You go after the ass-holes. You were supposed to jack up their operations and instead you fucking prosecute them. Edgar warned you. Hell, I warned you. I'll bet your daddy warned you. And you insisted. You want blame for your brother's death? Look in the goddamn mirror."

Kennedy felt his own face flush. "There's no proof that the Syndicate was behind my brother's death."

"There's no proof of anything because Edgar buried it. Edgar decided a lone gunman was best for the country. So he's been cocking up the evidence. He's had his hands in things that he shouldn't've, and goddamn if he ain't dead now."

Kennedy shook his head. "Don't blame me for anything that happened tonight. Your friend Edgar had been mobbed up for years."

"Bullshit," LBJ said.

"Bullshit?" Kennedy asked. "He'd breakfast at the track with Dub McClanahan who partners with Carlos Marcello. Hoover used to play golf with Johnny Rosselli, for God's sake."

"Rosselli," LBJ said. "Your father's favorite golfing buddy in Florida."

Kennedy ignored that. "If this murder has ties to the Syndicate, it's not because of me. It's because Hoover pissed someone off."

"You think?" LBJ asked. "Or you think maybe someone's had enough of your little tricks, taking down the country's business interests, and has decided to take out the government, person by person?"

In spite of himself, Kennedy shuddered. That wasn't possible, was it? If someone tried to do that—if someone wanted to do that—he could destroy the entire country.

"I'm the one with the enemies," Kennedy said softly. "If the Syndicate was going to kill anyone, they'd kill me."

"You goddamn arrogant prick," LBJ said. "You want to know Carlos Marcello's favorite saying? Hmm? Yeah, I've met the bastard—and he's from Louisiana, Mr. Holier Than Thou crime fighter—"

"He's from Tunisia," Kennedy said. He'd had a lot of run-ins with Marcello, including trying to get the man out of the country. He hadn't been born here and his visa had run out.

That trick had failed, miserably, and Marcello had had a grudge against Kennedy ever since.

"He's from Louisiana now, New Orleans to be exact, and he always said, 'You want to kill a dog, you don't cut off its tail. You cut off its head.'"

LBJ's words echoed in the crammed room. They had both raised their voices considerably, and the conversation hadn't started as a soft one.

Kennedy took a deep breath, but it didn't calm him. "If what you're saying is true, why kill Hoover?"

"As a warning to me," LBJ said. "A reminder that they can get to anyone, even the most protected man in government."

Kennedy leaned all his weight against the desk. His exhaustion had returned. He made himself pause, separate out the anger that LBJ always aroused in him, and then said, "This is all speculation."

"That's right," LBJ said, "and the answer to these questions is in the files."

In spite of himself, Kennedy laughed. LBJ always was a good bullshitter and for a few minutes, he had had Kennedy going. "The answer to what happened tonight is not in those files. In those files is some damning stuff about you and about my family. About Richard Nixon and Barry Goldwater and anyone else who might become President of the United States. It's the files you want not to solve any crime, but to help you stay in power. You'd use them the way Hoover did. They'd be your personal blackmail stash."

"I'm not going to blackmail anyone," LBJ said. "And I'm not going to lie to you. I want those files. As the head of this government, those files belong to me."

Kennedy's smile grew. "You're the head of this government for less than a year. Next January, someone'll take the oath of office and it might not be you. Do you really want to claim these in the name of the Presidency? Because you might be handing them over to Goldwater come January."

LBJ leaned on that file cabinet so hard it nearly fell again. This time, Kennedy had to step forward to help keep the damn thing upright.

Then someone knocked on the door. Both men jumped. Kennedy frowned. He couldn't think of anyone who would have enough nerve to interrupt him when he was getting shouted at by the President of the United States. But someone had.

LBJ moved the chair and pulled the door open. Helen Gandy stood there. She looked particularly small as she faced him.

"You boys can be heard in the hallway," she said, sweeping in as if the leader of the free world wasn't holding the door for her. "And it's embarrassing. It was precisely this kind of thing the Director hoped to avoid."

Then she nodded at LBJ. Kennedy watched her. The Dragon Lady. Jack, as usual, had been right with his jibes. Only the Dragon Lady would walk in here as if she were the most important person in the room.

"Mr. President," she said, "these files are the Director's personal business. He wanted me to take care of them, and get them out of the office, where they do not belong."

"Personal files, Miss Gandy?" LBJ asked. "These are his secret files."

"If they were secret, Mr. President, then you wouldn't be here. Mr. Hoover kept his secrets."

Mr. Hoover used *his secrets*, Kennedy thought, but didn't say.

"These are just his confidential files," Miss Gandy was saying. "Let me take care of them and they won't be here to tempt anyone. That's what the Director wanted."

"These are government property," LBJ said with a sly look at Kennedy. For the first time, Kennedy realized his Goldwater argument had gotten through. "They belong here. I do thank you for your time and concern, though, ma'am."

Then he gave her a courtly little bow, put his hand on the small of her back, and propelled her out of the room.

Despite himself, Kennedy was impressed. He'd never seen anyone handle the Dragon Lady that efficiently before.

LBJ grabbed one of the cabinets and slid it in front of the door he had just closed. Kennedy had forgotten how strong the man was. He had invited Kennedy down to his Texas ranch before the election, trying to find out what Kennedy was made of, and instead, Kennedy had realized just what LBJ was made of—strength not bluster, brains *and* brawn.

He'd do well to remember that.

"All right," LBJ said as he turned around. "Here's what I'm gonna offer. You can have your family's files. You can watch while we search for them and you can have everything. Just give me the rest."

Kennedy raised his eyebrows. The exhaustion was gone. Helen Gandy had given him enough of a reprieve to gather himself. No matter what argument LBJ made, he wouldn't defeat Kennedy.

No one would.

Not again.

"No," Kennedy said.

"I can fire your ass in five minutes, put someone else in this fancy office, and then you can't do a goddamn thing," LBJ said. "I'm being kind."

"There's historical precedent for a cabinet member barricading himself in his office after he got fired," Kennedy said. "Seems to me it happened to a previous President named Johnson. While I'm barricaded in, I'll just go through the files and find out everything I need to know."

"When Edward Stanton barricaded himself in his office, he caused a constitutional crisis," LBJ said. "This country can't afford such a thing."

"It wouldn't break my heart to see you impeached," Kennedy said.

LBJ crossed his arms. His face was covered in sweat. The room was hot. The pressure of the cabinets, the winter heating system, and the unintentional closeness of the two men made it seem worse than it probably was.

"You'd do that, wouldn't you?" LBJ said after a minute.

"Yes," Kennedy said.

"And I'd fire your ass, and it would play out just like it did a hundred years ago."

"Only worse," Kennedy said. "Everyone who knows about these files, everyone who suspects he's in them, would pick a side. We'd have teams, Lyndon. My side would think I could protect them better, and your side would think you could."

"And the Republicans would be running scared." LBJ chuckled. Then he shook his head. "Hell of a mess. Helen Gandy's right. These files are poison."

"I'm not going to let her destroy them."

"Neither am I," LBJ said. "And I'm not going to let you use them to knock me out of the running this year. I'm running for President. Hell, I'll be President come January, whether you like it or not."

With the files, LBJ could guarantee it. Even without them, if his poll numbers stayed where they were, he could guarantee it. LBJ, to Kennedy's surprise, had become one of the most popular Presidents in this century because he knew how to play the people.

He was different than Jack, but in some ways—especially when it came to the down-home folks—he was better than Jack. He could connect. He could fish out what people wanted as well as what they hated. He could promise it for them, and if he ran the country the way he ran Texas, he would get it for them, the cost be damned.

This was a stand-off and neither Kennedy nor LBJ had a good play. They only had a guess as to what was in those files—not just theirs but all of the others as well. They did know that whatever was in those files had given Hoover enough power to last in the office for more than forty years.

The files had brought down presidents. They could bring down congressmen, Supreme Court Justices, and maybe even the current President. Kennedy could use the files too. He could use them to help his own Presidential bid.

But, in a way, he was as trapped by his brother's memory as LBJ was. Kennedy couldn't play dirty politics with the files, not and retain the Kennedy sheen. Right now, he was the brother of a martyred President. But if he used those files, he'd be Bobby Kennedy, the hatchet man for his brother, the man who ran anti-crime committees with a harshness that made all of Washington and half the country wince.

LBJ would use that. And he wouldn't hesitate to smear Kennedy in the press.

It would be the ugliest primary season on record. And it would destroy everything.

He couldn't do that, any more than LBJ could.

They had to have another solution.

One he hadn't been willing to consider until now.

"These are our files," Kennedy said after a moment, although the word "our" galled him, "yours and mine. Right now, we control them."

LBJ nodded almost imperceptivity. "What do you want?"

What did he want? To be left alone? To have his family left alone? At midnight, he might have said that. But now, his old self was reasserting itself.

He needed a bullet-proof position. LBJ was right: The Attorney General could be fired. But there was one position, constitutionally, that the President couldn't touch.

"I want to be your Vice President," Kennedy said. "And in 1972, when you can't run again, I want your endorsement. I want you to back me for the nomination."

LBJ swallowed hard. Color suffused his face and for a moment, Kennedy thought he was going to shout again.

But he didn't.

Instead he said, "And what happens if we don't win?"

"We move these to a location of our choosing. And we do it with trusted associates. We get this stuff out of here."

LBJ glanced at the door. He was clearly thinking of what Helen Gandy had said, how it was better to be rid of all of this than it was to have it corrupting the office, endangering everyone.

But if LBJ and Kennedy controlled the entire cache, they also controlled their own files. LBJ could destroy his and Kennedy could preserve his family's legacy.

If it weren't for the fact that LBJ hated him almost as much as Kennedy hated LBJ, the decision would be easy.

"You'd trust me to a gentleman's agreement?" LBJ asked, not disguising the sarcasm in his tone. He knew Kennedy thought he was too uncouth to ever be considered a gentleman.

"You know where your interests lie. Just like I do," Kennedy said. "If we don't let Miss Gandy have the files, then this is the only choice."

LBJ sighed. "I had hoped to be rid of the Kennedys by inauguration day."

"And what if I planned to run against you?" Kennedy asked.

LBJ didn't answer that question. Instead, he said, "You can be an incautious asshole. Why should I trust you?"

"Because I saved Jack's ass more times than you can count," Kennedy said. "And right now, I'm saving yours."

"How do you figure?" LBJ asked.

"Your fear of those files brought you to me, Mr. President." Kennedy put an emphasis on the title, which he usually avoided using around LBJ. "If I barricade myself in here, I'll have the keys to the kingdom and no qualms about letting the information out when I go free. If you work with me, your secrets remain just secrets."

"You're a son of bitch, you know that?" LBJ asked.

Kennedy nodded. "The hell of it is you are too or you wouldn't've brought up Jack's death before we knew what really happened to Hoover.

So let's control the Presidency for the next sixteen years. By then the information in these files will probably be worthless."

LBJ stared at him. It took Kennedy a minute to realize that although he'd won the argument, he wouldn't get an agreement from LBJ, not if Kennedy didn't make the first move.

Kennedy held out his hand. "Deal?"

LBJ stared at Kennedy's extended hand for a long moment before taking it in his own big clammy one.

"You goddamn son of a bitch," LBJ said. "You've got a deal."

The Cover-Up

If we do not attack organized criminals with methods and techniques
as effective as their own, they will destroy us.

—Robert F. Kennedy

21

WALTER CAIN CLUTCHED his *New York Times*. He hadn't opened it, preferring to stare out the train's window instead. Spindly trees stood near the railroad tracks. Through them, he could see pristine snow and smoke coming from a chimney not too far away.

He had deliberately taken the local to New Haven. He figured if someone recognized him, he could get off at any station and disappear into a New York suburb or one of Connecticut's more rustic towns. He would look out of place until he got a change of clothes, but he had a plan for that.

He had a plan for everything.

He sat in the middle of the car, holding his *Times* so hard that his hand hurt. He'd had the presence of mind to grab a briefcase before he left his apartment. He'd stuffed the case with underwear and toiletries, then locked it so that it wouldn't snap open at the wrong time.

So far, no one had recognized him. The only people who had talked to him had been the clerk at the ticket window, the porter who'd punched his ticket, and a portly gentleman who asked if the seat across the way was taken.

The portly man got off before the train crossed into Connecticut. Cain didn't see where and didn't care. He was counting on the other passengers to have that same sort of disinterest in him.

He'd only chosen New Haven because he'd been there once, with some friends for the Yale/Harvard game. He leaned his head against the filthy window. The snow deepened as he got farther north—apparently that warm spell, which had hit New York a week or so ago, hadn't been as severe here. But the northern communities always got more snow and a deeper, colder winter.

He was leaving everything behind.

The thought should have been freeing. But it wasn't. In the past week, he had become a completely different person, one he knew lurked inside him, but which he'd never thought would emerge.

He'd thought Essie would protect him. Essie, with her sad, pretty face and her understanding ways. Essie knew the power of redemption. She said God could forgive anything.

She had almost convinced him.

And then she died.

But before she died, she'd had to suffer humiliation that he couldn't even imagine. His own people had investigated her. Maybe, if Essie had been a graduate of Vassar or even someone who had gone to secretarial school, then the FBI wouldn't have cared.

Hoover wouldn't have cared.

That old fat fuck had ruled on Essie himself. That's what SAC Hart said when he called to apologize. The fat fuck had said that such a woman would compromise an FBI agent. The KGB could use her past to buy him and make him a double agent.

Someone should have asked Cain. No one could have turned him. And if the FBI knew what she had been, then they wouldn't have been shocked at the revelation if it ever came from the KGB. He didn't understand how he could have been compromised, even if he had been a weaker soul.

Essie. He closed his eyes for a moment. She had come to his apartment just a day ago before he even went to work. Her face was dry, but her cheeks were chapped. She had clearly been crying, but she wasn't crying then.

152

He let her inside. She stood nervously in front of the door. Then she handed him a red velvet jeweler's box. He recognized it. He'd given her that box at Christmas. With his thumb, he flicked it open.

The diamond that had cost him two months salary glinted inside. *I can't*, she had said. *I'm not worthy of you.*

That's for me to decide, Essie, he'd said.

She shook her head. He closed the box and then put it back into her hand. He gently closed her fist around it.

I think you're the most admirable person I've ever met, he said. *You have taken a tragic life and made it something rich. I love that about you. I love you.*

Then her eyes filled with tears, but the tears didn't fall. *I can't, Walter. I can't take the pressure. I can't be a wife to you. I'm so sorry.*

Then she set the box on the table beside the door, and let herself out. She was sobbing. He followed, calling her name, but she didn't stop.

He ran after her, all the way to the subway station, but missed the train she'd gotten on by a matter of seconds.

Then he'd stood there—coward that he was—and thought he'd see her after work. He'd see her after work and he would take the ring and he would talk to her, gently and without pressure.

Like he had done so many times before.

That was the strange thing. She'd done this before, told him that she wasn't worthy, tried to give the ring back. She'd done it, and he'd let her cool off, and then he'd reminded her how much he loved her, how much she had changed, how much he *admired* her.

And she would give him that hesitant smile, then crawl into his arms, letting him hold her, letting him treat her like the precious woman she was.

He had no clue that yesterday morning had been different.

Not until Frank Bryce had insisted on walking him home. Frank Bryce, looking exhausted and ravaged, had told him about Essie, about what she had done.

Why she had done it.

Oddly, Cain didn't blame Bryce. The man had just been trying to save his job.

He blamed Hart. Hart had called her. After reading Bryce's report. After checking with the fat fuck, who had said that such a woman had no place anywhere close to his agents.

Such a woman.

Hoover had no idea about women. That hypocrite had destroyed Essie when he couldn't even control himself.

There might not be a god, but there certainly was a devil. And when he whispered in Cain's ear, like he had off and on all of Cain's life, Cain finally listened.

The Devil had put Hoover in Hart's city. The Devil had sent Hoover to one of his little gatherings, the fat fuck indulging in his hypocrisy.

Which Cain decided to expose.

He was getting his revenge.

It would be slow, but it would destroy everything the fat fuck stood for. The world would soon learn what Hoover really was.

And Walter Cain would watch.

22

BY HIS COUNT, JOHNSON was on his fifteenth cup of coffee of the day and it was only eight a.m. He'd also had half a dozen Danishes—and he had to make the White House staff promise that no one would tell Lady Bird. She'd watched his diet closely since his heart attack. She would hate to know how much caffeine and sugar he'd already consumed this morning.

But the jittery food added to his jittery nerves. He'd gotten his files from Bobby Kennedy's clutches before leaving Justice. Then Johnson had to find a place to lock them up. At the moment, they were locked in his lower desk drawer just a few feet away, but he needed some place more permanent.

He also needed a way to confirm that he had *all* the files. He hadn't had time to double-check before coming back here.

He paced the Oval Office as the morning meeting started. He usually sat in the armchair at the edge of what he called the living room grouping—two sofas, some arm chairs, and some end tables, far from the television sets, which he always shut off for the meeting.

A few of his aides were smoking, including a few who had been trying to quit. They watched him walk, hands clasped behind his back. Pierre Salinger, one of the many remnants of JFK's staff, stood behind the couch, a frown on his meaty face.

Salinger usually didn't attend the morning briefing, but Johnson needed him today. Salinger was the press secretary, an intense, witty man whose closeness to Kennedy made Johnson nervous.

Everything about Salinger made Johnson nervous. The man was portly, with big bushy eyebrows that hung over his intense eyes. He was brash and urbane, an intellectual's intellectual, who liked a good glass of wine and an even better cigar.

He'd been a raconteur when JFK had been President. Since the man died, Salinger had mostly been silent. His press conferences were morose affairs and his deep voice now had a tendency to sound lugubrious.

"It's like bringing in a goddamn funeral director," Johnson complained to George Reedy, one of the rotating group of aides who served him instead of a chief of staff, when Reedy suggested that the press secretary attend the morning briefing. "Like we need a goddamn funeral director today."

"We need one today of all days," Reedy had replied.

Reedy sat in his customary perch at the edge of the couch, legs crossed, thin face somber. Moyers fidgeted beside him, and Johnson's newest aide, Jack Valenti, made sure everyone's coffee cup was filled.

Buzz Busby, who wrote most of Johnson's speeches, thumbed through a stack of papers on his lap. His hands were shaking.

Only Walter Jenkins remained calm. Jenkins had been with Johnson damn near from the beginning. They had started working together in 1939 and if anyone could anticipate Johnson's thoughts, it was Jenkins.

"We can't keep this quiet for long." Salinger held a cigar, but he hadn't lit it. The cigar seemed more like a security blanket, a prop, something to keep his hands busy. "For all we know, it has gotten out already."

"We've got New York wrapped up tighter than a nun's asshole," Johnson said. "Everyone knows if this leaks before we put the information out, whoever leaks it won't just lose his job, he'll lose the possibility of getting hired anywhere else."

He sounded confident, but he wasn't. He knew that this story was too juicy to hold on to for long, and some cop or some bystander would report to the New York press that J. Edgar Hoover had died in some piss-filled alley behind a queer club.

"No offense, Mr. President, but those kinds of threats aren't going to hold us forever." Salinger set the cigar back in the pocket of his suit coat. "I think we should announce now."

"And say what?" Jenkins asked. "There's no way in hell we can release the real story."

"We don't know the real story," Jenkins said in a tone that told everyone that he was reminding them of this.

"We know enough to know it's not good," Moyers said. "The nation's top cop gunned down in the nation's most dangerous city? We have a few choices here. We can say that the shooting was random, which makes everyone look like a buffoon, or we say that we have leads on the killers, which isn't true."

"Besides," Reedy said, "the whole nation's going to think it's a conspiracy."

Johnson stopped pacing. He'd said as much to Kennedy. Hell, he believed that much. The possibility that someone was gunning for the major figures in the government had him terrified. He couldn't hide in the Rose Garden from now to the end of his term. It was an election year. He had to go shake hands, meet people, kiss a few babies.

The Secret Service wouldn't let him out of an enclosed bullet-proof car if he wasn't careful.

And there he was, thinking too far ahead. Lady Bird would chastise him. He needed to keep on the matter at hand.

But the matter at hand made him more jittery than the sugar and caffeine had.

"We could say he died of natural causes," Valenti said. Valenti was a former ad man and knew how to make information dance. His word was "spin."

"And when the word gets out that we were lying?" Moyers snapped.

"It's natural to die when a bullet punctures your aorta," Valenti said.

"Enough!" Johnson snapped. "I want realistic choices. I think Pierre's right. We gotta announce this. I think we tell the truth."

The entire staff turned toward him as if he'd said he was going to go outside in pink dancing slippers and do the tango.

"What's the truth?" Reedy said. "We know he was shot. That's all we know. Along with Tolson and three other agents. That's going to scare the entire country, especially after the assassination last fall."

Johnson nodded. "I wasn't thinking of presenting the gory details. I was thinking we have Pierre go out and make one of those breaking news announcements. We just received word that the Director of the FBI J. Edgar Hoover has died in New York. We don't know the circumstances, and we will tell you everything we know as soon as we know it, something like that."

"Every cub reporter from every podunk weekly will get on the phone and try calling the New York Police Department," Salinger said. "We can't contain anything if we make that kind of announcement."

"You're right," Reedy said. He leaned on the papers in front of him. "Everyone'll be burning up the phone lines to New York City. Everyone'll be fishing for information."

Jenkins smiled. "And no one'll know anything."

"The people who give accurate reports are going to have as much credence as the folks who make it up as they go," Moyers said.

"That'll give us some time to come up with something," Johnson said.

"An hour or two at the most," Salinger said.

"An hour or two might be enough," said Jenkins.

Johnson had stopped pacing. He was beginning to feel a little calmer. He liked plans.

"We tell the American people I'm going to talk to them tonight, calm them down, make sure no one panics. Then we have meetings all day, figure out how to handle this."

"There's no good way," Reedy said.

"I still like natural causes," Valenti said.

"I wish it was natural causes," Johnson said. "I wish the old queer had died alone in his bed. But he didn't. And now we have to cover up his relationship and where he was before he died."

"Maybe we shouldn't do that," Moyers said. "Maybe we should tell the country—and profess shock. Maybe that'll get them to focus on something else."

"Something else?" Busby asked. It was the first time he spoke up. "What else is there? J. Edgar Hoover is dead. They're not going to care if he was screwing Jackie Kennedy. They're gonna want to know why the hell the most important men in this country are being murdered. And I think that's a valid question to ask."

Johnson took a deep breath. He'd been asking it since he got the news. Part of him believed what he said to Kennedy, that this death was tied to JFK's. There was no proof yet, as Kennedy said. But that meant there was no proof either way.

"That commission you started isn't going to fly anymore," Reedy said to Johnson. "We need some real police work to investigate this case, not some Presidential Commission headed by a Supreme Court Justice."

"We won't worry about that," Johnson said. "Earl Warren might still be useful. We're in the early stages here."

"We can't cover up that Hoover was shot," Moyers said. "It's too easy to refute. We have to admit that much."

"But not right now," Reedy said. "I agree with the President. Let's make the announcement. Let's let the press run with the story for now. We can deal with the rumors later."

"I'm more worried about the country," Johnson said. "They're not going to take it well. Whatever people thought of Edgar, he made them feel safe."

"They're not going to feel safe after this," Reedy said.

"Unless we keep them feeling that way. Keep up the Director's press." Busby tapped his fingers on the armrest. "That's the key. How would Hoover like to have gone out?"

"In a blaze of glory," Johnson said. "Hell, Edgar believed his own press half the time."

"Think we can give them that blaze?" Busby asked.

"You saying that he was in that alley on purpose? Working a case? Saving America from the Communists and the criminals, like he always did?" Johnson asked.

Busby nodded. Reedy leaned forward. "It might work."

"It might come back to bite us," Salinger said.

"Who's going to contradict the FBI?" Valenti asked. "We present it right, and no one'll contradict it."

Except one man. Johnson let out a small sigh. "We need Bobby on board. Go make the announcement, Pierre. Tell the press Edgar is dead and we're not sure of the circumstances. *Do not* say that he was shot. Tell them we'll have more facts as we know them. Tell them we think Edgar went to New York to follow an important lead."

"Think?" Salinger said.

"Tell them he did."

"They'll want to know what it is," Salinger said.

"It's confidential. We don't want to get into the middle of an active investigation. We'll have briefings all day. Fortify yourself. You're going to be handling a rabid group of dogs for the next week or so."

Salinger nodded. He looked tired already. Maybe he was.

But Johnson didn't feel that way anymore. He liked Busby's suggestion. The lie wouldn't be that big a lie—nothing more than Hoover would have done in the first place. He could almost hear Edgar chuckling over it.

"Thank you, Pierre," Johnson said. "Go make the announcement. The rest of us, we've got a lot of work to do. We need a cabinet meeting to set up, some Congressional bigwigs to calm, and a lot of phone calls to make. Anyone have a list?"

Salinger remained behind the couch. He was frowning.

"You got a problem, Pierre?" Johnson asked.

"Mr. President, I'm sorry to be an alarmist, but what if this truly is part and parcel of what happened to President Kennedy? What if we're facing some kind of conspiracy? Or what if some foreign government is trying to control the country through assassination?"

Like the Kennedy brothers did? Johnson almost asked, but didn't. They weren't the only Presidents who had tried to control some foreign nations through assassination. Even Roosevelt had wondered if he could get an assassin squad into Germany to kill Adolf Hitler.

"We'll deal with it then, Pierre," Reedy said as he stood. "Now get out there. We have to get ahead of this story."

Johnson nodded his thanks to Reedy. Reedy knew how hard it was for Johnson to deal with Salinger sometimes, especially when the man was being difficult.

Salinger walked slowly out of the office. Reedy closed the door behind him.

"This is going to be a hell of a week," Reedy said.

"A hell of a year," Johnson corrected. "And it's only just beginning."

23

BRYCE ARRIVED AT THE OFFICE carrying a greasy bag. Inside: one cup of coffee and two bagels slathered in cream cheese. His sour stomach had become a permanent condition. He decided he wasn't going to cater to it.

He went into his office. Thurman Whitson, one of the junior agents, followed him inside. Bryce had called Whitson before he left the scene, asking Whitson to look into a few things for him.

Hart had assigned Whitson to Bryce since Bryce no longer had a regular partner. Whitson had been in this field office for only two years. His big bright blue eyes and botched crew cut made Bryce think of the Gerber baby.

Bryce ignored Whitson for a moment. Bryce set the greasy bag on his messy desk, pausing long enough to move some of the less important papers. The fact that he still rated an office surprised him; it showed how strong his work had been in the past.

It also showed how sloppy he had gotten in the present. He had law books on a back shelf, some books on the history of New York, and phone books for the past five years on the bottom shelf. Case files were stacked haphazardly on the radiator cover. At some point, he should send a request to the secretarial pool for someone to clean up his mess.

He took the Styrofoam coffee cup out of the bag and removed the lid, setting the cup on his already ruined blotter. The coffee was his first rebellion against Hoover. If Bryce were here alone, he'd toss his hat into the wastebasket. But he didn't want Whitson to see it, in case someone decided to maintain the stupid dress code.

Finally Bryce took out a bagel slice and plopped himself behind the desk, pretending a jauntiness he didn't feel.

"What do you got?" he asked Whitson.

"I went to the motor pool," Whitson said, "and everything checks out. It was definitely Cain who took the sedan last night. No one's brought it back."

Of course no one brought it back, you idiot. It's now part of a crime scene. Miraculously, Bryce managed not to say that. He had vowed on the way to the office to contain as many of his offensive comments as he could.

Whitson glanced at some notes he'd scrawled on a yellow legal pad. "The night janitorial staff remembers seeing Agent Cain. He looked distracted. He frightened one of the janitors and didn't apologize."

"Frightened how?"

"He had several guns on his desk. He was hefting them, then turning them in his hand, as if testing for something. The janitor thought if he startled Cain, he might get shot."

"The janitor didn't think to report this?" Bryce asked.

"He says he's seen a lot of strange things in this office at night and that was not the strangest."

Bryce didn't push it. "What else do you have?"

"Agent Cain is not in his apartment, and no one has seen him since he left here last night."

"Any other hangouts, places he might be?"

"No, sir, not that we know of, sir. The problem is that one of Agent Cain's closest friends is Agent Nolan and, well—you know, we can't ask him."

Bryce nodded. He wondered if Nolan and Cain were actually close or if Cain had been another of Nolan's projects, like Bryce occasionally was.

He would never know the answer to that either.

"Did you go in the apartment?" Bryce asked.

"I had the super open the door," Whitson said, "you know, just in case Cain had been injured or something and couldn't get up, but he wasn't there."

"Did you see anything unusual?"

"I didn't know what to look for, sir. It looked like a bachelor's place. Messy, but normal, you know?"

Like Bryce's place now that Mary was gone. "I need a warrant for the apartment. I also need every personnel file on Cain and every file on Cain's desk. I want all his open and active cases, and I want to talk to anyone who saw him yesterday. Anyone at all."

"Yes, sir."

"The files first, then the warrant, all right?"

"Yes, sir."

"And Whitson?"

"Yes, sir?"

"Find out if anyone was with Cain when he left the office late last night."

"No one was, sir."

Bryce frowned. That was important information. How come Whitson hadn't told him that first?

Then he realized the answer. No one except himself and SAC Hart knew why they were searching for Cain. Everyone thought that Cain was missing and presumed dead, not that he'd been involved in the shooting.

Whitson was standing, about to leave and finish his assignment. Bryce waved at him to sit down.

"One more thing, Whitson," he said. "What do you make of Cain's behavior yesterday?"

Whitson shrugged. "What am I supposed to make of it, sir?"

"The janitor said he acted strange. He took a car out of the motor pool when he wasn't on duty. He was looking at guns. Did you draw any conclusions from that?"

Whitson took a deep breath. His fat baby cheeks were flushed and his eyes a little too bright. "He sounds like a man on a mission, sir."

"Any idea what that mission was?"

"It sounds like he went to relieve one of the agents on duty."

That seemed like as good an interpretation as any. Bryce decided to let it stand.

"Then that's the assumption we'll operate under. You inform me if there's any word from the field about Cain's whereabouts."

"You think the killer has him, sir?" Whitson asked.

Bryce hesitated just a moment before answering.

"Yeah," he said, his voice soft. "I think the killer has him. I think the killer has him good."

24

WALTER CAIN STOOD in the household appliances section of Malley's Department store, along with half a dozen other shoppers, four clerks, and one of the store managers. In one hand, Cain held a shopping bag filled with clothes—plaid shirts, dungarees, some workman's trousers, and seaman's sweaters. He was going to change into them before he went to the cemetery. He figured a man in a suit would be memorable if he stood in a cemetery on a cold February morning, but no one would notice a man dressed like a worker.

Especially if that man was looking at babies' graves. He needed a new identity. Finding some unfortunate who hadn't made it out of infancy would give him the needed birth certificate. Once he had his documentation, then he could go to Canada.

He had been almost out of the department store when the *Breaking News* graphic appeared on all of the television sets. On the large black-and-white sets, the graphic looked important. On the new color sets, the white words on the dark blue background looked silly—almost like a child's cut and paste.

People stopped around him, so he stopped, even though he knew what the announcement would be. *The Director of the FBI, J. Edgar Hoover, was shot to death in an alley next to his long-time lover, Associate Director Clyde Tolson, after they emerged from a party for degenerates held every Thursday night at that location. Hoover had frequented that party every single time he was in New York. Sources believe that Hoover had been targeted by a mugger uncertain of his identity or by a citizen who had been trying to clean up the mean streets of New York.*

Cain was so convinced he'd hear those words or something like them, that he was surprised to see not Walter Cronkite, but the White House Press Secretary Pierre Salinger. Salinger looked ill at ease as he walked up to the podium.

Cain suppressed a smile. It was hard for regular men to talk about people like Hoover, but it had to be done. Obviously, Salinger knew that.

"I have terrible news," Salinger said, his voice out of sync on the various televisions. "We have just received word that the Director of the Federal Bureau of Investigation, J. Edgar Hoover, died this morning in New York City. We do not yet know the circumstances. As soon as we have that information, we will present it to you."

Cain took a step forward. What did Salinger mean that they didn't have the information? Of course they had the information. Cain had laid it out for them like breadcrumbs. Whoever investigated the shooting would know about that party. It was an open secret in New York's law enforcement community.

Everyone knew. Why weren't they saying anything?

The White House Press Corps was shouting questions at Salinger, but the people around Cain were strangely silent. One young woman put her hand against her mouth. Tears were filling her eyes.

"We don't know the circumstances," Salinger said. "We do know that the Director had gone to the City on important FBI business. There is speculation that the two items are related."

"What?" Cain asked. "It wasn't related."

Two people looked at him.

"Not again," said the clerk beside him, a middle-aged man with thick dark glasses. "What is this country coming to?"

"This is some kind of war," said the man beside him.

Cain moved away from them. He wanted to hear Salinger.

"How did Director Hoover die?" asked a woman in the front row of the press conference.

Salinger shook his head. "We have almost no information at the moment. We decided it was better to let the country hear the moment we received word. We are gathering the facts right now, and I will be briefing you all day as I learn what's going on."

Reporters continued to ask questions, but Cain wasn't really listening any more. Instead he looked at the handful of people gathered around the television sets.

They all looked upset. They all seemed to think this was a sad event. And they would continue to think that as long as the circumstances of Hoover's death were kept secret.

He clutched the bag so tightly that its handles bit into his hand. Mistakes. People made mistakes when they got emotional, and he was being emotional now.

At the moment, no one had tied his name to the investigation. Maybe no one had checked the registration of the two sedans. Maybe no one knew about him.

There was no "wanted" bulletin to accompany that breaking news. And there should have been if they were looking for him.

They weren't yet.

He still had time. But he had to keep his profile low, and his demeanor even. He had to seem like these other sheep, mourning a deceptive hypocrite who had used them and their belief in his investigative abilities to further his own ends.

And that might be the hardest thing of all.

25

KENNEDY SAT CROSS-LEGGED on the floor of his office, the index card box open and resting against his ankles. He had finally located the cabinet with the labels that matched the key—or at least what he thought was the key—for his family's files.

The doors to his office were locked. Outside, a few agents stood guard. Kennedy had already assigned Angie Novello to rearrange offices on this floor so that the files could go into a room near his.

He knew LBJ wouldn't allow Kennedy to keep the files in his own office, but he probably wouldn't object to them remaining at Justice— at least, not without another pissing contest.

Kennedy had won the first contest. And he'd been magnanimous: He'd helped LBJ find his own files and remove them.

There were less than he would have thought. The ones Kennedy had taken from the cabinet—and LBJ had plucked from his hands when he saw Kennedy thumbing through them—were about Bobby Baker, LBJ's former aide on Capitol Hill who was once known as Little Lyndon. Baker had used his ties—both legal and illegal—to make himself into a multi-millionaire. In the last few years, the FBI had conducted an official investigation of Baker, and Hoover had reported all of those findings to Kennedy. The Bobby Baker case had made the front page just before Jack's death, and it looked like it would result in a conviction and prison time for Baker.

What was in these files had to be the information Kennedy had been pressing Hoover for last November. The links between Baker and LBJ—the rumors, the compromising photographs, the financial breakdowns.

Kennedy knew Hoover had been holding out on him; Hoover liked LBJ a lot more than the Kennedy brothers. And after Jack's death, Hoover had no reason to help Kennedy and every reason to support LBJ.

But that didn't stop Hoover from keeping dozens of files on the Baker-Johnson-Texas underworld ties. And it galled Kennedy to give those files away.

Losing them, however, was the price he was going to pay to remain at LBJ's side from now until the 1972 election. When Kennedy would lead the Democratic ticket.

The other files, so far as he could tell from looking over LBJ's shoulder, were mostly photographs of LBJ and women other than Lady Bird. Most of the photos were taken with a telephoto lens into hotel windows.

Kennedy didn't care so much about those. Those matched the ones in his brother's file and maybe one or two in his own. He wanted to see what else was in the Baker files, and knew he never would.

But he hadn't said a word to LBJ about the possibility of other files—files on Baker himself, files on the aides who had been with LBJ since his days in Texas politics.

Once Kennedy had removed his family's files, he would remove those files as well.

The entire bottom drawer of the first cabinet seemed to be about his parents. He couldn't tell from all the notations—the numbering system was extremely complex—but he could tell that the files went back for decades.

Kennedy got up. He needed a box, but he didn't have any—and he wasn't going to send for one.

He had just unloaded a bin with files on Everett Dirksen when the phone rang.

Kennedy cursed. He hadn't asked to be left alone—this was too important a day to remain out of touch—but he had made it clear (he thought) that he didn't want to be disturbed unless it had something to do with Hoover.

He brushed his hands on his pants, and grabbed the receiver. "Yeah." He let his tone carry his annoyance.

"Mr. Attorney General," Angie said, using that phrase even though he had always told her to call him Bobby, "I have Eugene Hart on the line. He's the Special Agent in Charge of the New York Regional Office. He said he was told to keep the national office apprised of his investigation, and he wasn't sure who he should report to."

Kennedy felt the hair on the back of his head rise. He'd been too focused on the files. He needed to pay attention to the Justice Department as well, particularly the FBI.

"Angie, from now on, refer every bit of business that would have gone to Hoover to me. How're you coming on those offices?"

"There's nothing available, sir."

"All right, then. Make a list of Hoover's right-hand men. Get Agent Haskell to help you. Make me a map of their offices in relation to mine."

"Yes, sir." She sounded confused. "Do you want to speak to SAC Hart?"

"Is this a secure line?"

"He says his is."

"Make sure mine is and patch him through."

She put Kennedy on hold for a brief moment. He used it to grab a legal pad and go to the other side of his desk, kicking his chair back with one foot. He pressed the receiver between his ear and his shoulder, and rummaged in his top drawer for a pen that worked.

By the time Hart came on the line, Kennedy was ready to take notes.

"Mr. Attorney General, sir," Hart said, "I didn't mean to bother you, but your secretary said—"

"I'm the person to bother," Kennedy said. "I'm going to handle the Director's duties until the President appoints someone new."

LBJ didn't know that, of course. He would learn it at the cabinet meeting he'd called for—Kennedy checked his watch—in less than one hour.

"I would fly to Washington to brief you, sir, but I think it's better for me to stay on site."

"I agree, Agent Hart." Kennedy hoped he was using the right title. He never really paid much attention to the rankings in the FBI, since the person he had to deal with all the time was Hoover. "Tell me now. We're on a secure line."

"Well, sir, I think we have a problem."

Kennedy smiled in spite of himself. "And I think, sir, that you have a gift for understatement."

Hart let out a dry chuckle. It sounded involuntary, and then he confirmed it by adding, "Sorry, sir, that wasn't appropriate."

Kennedy let it go. He didn't think anyone should be grieving Hoover, but he had a hunch that was not a popular opinion at the moment.

"Sir, so far, the NYPD refuses to relinquish the investigation to the FBI. They're claiming jurisdiction, and they're right." Obviously that bothered Hart a lot for him to mention it first.

"We'll deal with that in a moment, Eugene—is it all right if I call you Eugene?"

"Of course, sir."

Good. That made the question of titles irrelevant and gave Kennedy less of a chance to make an ass of himself. "Tell me what you found and what you believe."

Hart ran through the crime scene. He stammered over the information about the party and the neighborhood until Kennedy said, "I understand the implications, Eugene. You're not shocking me. I've known Edgar's predilections since the late 1940s."

"Good, okay, sir. That makes this a bit easier. Here's what we think happened. He always kept his bodyguards too far away when he went on his personal visits. I don't think he was protecting himself. I think he was protecting his friends."

Probably from people like Hoover, people who wanted compromising photographs. But Kennedy remained quiet.

Hart described the crime scene, where the other agents were found and how they were killed.

"Right now, the NYPD is going on three assumptions. The first was that this was some kind of spree killer, you know, like that Richard Speck out in the Midwest a few years ago—the guy who just randomly shot half a dozen people."

Kennedy barely remembered the case. But he didn't need to know much about it. He understood what a spree killer was.

"The NYPD started with the premise that this was a mugging gone wrong. Or maybe a fag killing and then the killers realized what they'd done."

That didn't sound likely to Kennedy. Hoover was recognizable no matter what he was wearing. Whoever shot him had to have seen him and known who he was.

"Now, though, the NYPD is leaning toward their third theory. They think the FBI or maybe Hoover himself was targeted by person or persons unknown. They've run a list from the local Communist Party to members of the Genovese crime family. They want a list of anyone we consider possible."

"They think that someone in organized crime did this?" Kennedy asked, feeling a chill.

"It looks planned," Hart said. "I was at the scene myself, and I have to say, this was one professional job."

Kennedy's heart was pounding harder than it had all day. If the Genovese family or anyone who was mobbed up had killed Hoover, that proved LBJ's point—that this was tied to Kennedy's work as Attorney General.

And to Jack's murder.

"But, sir," Hart was saying, "I don't think that's what happened."

It took a moment for his words to register. "What do you mean that's not what happened?"

"The moment we got the news, I sent an agent there who lived nearby. He was supposed to lock down the scene. Well, he discovered that the scene was larger than he expected and it covered several blocks. He worked his way backwards from that alley to the place where he be-lieves—and I agree—the first shots were fired."

Kennedy clutched his pen. He hadn't written much on the legal pad so far. He wasn't sure he was going to write anything at all.

"There the agent found a second sedan registered to the FBI. One that shouldn't have been there. You see, the NYPD believes that the second car arrived to relieve the men in the first car, and the men from the second car are missing. The NYPD even did a canvas to see if they could find the men from the second car."

"But?" Kennedy asked.

"But we believe there was only one man in the second car. We be-lieve he's the one who committed the five killings. Everything we've found so far backs that conclusion."

Kennedy frowned. He set the pen on his desk. "You're saying that someone stole an FBI vehicle—"

"I'm saying that an FBI agent committed the murders."

Kennedy's breath caught. "What?"

"He had just found out that his fiancée had killed herself. Do you know the department's policy on marriage?"

"No," Kennedy said.

"It's one I think your new director should change. In a nutshell, po-tential spouses have to be vetted through the FBI and if they fall short, the agent is told not to marry them."

"And if the agent does?"

"Most likely, he'll be fired. The Director believed that sexual black-mail was the easiest and the most vicious kind."

Kennedy stared at the files all around him. He was beginning to understand Hoover's point in an entirely new way. The old man loved getting sexual information on everyone he knew.

"So something was wrong with the fiancée," Kennedy said.

"Yeah," Hart said. "The long and short of it is when this all came out, she committed suicide. And the agent, a Walter Cain, blamed Di-rector Hoover."

"That I don't understand," Kennedy said.

"Agent Cain used to work HooverWatch, sir. He knew about the Director's…um…proclivities."

Kennedy set the legal pad on the pen and it nearly rolled off the desk. He caught the pad with one hand. "You're saying this Cain murdered five people because Hoover was a hypocrite?"

"Yes, sir. We think Cain snapped."

"Snapped." Kennedy let out a puff of air. He tried to turn the information over and over in his mind. It didn't quite make sense. "Are you sure this man wasn't turned? Are you sure he wasn't working for the KGB or Castro or something?"

"We're not sure of anything right now. But I can tell you that Cain used to be a Green Beret, and there are instructions in his file to keep him away from international cases. He came to the FBI because he was a better fit for us. It seems he didn't accept other cultures well."

Green Beret. Kennedy suppressed a sigh. The term had caught on after Jack had visited the highly trained special squad and asked them about their green berets. Jack had been the one to expand the force. He had loved the very idea of a secretive special squad.

Kennedy had taunted him about it, saying Jack had absorbed the wrong things from those Ian Fleming spy novels he loved so much.

"You're telling me," Kennedy said slowly, "that this Cain wasn't a likely double agent."

"Yes, sir," Hart said. "That's exactly what I'm saying, sir."

"Aren't most double agents unlikely double agents, at least on paper?"

"Sir?"

"The successful ones," Kennedy said. "The Kim Philbys of the world. Aren't they successful because no one suspects they would ever be double agents?"

"I can't answer that, sir," Hart said. "It's not in my area of expertise."

Kennedy leaned his chair back. Bureaucrats. So unwilling to take any kind of risk, even in conversation.

But that meant that Hart truly believed Cain had killed Hoover, or Hart wouldn't have said much about the agent. He would have said simply that they had a possible suspect.

"Could Cain be working for the Syndicate?" Kennedy asked.

"The Mafia?" Hart sounded so shocked that Kennedy didn't want to correct him. The Mafia was a small part of the Syndicate, even though the media thought it was all one and the same. The Syndicate contained organized crime families from all walks of life, from Jews to Italians to Cubans. *The Mafia* referred only to the Italians.

"The Syndicate, yes," Kennedy said. "Could he have been turned by them?"

"Why?" Hart said. "The Director never really believed the Mafia was a threat. Even after 1957—"

When the Syndicate held a big meeting of all the bosses in upstate New York. Hoover had been shocked to learn of this, even though his agents—and members of Kennedy's Senate Committee—had been warning him about this for years.

"—he thought it was a small threat. He kept calling them *gangsters*, and believed they were getting in the way of the war against the Communists. There'd be no point to take one of our agents and have him spy for the Mafia."

"Not even in New York, a Syndicate stronghold?" Kennedy asked.

"I can think of a lot better candidates. Guys with pull who needed the money. Guys who were hooked into the system. An agent like Cain, he couldn't get specialized information any more than some reporter could."

"But you'll check that for me, won't you?" Kennedy asked.

"Yes, of course we will, sir. But I don't think we'll find anything."

Kennedy sighed and rubbed his face with his hand. The lack of sleep was starting to catch up to him. "If your scenario is true, Eugene, this is a public relations nightmare."

"It gets worse, sir. We have enough evidence now that if Cain were some random criminal, we would put out an all-points bulletin so that law enforcement all over the country could look for him. We'd let the media know. We'd do a large campaign so that this man couldn't hide. We can't do that. At least, I can't order it. You could, sir."

Kennedy wasn't sure he wanted to. "What about the NYPD? Can't they say they're looking for him?"

"Sure, but in New York. Cain is a trained investigator, sir. He's going to know what we're going to do before we do it. I'm pretty sure that the only way we can catch this guy is to let the public help us search."

"Let me run this through channels," Kennedy said. "I'll see what we can come up with."

"All right, sir." Hart didn't sound all right. "But the problem is a pretty simple one. If we don't do something soon, we'll lose him. He'll vanish and we'll never find him."

"No one's that good," Kennedy said.

"It's his training, sir. He used to go into foreign countries, blend in and do—what the Green Berets call wetwork. Do you know what that is, sir?"

Kennedy had heard the term a lot when he was on the McClellan Committee. He'd used the word himself before the Bay of Pigs, when he and Jack decided to get help eliminating Castro. It hadn't worked—their wetwork specialists who were, ironically, with the Syndicate—had failed, starting the chain reaction that created the whole nasty disaster—one that brought the world to the brink of nuclear war.

"Yeah," Kennedy said curtly. "I know the term."

"Then you understand, sir. If we don't move quickly, he's gone for good."

"I understand," Kennedy said. "I'll get back to you."

Then he hung up. He kept his hand on the receiver for a moment, as fear swept through him. He hadn't told Hart to keep the conversation confidential.

But Hart would. He was talking to his boss—briefing his boss—who was Kennedy now.

Kennedy made himself breathe. All of this information was his and his alone.

He rested his hand on the legal pad. He still had forty minutes before the Cabinet Meeting. If he went to the White House beforehand, he might get a short audience with LBJ.

But Kennedy had some facts to check first. Thinking about the Syndicate and the Bay of Pigs brought back other memories, as well as some information that Kennedy had blocked until now.

He'd purposely avoided anything to do with Jack's assassination. Once Kennedy had the body back from Parkland Hospital in Dallas, once he had all the secret documents and tapes from the Oval Office secured, once he had the family calmed, he had disappeared into his own office and closed his eyes.

He hadn't wanted to know who killed Jack because, if he thought about it, he already knew.

LBJ had been right.

The person who killed Jack Kennedy hadn't been Lee Harvey Oswald.

It had been Jack's most trusted advisor, and his best friend.

Kennedy had killed Jack. As surely as if he had stood in that Texas Schoolbook Depository window and pulled the trigger on the gun himself.

Kennedy had alienated the Syndicate, and then he had betrayed them. He had tried to destroy them, and instead of destroying them, they had destroyed him.

Or nearly had. Would have, in fact, if Hoover hadn't died.

But now Kennedy was back.

He pressed the intercom on his phone. Angie answered.

"Angie, tell the President that I'm being briefed on today's events, and I'll need an extra half an hour or so to get the information together before the Cabinet meeting. Ask him if it can be postponed—and ask him if I can have a few minutes of his time just before it."

"Yes, sir," she said.

"And do me a favor. Have Agent Haskell bring me all of the files that Hoover kept on my brother's assassination. Including the most current ones."

"All right, sir," Angie said.

"I want notes, too. Handwritten stuff, anything Hoover might have left. The stuff he wanted the staff to give to that commission LBJ set up—what's that called?"

"The Warren Commission, sir."

"Yeah, that," Kennedy said. "I need all of that information pronto."

"Yes, sir."

"With enough time for me to do a brief review before my meeting with the President."

"Sir, I don't think you'll have enough time. Would you like an agent to brief you on all of this?"

Kennedy didn't want anyone's interpretations of the facts. He wanted the files. He wanted to see what Hoover had seen.

"No," he said. "I just need the files. Now."

Then he let go of the intercom.

After the click, the office was completely silent. From where he was sitting behind his desk, he couldn't see the windows or the doors. He was lost in a forest of secret files.

And he wanted more.

He needed Hoover's knowledge.

Kennedy had to know if his suspicions were right.

If the Syndicate had killed his brother, then Kennedy had a chance, a small chance but a chance nonetheless, to get back at the Syndicate, maybe even completely destroy them.

Everyone in my family forgives, the Ambassador used to say with pride, *except Bobby*.

Kennedy nodded as his father's words rang in his head. He had forgotten who he was for a while.

But now he was back.

And this time, no one would get the better of him.

This time, he would win.

26

MIDMORNING, AND THE OFFICE had grown quiet. Agents had left to search for Cain on the assumption that the man was being held by a killer. Hart had locked himself in his office, and Whitson was following Bryce's instructions.

Bryce sat at his desk. The transistor Mary had given him two Christmases ago was on. He'd heard the announcement of Hoover's death, thought it particularly bad form on the part of the White House, and didn't pay much attention to the comments that followed.

He was too focused on the papers Whitson had brought him. Surprisingly, Cain's personnel and case files covered most of Bryce's desk.

Bryce started with the personnel file. It made for much more interesting reading than he had expected.

Cain was ten years younger than Bryce would have guessed by looking at the man. Cain had gone through Quantico straight out of high school, one of the few recruits to ever do so. Hoover insisted on having a college-educated force. In fact, early on, Hoover insisted that all FBI agents have law degrees.

Hoover had quietly discarded that requirement, although he preferred lawyers right to the end. However, Bryce had thought the college requirement was hard and fast.

Apparently it wasn't.

Bryce found letters of recommendation from various field agents, some of whom quite high ranking, praising Cain's intelligence and drive. A few mentioned Cain's impoverished background and his inability to pay for college.

Bryce had known a lot of impoverished agents who had somehow paid for their own college. They'd taken the six-year plan and finished only a few classes a semester while working or they got scholarships or managed to wrangle a few grants for specialized work.

No one that he knew of had ever come straight to Quantico before.

Bryce almost skipped ahead to the transcripts from Quantico, but didn't. He wasn't sure he wanted to know how hard that place was for someone who hadn't spent time at an institute of higher education.

Instead, he paused, reached into the greasy bag on the floor beside his chair and grabbed the second bagel. It had gotten cold and the cream cheese had congealed, but Bryce didn't care. He ate slowly, not sure when he was going to get his next meal.

It took some digging through the voluminous paperwork, but he finally found some early records. Cain had attended high school in rural Pennsylvania. He hadn't graduated. Instead, he enlisted when he turned eighteen and spent the next two years in West Germany.

When he had come home, he could have gone to school on the G.I. Bill—and he did use that at a community college in upstate New York to get his high school equivalency.

But then he applied at the FBI training facility, got his letters of recommendation, and was accepted into Quantico on a provisional basis.

Bryce had to do even more thumbing through papers—the entire damn file was messier than his desk—before he found the application itself, along with the notations of the accepting agent.

Apparently Cain hadn't been on cushy city duty in West Germany. He'd had Green Beret training. He'd shown an aptitude for all levels of the work, including solo reconnaissance.

He was the best sniper in the entire division, maybe the best in West Germany.

And he occasionally got special assignments.

Some of his military file had been appended onto the application. But the information about Cain's actual work in West Germany was redacted. Only the notes that the agent who approved the application provided a clue.

Served with distinction. Finished dangerous missions alone. Proved to be one of the most valuable assets in Germany. Did not resign—got discouraged when he didn't agree with an assignment; thought the high value target redeemable.

Redeemable. Bryce stopped when he saw that word. He set the remains of his bagel down and wiped off his fingers. *Redeemable* was an interesting word for a "valuable asset" to use about his "high value target." It was a religious word, perilously close to *redemption*, and filled with a kind of hope that Bryce had never seen in the FBI, let alone in Green Berets.

If he was reading between the lines correctly—and he had a hunch he was—Cain was trained as an assassin and used on a mission that took him into East Germany, maybe deeper into the Soviet Union than Bryce wanted to think about.

Bryce tapped his forefinger against his teeth. *Redeemable.*

If nothing else, the word was a link to Essie Seward and a window into Cain's mind. Not only had Essie been redeemable, she had been redeemed. Like Mary Magdalene, she had gone from being a prostitute to a woman who served God.

No wonder her death had set Cain off. Not only had he lost the woman he loved, he had lost her for the very reason that he had probably fallen for her—she had been redeemed.

But in order to be redeemed, a person had to be a sinner first.

And it was her sins that made the FBI reject her as a choice of fiancée for one of their agents. Her sins that had caused Hart to make that awful call, telling her she would never be worthy of an FBI agent, that she would ruin him and his career.

In other words, the FBI had said the redemption didn't matter. Only the sins.

Bryce sighed heavily and picked up his coffee cup. It was empty, but he didn't get up to get another.

Instead, he continued digging.

He would have thought that a "valuable asset" who judged one of his own targets wouldn't have been of any use to the FBI. But Bryce gleaned from more search in the file that Cain had gone ahead and eliminated the target, despite his misgivings.

The misgivings provided the basis for his refusal to re-enlist, which was rare for Green Berets. In fact, it was rare for them to go after only a few years. So much had been invested in their training that it wasn't cost effective to have them serve for only two years.

And that was the answer Bryce had been looking for. Cain had been brought in not as a charity case or as a high achiever, but because the government wanted a return on its investment. They probably decided against the CIA because, given Cain's background, he might have to do some of the same work for the CIA that he had been doing for Green Berets.

In fact, there was a greater chance that he would, since a lot of the CIA's clandestine operations had an illegal edge. Many CIA operatives had been abandoned by their superiors, something that Cain, just from his personnel file, couldn't handle.

Bryce pulled out a legal pad and made a note of that thought. Then he continued his own personal analysis.

They had made Cain an FBI agent, figuring he wouldn't have to do what some in the spy business called wetwork. That his training would make him suitable for surveillance and lower level investigations, as well as protection duties.

And, thanks to Hoover, FBI agents did judge their targets—often, in fact. Hoover insisted on a moral agency, one that looked at everything with an eye to redemption.

Cain must have seemed like a perfect fit.

Bryce thumbed through the file, then stopped and looked at his legal pad. He had written that Cain couldn't handle being abandoned by his superiors. That had come from his reading of the personnel files and what Bryce saw between the lines.

And if that analysis were true, then that added some insight into the events of the past twenty-four hours.

Cain felt abandoned by the FBI. The FBI had brought him in, trained him, promoted him, and made him feel at home. Then it had taken the woman he loved and destroyed her.

Bryce tapped his pen on the legal pad. The FBI hadn't just abandoned Cain. With a single action, it had ruined his life.

An action that Cain—a good military man—didn't blame on the guys carrying out the orders, but on the man who issued them.

A man he didn't consider redeemable. A man he considered a degenerate, and someone unworthy of judging a woman like Essie—a successfully redeemed woman, the kind that Christ held in the highest esteem.

Bryce tapped his pen on the page. Was that enough for a man to go off the deep end and kill five people? Or did something else happen?

Bryce sighed. The file gave him some answers but even more questions. And he had only just started into it. He hadn't even looked at the various cases Cain had been on.

He needed to stop reading, however. He needed to get out into the field, to see if he could find evidence of Cain's trail.

He needed some time to think.

27

THE FILES WERE DEVASTATING.

Kennedy sat at his desk, paging through report after report. Some were from the Dallas Police Department, some were from local Texas FBI agents.

All made that day his brother died come back with such clarity that Kennedy's heart ached.

He had never watched the Zapruder film, although Hoover had his own copy of it. Hoover also had copies of photographs from various amateur photographers around the parade route, and a few from professional photographers who had stationed themselves on that corner.

The files also referred to footage from a Dallas television station. Apparently one of the station's reporters was getting film in Dealey Plaza for that evening's news.

A man with Secret Service identification that the reporter inspected with amazing vigor claimed the Secret Service needed the footage so that it could catch the killer, and the reporter handed over the film.

No Secret Service agents remained on the ground in Dealey Plaza after Jack's limosine zoomed off to Parkland Hospital.

Yet the reporter wasn't the only person who had talked to Secret Service agents. A number of bystanders near what was now being called the Grassy Knoll had their cameras confiscated by other Secret Service agents as well.

Hoover had made a notation on one of the files—*Fake identification? Where had it come from?*

But Kennedy knew. Through some back channels, he had provided real Secret Service identification to the mobsters hired to do wetwork in Cuba. The Administration—his brother's administration—had believed the Secret Service identifications would open doors that would remain otherwise closed.

The ID hadn't opened any doors. All the plots to assassinate Castro and the people high up in his government had failed.

But the IDs had never been returned.

Kennedy leaned back in his chair and rubbed his eyes. That despair he'd been fighting for months threatened to return.

But he couldn't let it.

He needed more.

He paged past the memos with notations in Hoover's handwriting—*essential that the evidence point to Oswald ONLY*—and onto the actual facts of the case.

The more he read, the more he realized there had to be several shooters, some on that grassy knoll, maybe one in a building near the depository.

Oswald's gun was mail order, and he wasn't a sharpshooter. Besides, according to gun experts for the FBI, there was no way a good shot would have been able to shoot Jack that many times from the window that Oswald supposedly used. A bad marksman with a handmade gun couldn't have hit Jack at all.

And then there was Jack Ruby, the man who shot and killed Oswald on national television. To shoot and kill another killer—or supposed killer—was a mob signature. The mob often set up a patsy, let its own boys do the killing, and then had someone else—a second patsy or a lower tier mobster—kill the fake shooter.

Kennedy had been familiar with Ruby for years. His name had come up many times in the organized crime investigations Kennedy had spearheaded. When Kennedy had heard the man's name and seen the footage of the shooting, he knew that the Syndicate was involved. He knew it to a dead certainty.

Ruby had been part of the Syndicate—first in Chicago, then in Texas—for decades. He was a bag man for Carlos Marcello and had traveled all over the United States doing odd jobs.

His name had come up several times in the McClellan hearings and more than once in Kennedy's investigations of Jimmy Hoffa. Ruby was so mobbed up that Kennedy didn't have to read the FBI reports in front of him, which confirmed it.

Jack Ruby was the guy who had made Kennedy close his eyes in the first place.

Now Kennedy forced himself to keep those eyes open.

Hoover had stamped dozens of reports and memos about Ruby as classified. He didn't want them to go to the Warren Commission.

Nor did he want any information about Marcello to get there either.

Marcello, whom the FBI had in taped transcripts making the very threat LBJ had repeated this morning. To kill a dog, you don't cut off its tail.

You cut off its head.

LBJ knew as well. He'd seen those transcripts.

Kennedy felt his face flush. He had to take a deep breath to remain calm. LBJ didn't want the Texas mob connections to come out, and Kennedy knew why.

That information was in Kennedy's own files, the files he planned to use in late November to convince Jack to take LBJ off the ticket. LBJ had received campaign donations from Carlos Marcello. LBJ had men in his organization who had also worked with Marcello.

LBJ's connection to the Texas part of the Syndicate was as deep—maybe deeper—than Jack's connections to the Giancanas.

But not, Kennedy knew, as deep as the Ambassador's ties to organized crime. Their father was what the experts called an above-the-ground mobster, someone who worked in plain sight.

That was why Kennedy had gone after some mob families and left others alone. He'd tried to end the scourge, but had tried to do so without implicating his father or his brother.

He had wanted to make sure his brother got reelected. Then he wanted to end the mob's ties throughout America completely.

Kennedy had thought it impossible after Jack died.

Kennedy had given up so completely, he no longer consulted with Robert Morganthau of New York about the upcoming Hoffa trials.

But now Kennedy had a chance to crush the mob.

And he had a reason.

He was going to get back at them for the murder of his brother—and he was going to use Hoover's death to do it.

28

WALTER CAIN LIVED in a sixth floor walk-up in a neighborhood not a lot better than the one in which he murdered J. Edgar Hoover. Frank Bryce looked out the hallway window and noted the only distinctive feature of the neighborhood—the spire of the Catholic church just down the block.

The church where Essie Seward had confessed her sins, found work and a refuge, and set about rebuilding her life. The church where Cain had met and fallen in love with her. The church that was, in a way the Bible never meant, the Alpha and the Omega—the beginning and the end.

"There's nothing there, sir," Thurman Whitson said from the door-way to Cain's apartment. "He didn't have anything in the hall."

Except that every time he came up the stairs, tired and worn out from his long day, he saw the church spire through the hall-way window.

For a man who believed in redemption, that might have been enough.

Redemption. Bryce frowned. Maybe the problem wasn't that the FBI had ignored Essie's redemption. Maybe it was that the FBI had ignored Cain's.

Essie would have given him hope. If a woman with her past could be saved, then maybe a man with his past could be saved as well. A man whose government had asked him to sneak into other countries and target people he'd never met. People on a list.

Bryce turned and walked into the apartment, not stopping at the door the way the FBI manual said that investigators should, but the way that someone who lived in the apartment would walk inside.

He wanted to see what Cain used to see.

What Cain used to see was a living room with a half-kitchen, a ratty couch with a blanket tossed over it, a small black-and-white television set with rabbit ears extended and covered with aluminum foil, and a transistor radio on top of the 1930s Frigidaire.

Papers were scattered all over the floor, but that looked like someone had knocked down a stack, not like Cain had normally lived this way. In fact, there were hints that the apartment was usually neat. There were no dirty dishes piled in the sink and no stench of untended garbage.

Bryce walked past Whitson, who was watching him as if he were the strange one. Bryce stepped into the small bedroom, noting the single bed made up military style and the open door to the bathroom.

There was another closed door beside that one, and Bryce pushed it open. A closet, which looked surprisingly neat. A man on the run should have ransacked his closet, shouldn't he?

Bryce let out a small breath. Maybe an average man. But what would a man on the run do with two matching black suits and a dozen white shirts?

He closed the closet door, walked to the dresser and pulled it open. There was the expected messiness. Cain had ransacked his underwear drawer. There were dress socks, but no white socks and no underwear at all.

Everything else was there: the ties neatly folded, the tie clips, some cufflinks for one of the dress shirts. Handkerchiefs and a military style watch at least a decade old. Other drawers revealed some medals, a few pictures of family, and some old letters. Nothing more.

Except a small red velvet box. Bryce opened it. A cheap diamond ring glittered in the morning light.

Bryce sighed and closed the box. Essie must have returned the ring before she killed herself.

Which would have been sometime yesterday. Cain had put the box away, but he hadn't returned the ring—and it had to be worth a lot for a man on his salary.

"I want the letters and pictures from this apartment," Bryce said to Whitson.

Whitson nodded.

Bryce slipped into the bathroom. It was tiny and mostly empty. There was a rust stain in the sink and a matching one in the bathtub, but no dirt.

Of course, Whitson had been wrong when he said that Cain had a typical bachelor's apartment, messy and empty. Normally this place wasn't messy at all. The toilet bowl was clean and the seat was down. Everything in its place.

Bryce frowned. *Everything in its place.* The only things missing in here were toiletries. They should have been on top of the shelf above the toilet, but that shelf was empty.

There was no medicine cabinet, nothing for things like toothpaste and a toothbrush except that shelf.

That empty shelf.

Above a full garbage can. Bryce upended the garbage can. It was filled with toilet paper, small pieces wadded up.

The way a man did when he was trying to clean tears off his face. Tears he couldn't stop.

Bryce whirled and saw the one other thing that was out of place.

Behind the door, a fist-sized hole so new that the plasterboard hadn't had time to yellow on the breaks.

Cain had come in here after he had gotten home. He had seen the church spire when he came up the stairs and that had started the tears—tears he couldn't stop.

He'd hurried inside, knocked down that stack of papers, whatever they were, as he rushed past them, and then went into the bathroom, closing the door behind him.

He didn't want anyone to know about his tears—not even himself, probably. Which was why he came in here, where he could be alone.

He'd cleaned off his face, tried to get control of himself, and couldn't.

Bryce turned again. One more missing item—no mirror. Every bathroom had a mirror. Every man's bathroom needed one. He had to shave somehow.

Bryce crouched, pushing the tissue aside. Sure enough, there were pieces of silvered glass on the floor. Little ones, the kind that were hard to get up with a broom and a dustpan.

"Give me your flashlight," Bryce said to Whitson.

Whitson leaned inside the bathroom and handed him a flashlight. Bryce turned it on. The light up close to the floor reflected the broken glass and found the other thing that Bryce had been looking for.

Small drops of blood.

Cain had cut his hand when he smashed that mirror.

What had he done? Seen his own tear-streaked face reflected back at him? Gotten angry at the loss of control?

Bryce stood and examined that hole in the wall. There was no blood on the plasterboard, and there would have been if Cain had hit this spot second.

So somewhere, in the midst of all those tears, Cain had gotten angry. He'd put his fist through the wall, which probably calmed the crying, then turned and saw his own ravaged face.

And destroyed it.

A shudder ran through Bryce.

He tried to imagine what Cain would have seen. An FBI agent whose life had just been ruined.

An FBI agent who never should have been an agent in the first place. Who was told he belonged here only because there was nowhere else for him to go.

Had he been told that?

Or had he been told that he belonged in the FBI because of his highly developed moral sense? That he had a level of ethics that few people possessed?

"Hey, Whitson," Bryce said. "When you had your meeting with the Director, did he talk to you about morals?"

Whitson peered into the bathroom, a frown on his face. "Why would you want to know that?"

"Humor me," Bryce said. "Did he?"

"God, I don't remember. I remember his hand, though, all soft and dry. I hated shaking it. Then he takes out a tissue and wipes it off, like I'm the dirty one."

Bryce remembered that too. "What else?"

"He talked about a lot of things. How important we all were to the department, how we needed to uphold the country's values. How we were—"

"That was it," Bryce said. "Uphold the country's values."

Which Hoover didn't do. Which, if one looked at Cain's personal history, he hadn't done either.

FBI agents: people who seemed to be one thing and actually were another. Something less, something not nearly as important.

Something that had to be destroyed.

"Jesus," Bryce said softly.

"You find something?" Whitson asked.

Not something he could explain. How did you tell a junior agent with little investigative training that you understood what had happened here in the hours before Cain went on his killing spree?

How did you explain that Cain wasn't just after Hoover, he was also after himself. The man who had gotten Essie into the position where the FBI could destroy her.

In this little room, Cain had split in half. He had become a man beyond redemption, and he had become the man who destroyed people who were beyond redemption.

He would function like a hunter, like a Green Beret operative, until something provoked him again. And because he wasn't rational any longer, it would be a lot easier to provoke him.

Cain was even more dangerous now than he had been when he returned to the office and went through his guns, looking for the right weapon for the job of murdering the Director.

Because in Cain's twisted mind, it was logical to go after the Director—and that was a logic even Bryce could understand.

But from there, Bryce wouldn't be able to predict what would set Cain off. Because he was already off. His rational mind was gone.

What proved it was that he had left a trail. Experienced investigators wouldn't leave a trail. Unless they meant it deliberately.

"You said he'd cashed a check at the deli next door?" Cain asked Whitson.

Whitson nodded. "It was pretty big. The owner wouldn't have done it if he hadn't known Cain was an FBI agent."

Everyone in the building had known Cain was an FBI agent. The neighbors hadn't thought anything of Cain leaving the apartment that morning in his usual black suit with a black overcoat and regulation hat. They had remembered the briefcase only because he didn't always carry one.

"Why don't you check other delis around here," Bryce said. "Let's see if he cashed more than one good-sized check."

"Wouldn't it have been easier to go to the bank?" Whitson asked.

"I have a hunch he did that too," Bryce said.

Cain had left his passbook in the top drawer of his bureau, along with a few coins and a five-dollar bill. Maybe he had thought that would make him look like he would return soon or he hadn't left at all.

That trail bothered Bryce.

It might have been a trail of breadcrumbs leading him in the wrong direction.

Which was why Bryce was going to be the one who took the passbook to the bank.

He sent Whitson out of the apartment, took one last look around, and then left. It took him a while to get to Cain's bank.

It wasn't far from Regional FBI Headquarters. The bank itself was old. It was one of those stone buildings with massive double doors, large glass windows, and old-fashioned teller's cages. Bryce walked around the line, going instead to the information window near the back.

"I need to talk to the bank manager," he said as he flashed his badge.

The manager seemed to appear in a moment. He was a balding man named Oliver Doyle, and he seemed nervous to have an FBI agent in his bank.

He led Bryce through the information door into the narrow back, up a flight of stairs, and down a hallway to some large offices. The offices overlooked Broadway. Even on a cold winter morning, the street below looked busy. Men hurrying to their jobs, most wearing black overcoats, clutching briefcases, and sipping from a Styrofoam cup filled with coffee.

Bryce winced. Cain *had* left a trail of breadcrumbs pointing in the wrong direction. Because Cain looked like every other middle-class male scurrying to his job. No one would notice him. He didn't look different enough.

"Agent Bryce," Doyle said, his voice quivering. "Please have a seat."

The office was large—larger than Bryce's. It was also neat. The metal desk—twice the size of his—had one single file on its blotter. The blotter was a calendar with removable pages. Right now, February stared up at him, with more than half the days neatly crossed off with an X.

Bryce sat across from Doyle and leaned forward, placing the passbook on the word "February" itself. "I need to know every account in this bank owned by Walter Cain. This passbook belongs to him. I need to know how much is in each account and if there's been any unusual activity today."

"May I enquire as to why?" Doyle asked, his voice still shaking.

"You may inquire," Bryce said, "but I'm not at liberty to tell you anything."

Doyle nodded as if he had expected that. He took the passbook and slid out of the office, closing the door behind him. Bryce stood up and went back to the window. Rays of orange morning light streamed through the gap between buildings. People hurried in and out of that patch of sunlight as if they were going through a small spotlight on a stage that they weren't even aware they were on.

Cain had written a series of checks, establishing a route. Bryce would have evidence of that route when Whitson was done with his canvas.

But Cain hadn't worn distinctive clothing (although, to be fair, it didn't look like he owned much distinctive clothing). He left his FBI sedan at the crime scene, and, like most people who lived in the five boroughs, he didn't own his own car.

His parents had died before he joined the Green Berets, and he listed no other family on his FBI or military documents. He had few friends, at least that Bryce knew about, and because Cain had been out of the country before going to Quantico, no real favorite haunts.

He was the perfect man to disappear. And he would be hard to find—provided he was thinking clearly and was deliberately trying to leave a false trail.

Bryce didn't know Cain well enough to get into his head. So the only question Bryce could ask was this: If he were disappearing, how would he do it?

He wasn't sure he would be smart enough to wear his FBI clothes. But he had a secondary wardrobe, one in which he was a lot more comfortable.

Assuming, though, he had been smart enough, what would he do?

He wouldn't rent a car. That would be—could be—memorable. He would take public transportation out of the city. Which meant busses or trains.

On a bus, a man in a suit with a briefcase would be noticed. But no one would notice a work-a-day guy taking the train to Jersey or Pennsylvania or upstate. If anyone gave the guy any thought, they'd assume he was on a sales call or going home from a business meeting. Or just heading to one.

Cain would probably look like a dozen other guys on the same train, guys who would get off at various stops without having said a word to their neighbor or anyone else on the platform. Guys who lugged their briefcases away from the train like men who were on some kind of mission.

The door opened. Doyle was back. His domed forehead glistened with sweat.

"It seems," he said, "Agent Cain withdrew all but five hundred dollars from this account."

Bryce slipped his hands into his pockets. Cain had cashed a fifty-dollar check at the deli. If he stopped at nine other places and wrote fifty-dollar checks before coming here, then those checks would clear in the next few days, effectively emptying the account.

"Did he have other accounts here?" Bryce asked.

"A savings," Doyle said. "He closed that account, and took the money in cash."

"He came here this morning and did all that?"

"Well, no," Doyle said. "He did it at one of our branches this morning. That's what took me so long to get back to you. I had to make a few calls."

"Which branch?" Bryce asked.

"We have one near the Port Authority Terminal," Doyle said. "Times Square. It's not our best branch, and according to our records, he's never used it before."

Bryce nodded. More breadcrumbs? Or did Cain simply not care?

"How much money are we talking about here?" Bryce asked.

"He took about four thousand dollars, all told," Doyle said. "Honestly, if he weren't an FBI agent, he wouldn't have been able to take it all in cash. We usually do bank checks for withdrawals that large."

Four thousand dollars. That was enough to buy a small house outside the city. One of those so-called starter homes.

"That's unusual, isn't it?" Bryce asked. "Most banks let people cash out."

"I didn't mean to mislead you, Agent Bryce. Agent Cain took out the money from a teller. Usually it takes a branch manager to approve sums that large. The manager wasn't in yet. The branch had just opened for the day. But since Agent Cain worked for the FBI, the teller and her immediate supervisor on the floor believed there would be no problem with the withdrawal."

"So they processed it," Bryce said.

Doyle nodded, swallowing hard. "Did we make some sort of mistake, sir? That was Agent Cain's money, wasn't it?"

"Yes, it was Agent Cain's money," Bryce said.

"That's an awful lot of money," Doyle said. "But he told our girl that he was getting married and needed the funds for the honeymoon and the down payment on a house. She offered to give him traveler's checks and advised him to use a real check for the house, but he just smiled at her. She thought that was a little unusual, but she figured an FBI agent would know what he was doing."

"He did know what he was doing," Bryce said.

He was disappearing. With cash, a briefcase, and a generic suit, he would be invisible and nearly impossible to trace.

Breadcrumbs—not setting a false trail, but leading nowhere. Bryce could send a dozen agents to the Port Authority Terminal, and not one would be able to find Cain's actual route. Not one would find anyone who had seen Cain.

If Bryce was going to find Cain quickly, he would need a lucky break.

Otherwise, he was going to have to do old-fashioned detective work, delving into Cain's past, his old friendships and his old haunts.

And then he would have to hope that Cain made a mistake by going back to his past. Because if Cain was smart about his disappearance, Bryce would never find him.

Cain would vanish into suburban America, become someone else, and live a quiet life.

Until someone—or something—set him off again.

29

The Cabinet meeting was going to be held in the Fish Room, probably to torture Kennedy. His brother preferred the Fish Room to the smaller Cabinet Room for meetings. Jack also liked the funky décor and wouldn't let his wife change it.

Franklin Roosevelt had taken that room—which was catty-corner across the hall from the Oval Office—and decorated it with his own fishing equipment as well as some fish he'd caught. Jack added a prize fish of his own and would often point to it proudly as the reason he preferred the room.

In reality, he liked the Fish Room best because there was enough room around the conference table for his most comfortable rocking chair. Jack's back had gotten progressively worse during his Administration, to the point where he was in near constant pain at the end. The back brace he wore—extended to the groin after an injury suffered in the White House pool (where he probably was swimming with one of the beauties Powers had procured for him)—was one of the things that made the second head shot possible. Most people, when shot in the back of the skull like Jack had been, would have fallen forward. A second shot to the front of the head wouldn't have been possible, and he probably would have survived.

But the back brace held him upright, making him so vulnerable to that killing second shot.

Kennedy put a hand to his mouth as he came into the hallway of the West Wing. Studying the details of the assassination this morning hadn't helped his mood. He felt slightly queasy and more than a little tired.

At least the depression wasn't coming back. He doubted it ever would.

He rounded the corner toward the Fish Room. He figured LBJ would talk to him in there, briefly, before the other cabinet members showed up. Instead, one of LBJ's assistants caught him in the corridor.

"The President wants to see you in the Oval, sir," the young man said.

Kennedy nodded, not trusting himself to speak. He'd only been to the Oval Office a few times since Jack died, and not at all in the last two months. He'd heard that LBJ had redecorated—that was the prerogative of every President, to make the Oval Office his own office—but Kennedy hadn't wanted to see it.

Word had probably gotten back to LBJ about that. LBJ was playing his own power games, reminding Kennedy who the President was now—and who the President would remain (if they were lucky enough to win) for the next four plus years.

Still, Kennedy made himself seem calmer than he felt as he walked into Mary Margaret Wiley's office. He had to walk through the Cabinet Room to do so. There were pitchers of water on the table and ashtrays scattered about. All of the curtains were closed. Fresh coffee sat in pots on the sideboard and someone had laid out donuts as well as sandwiches.

Maybe LBJ had changed the venue of the meeting. Maybe he'd made certain that Kennedy had been told to expect the Fish Room, just to screw with his mind.

Kennedy made himself take a deep breath as he turned right into Mary Margaret's narrow office. She had redecorated it. It looked nothing like it had three months before. For one thing, it was neater. For another, the desk had been moved so that it faced the door. No one could get to the Oval Office without first going past Mary Margaret Wiley.

Mary Margaret had been LBJ's secretary during his Vice Presidential days. She was a good-hearted woman who ran LBJ's office with an efficiency that Angie Novello—who was the most efficient secretary Kennedy had ever had—could only dream about.

Mary Margaret looked up as Kennedy entered. She was wearing a black dress with a little jacket over it, and her makeup was muted. Her desk was clear, although the credenza beside her was covered in files.

She looked Kennedy over when he appeared in the doorway as if she couldn't quite believe he had come to see the President dressed like that. She often gave Kennedy those looks. Back when LBJ was Vice President, Kennedy often forgot his suit jacket in his own office and wouldn't go back no matter who he had a meeting with.

This morning, Kennedy hadn't had time to change out of the ratty sweater that was coated in Brumus's hair and didn't match his brown pants. His hair, which constantly gave him trouble, was probably standing up on all sides. He hadn't looked in a mirror since he shaved yesterday morning.

"He's waiting for you," Mary Margaret said, and then she smiled. "I do have an extra jacket in the back closet, if you want it."

She'd said that to Kennedy the morning he first met her, and several times since. Each time, she'd meant it.

She meant it now.

But he wasn't going to change tradition and accept. He smiled, making sure the smile was a bit on the rueful side.

"I've been up all night, Mary Margaret."

Normally she would have made a dry, witty comment in return. Instead, her smile faded.

"I know," she said. "It's a terrible day. I'm not sure what we're going to do. Something has gone very wrong."

Kennedy nodded, careful to look away as he headed through a side door leading into the Oval Office. If she thought something had gone wrong, then so did the rest of the country. And that slight sense of panic she was exhibiting had to have come from LBJ.

All of which suited Kennedy well.

He knocked on the door leading into the Oval just to be cautious, then opened it and stepped inside.

The room was different. Jack's rocking chair was gone. LBJ had removed the desk that John Junior used to climb under and replaced it with one that Kennedy didn't recognize.

The focal points of the entire office used to be the fireplace on one wall and the desk and windows on the other. The oval shape took some getting used to, but it had become comfortable over time.

It was comfortable no longer.

LBJ had repainted the room a puke yellow, apparently so that his giant television console would match. The three television screens, each tuned into a different one of the three networks, dominated the room, even with the sound off.

The books above that ugly console now looked like decoration, rather than volumes a President needed to complete his daily tasks.

Behind the desk, near one of the old American flags, were two teletype machines, clacking away as the days' news stories filed through. The sound was nearly unbearable. Kennedy had no idea how LBJ could spend his time here, let alone listen to that clacking all day long.

LBJ sat at his desk. He was leaning toward the televisions, but he was on the phone, his right hand on the cradle, ready to push the button to hang up. He didn't acknowledge Kennedy, who hovered near the desk, waiting for Presidential permission to sit down.

They were playing power games, and Kennedy knew it. He wanted to pick up the small sculpture of a beagle on LBJ's desk and shake it at him. LBJ was protective of that little sculpture. He said it looked just like his dog, the dog that had already gotten him in trouble with the press because LBJ liked to hold the damn thing up by its ears.

It was one of those silly tempests—anyone could see how much the man loved his dog and how much the dog loved him—but LBJ's critics had seized on it. And if Kennedy picked up that sculpture by its ears, LBJ would get furious at him.

But Kennedy didn't. He was here on serious business. He could wait until LBJ deigned to turn toward him.

Finally LBJ hung up the phone and leaned back in his large chair. He motioned Kennedy to sit. It took Kennedy a moment to find a chair. The only one close to the desk was a crappy office chair that someone had placed near the television sets.

Kennedy picked it up and moved it on the opposite side of the desk from the televisions. If LBJ wanted to see the network coverage, he'd have to look away from Kennedy.

Kennedy knew that was a pissy little game, but that was the way the relationship had evolved.

"You didn't bring me any files, Bobby," LBJ said. "I thought you'd have files."

"You took yours," Kennedy said.

"I'm sure there's more," LBJ said. "If you're not here to give me files, why are you here and why did you want to meet a half an hour later than the President decided to meet?"

Kennedy hated it when LBJ referred to himself in the third person. He used to do that as Vice President as well, so it wasn't a new affectation. But it was an annoying one, as if Kennedy had forgotten LBJ's position in the world.

"I came to brief you," Kennedy said. "I heard from New York, and we have a problem."

"We have a lot of problems. You know how many phone calls my staff has been fielding about Hoover's files? Everyone wants a favor in exchange for his own personal file. You think we can do that?"

"No," Kennedy said. "I think we do what Edgar did. We give them a sample of what's in the file. If they want us to look through it, we will and tell them what we found. But we're not giving anyone the documentation."

LBJ leaned back in his chair. The metal base squeaked. His eyes narrowed. "You're one vicious son of a bitch, you know that, Bobby?"

"Yes, sir," Kennedy said. "Would you like to hear the briefing now?"

"Only if you stop saying stupid things like we have one hell of a problem. I know we have one hell of a problem. We've had it since Edgar got gunned down. And now we're going to have to tame that lion ourselves. So tell me what the new problems are."

"New York believes an FBI agent is the one who assassinated Hoover."

LBJ didn't move for a long moment. He seemed to be holding his breath. Then he glanced at the windows behind his desk, at the Secret Service agents standing outside.

Kennedy could see how LBJ was thinking. He was wondering if the agents around him would assassinate him.

Kennedy held the pause for a long moment. He hadn't expected that sentence to scare LBJ, but now that he thought about it, it made sense. LBJ was the one who locked himself in the bathroom on Air Force One flying back from Dallas—he said because the entire event made him ill. But more than one observer reported that he looked terrified and he went inside to be alone so that he could calm himself down.

"They think," Kennedy said when it was clear that LBJ wasn't going to ask him any questions, "that this agent was turned by the Syndicate. Seems he fell in love with a hooker and wanted to save her by marrying her. The Syndicate found out and extorted him. Once he was in, he became their man."

"No man would kill for that," LBJ said. He turned his chair back just a little. "Sounds like cockamamie Freudian bullshit."

"Yeah, it did to me too," Kennedy lied. "Until they told me that the Syndicate threatened the girlfriend and told him he had to murder Hoover to save her life. They killed her anyway, but I don't think he found that out until after he'd killed Hoover."

LBJ let out a small whistle. "He's on the run, then."

Kennedy nodded.

"We got one rogue guy murdering five people. How does that happen?"

This time, Kennedy described the scenario precisely the way Hart had given it to him. He told LBJ about the shootings and the sedan as a single mistake.

"Seems we trained him as a Green Beret," Kennedy said. "He'd been in East Germany, doing some work for the Eisenhower administration."

LBJ closed his eyes, then rubbed the bridge of his nose with his index finger. "You're telling me we trained the son of a bitch to be an assassin?"

"I'm afraid so."

"We trained a man to kill other people, then put him in the FBI, let him get compromised, and he shoots Hoover? Why the fuck would the Mafia want Hoover dead?'

Kennedy swallowed. This was the part he hated. "You told me why this morning."

"Because of your damn fool persecution of Hoffa? Because of what you did to Marcello? Next thing you're gonna tell me is that they murdered Jack."

"You know they did," Kennedy said softly. "What took me so long was I read all of the memos Hoover sent you about Jack's death. I particularly like the repeated scrawls about making sure everything points to one shooter. I can just imagine the conversations you had with him. Did you want Earl Warren heading up that commission of yours because you knew no one would contradict his findings or because you thought you could control him?"

LBJ opened his eyes. He hadn't moved his index finger, so he was peering at Kennedy over his hand. "What exactly are you saying, Bobby?"

"I'm saying you and Hoover decided to cover up what really happened to my brother. You decided to tell the world that Oswald acted alone. I have evidence of it."

LBJ took a long breath. Then he sat up, letting his hand fall onto the desk.

"Hell, yes, we decided that," LBJ said. "The last thing we want is the country to think there was some kind of conspiracy, that the mob was so powerful it could kill a President."

"Well," Kennedy said. "Now it's powerful enough to kill a President and the Director of the FBI. How many more people are they going to kill before you admit what's going on?"

LBJ's hand had become a fist. "What exactly is going on, Bobby?"

"We're at war. We're at war with the Syndicate, and they're winning. I say we let people know that this FBI agent, this Cain, killed Hoover for the Syndicate and that the killings were tied to Jack's death. We let them know that we will put every dime we have toward catching and incarcerating the heads of these families and—"

"Incarcerating?" LBJ leaned forward. "That's a pretty prissy word. Don't you mean killing?'

"You want to admit that we're going to gun down every single mob family? That won't play well in the press."

"Why not, if they did what you say and killed Jack and Edgar?"

Kennedy's stomach clenched. Had LBJ been briefed too? Did he know Kennedy was lying to him about the mob involvement? If so, Kennedy was going to have to find a hell of a way to cover his own ass.

But he couldn't look nervous. He'd been around LBJ enough to know that the man pushed to see if he could break someone, whether he had the right information behind the push or not.

"You don't out-and-out say you're going to kill someone," Kennedy said.

"Why not?" LBJ's tone was flat. "You and Jack said that about Castro. You don't think maybe this is Cuban revenge and not Syndicate at all?"

Kennedy almost let out a sigh of relief. LBJ hadn't been briefed. He was pushing Kennedy without any real information.

"No, I don't think that," Kennedy said. "The New York office has evidence of the man's mob ties. One of the senior agents had recommended just yesterday afternoon that the man be relieved of duty."

"Shit on a stick," LBJ said. "What are we gonna do?"

"I've been thinking about that too," Kennedy said. "The country's already scared. Have you talked to people? They think it is a conspiracy already. They might not believe you if you tell them otherwise. So we'll be as honest with them as we can be."

LBJ watched him, but said nothing.

"We let them help us find the bastard, this Cain. See if he can hang himself. Maybe he'll give up Marcello or Giancana or whoever it was ordered the hit."

"We're just making him a target," LBJ said. "The mob'll go after him too."

"You don't think they aren't already?" Kennedy said. "Why do you think he went to ground? He's not afraid of us. He's afraid they'll kill him like Ruby killed Oswald."

LBJ picked up that clenched fist, then set it back down on his desk top, very slowly. "That still doesn't explain what Hoover was doing in that neighborhood."

"Sure it does," Kennedy said. "This time we tell a tiny lie."

LBJ looked at him sideways.

"You remember in the '30s how Hoover was getting complaints that he wasn't doing the actual job of arresting the bad guys?"

As a young man, Kennedy had followed Hoover's career with awe, just like other children the same age had. It was only as he got older, and met the man at the family's Palm Beach estate, that he realized Hoover couldn't handle a barbed comment, let alone a criminal with a gun.

"I remember more or less," LBJ said.

The *more or less* gave Kennedy permission to explain the details. "He let his agents call him when there were some arrests to be made and he went in after the target was secured. That way, the press could take pictures of him arresting the bad man, and he would seem like the conquering hero."

LBJ's frown deepened. "You're saying he went to that filthy little alley to arrest a lowly FBI agent? That's our cover story?"

Kennedy shook his head. "I'm saying that our story is this: That lowly little FBI agent called him, saying that Marcello or Giancana or someone was going to meet with him, and that there was enough material to arrest him. Hoover went to arrest a big fish and instead got betrayed."

LBJ didn't move for the longest time. He just stared at Kennedy. Kennedy wondered if LBJ was trying to see through Kennedy, to see how truthful Kennedy was being.

LBJ was good at judging people, but he was also paranoid and he knew they needed some kind of cover story, some reason for Hoover and Tolson and three other FBI agents to be in that neighborhood.

"We can't give out a name," LBJ said.

It took Kennedy a moment to understand what LBJ was referring to. "You mean of a mobster?"

LBJ nodded. "We say that no one knew who the big fish was except Hoover and Cain and maybe Tolson. That they had set this up—outside the system—and Hoover thought that the New York Bureau was in on it, even though they had no idea. Then we stick to that, no matter what."

Kennedy almost said that he knew how to manage a cover story, but he didn't.

He didn't dare.

"You think this'll fly?" LBJ asked.

"You got a better idea?" Kennedy said.

LBJ shook his head. "This story has the blessing of being consistent. It gives Hoover a real reason to be in that alley and it makes it clear why the mob would want to get him without bringing Jack into it."

Kennedy didn't like the sound of that last. "We're bringing Jack into it. They killed my brother. You know it, for God's sake. You probably knew it the minute Jack Ruby showed up. He worked Dallas for a long time."

"I had nothing to do with Ruby."

"But you knew who he was." Kennedy stood, put his hands on the desk, and leaned toward LBJ. It was an LBJ trick—to get into your opponent's face—and usually Kennedy hated it. But he was going to use it now. "Don't lie to me, Lyndon. I know you knew who he was. He was a bagman for some of the men who funded your campaigns. I mean, this all could be twisted a completely different way. The shootings happened in Dallas, in your home turf, with men who had associations with you, and with Bobby Baker cleaning up some of the mess."

LBJ's face flushed. "I had nothing to do with your brother's death."

"I know that, Lyndon," Kennedy said. "You know it. But you also know how information can be presented to promote a certain viewpoint. I know that you're afraid of the Dallas connection, which is why it benefited you to have Oswald work alone. But it doesn't benefit you anymore. The Syndicate is going to continue killing until it gets the credit it wants. So let's bring the war to the surface. Give me men, give me funding, give me resources. I'll turn Hoover's FBI into a true force of G-men against organized crime. The Carlos Marcellos of the world won't know what hit them."

"You want to run the FBI?" LBJ asked. "That's a step down from A.G. I thought you were angling for Veep this morning."

"I'm not angling," Kennedy said. "We had a deal. I am your Vice Presidential candidate. And as Attorney General for the next ten months, I'll be the one to run a bureau in my department. That'll give you time to find the right replacement for Hoover. No one wants a director who's just put in there for show. You need someone tough and good."

"You already have a name," LBJ said.

Kennedy nodded. "I'm thinking Robert Morganthau after he finishes off Hoffa. But you have to give him time to win that thing."

"Morganthau's *your* guy."

"He's an anti-crime guy. It'll be perfect for our little war."

LBJ put that fist against his mouth. "You're enjoying this too much."

The glee Kennedy had been feeling all night was beginning to show.

"Look," he said as he took his hands off the desk and stood up. "I know I share a lot of the blame for Jack's death."

"And Edgar's," LBJ said.

Kennedy shook his head. "That one's on you. If you'd handled Jack's investigation differently…"

He let his voice trail off. He couldn't get into recriminations and blame at the moment. He needed to continue his earlier thought.

"I do share the blame for Jack's death, and it nearly destroyed me." Kennedy shoved his hands in his pockets. He hated being vulnerable, particularly with a man like LBJ. "But Hoover's death has given me an opportunity.

Don't you see? This is the mob's big mistake. They shouldn't have gone after Hoover. We can get them now. The country'll be behind us."

LBJ tapped that fist against his teeth.

"And they won't question the conspiracy," Kennedy said. "They won't focus on Dallas or you or Bobby Baker. This murder occurred in New York, for God's sake. Where could the next one happen? Miami? Chicago? Las Vegas? Those towns are mobbed up too. Do you want to avoid all of them in the 1964 campaign?"

"Shit," LBJ muttered, and Kennedy knew he had him.

"Let's fund this thing. Let's declare the war, put the money and manpower behind it, and clean house. We can do it, you and I."

"They'll come after us," LBJ said. "I'm the head of the dog now."

Kennedy nodded, trying to remain calm even though the analogy pissed him off. LBJ was not his boss, not really. Nor was he Jack's equal in any way.

Jack wouldn't have fallen for this. Jack could always see through Kennedy's maneuvering. Sometimes Jack allowed it. Sometimes he didn't.

"Yeah," Kennedy said. "They'll come after us. But we're finally prepared."

"How many of our agents are compromised?" LBJ asked. "How many could shoot us in some dark alley?"

"I'll go through the files," Kennedy said. "I'll clean house. Anyone suspicious gets tossed. It'd take the mob years to put someone new in place."

"And if you miss one?"

Kennedy didn't believe that anyone had been compromised, but he didn't dare say that. He needed LBJ to believe this fiction.

"Even if I miss one, he'd have to be crazy to act after we fire all the others."

"Unless they kidnap his girlfriend, like they did with the guy in New York."

Kennedy felt his face heat. "We can't protect ourselves against a guy who's got nothing to lose. But we can set procedures in place for guys in trouble. Those procedures don't exist right now. We need to neutralize anyone who remains, and make sure all he can do is feed information to his contact, whoever that might be. And if he does things like that, eventually we'll catch him. We'll be diligent about it."

LBJ kept tapping his fist against his mouth. He was clearly still thinking about the possible double agents.

Kennedy felt a surge of annoyance. He just wanted LBJ to act, not to think about it. He'd thought the short meeting would force his hand. Instead, LBJ didn't seem to care that his entire Cabinet was waiting—and Kennedy couldn't push it. He didn't dare. LBJ might wonder why Kennedy was being so impatient.

"Would you like to leave things as they are?" Kennedy snapped, unable to remain silent any longer. "Because right now we have no idea how many other double agents we have. Right now, we're all at risk. At least if we follow my plan, we can clean house and make sure everyone who works for us believes in this country and this government."

LBJ's fist kept tapping. Finally he stopped, sighed, and nodded. "I can't think of anything better. At least not short term. We'll brief the Cabinet, then let Salinger talk to the press. I'll give a speech tonight promising solutions, and a major policy speech later in the week, maybe in front of Congress. We'll declare your war, and see if we can get them to pony up the resources to fight it."

"It's not my war," Kennedy said tightly.

"What?" LBJ seemed confused by his reaction.

"You can't call it my war. I've been fighting this fight for nearly a decade. No one'll pay attention to Bobby's Fight Against the Mob. It has to be *our* war. It has to be the War Against Organized Crime. And we both have to stand behind it."

LBJ looked down. For a moment, Kennedy thought he would backtrack and wouldn't support it at all.

LBJ had mob ties, just like Kennedy had, just like Jack had, just like the Ambassador had. Hell, a man couldn't get into politics right now without them.

"You have the files," Kennedy said. "Burn them if you want. There'll be no paper trail, nothing to tie you to Marcello except testimony of some made men, most of whom we can impeach easily."

LBJ ran his fingers along the edge of the desk, not looking up.

"Stop worrying, Lyndon," Kennedy said. "You've got to act on this."

LBJ finally looked up. "I don't think you understand how ugly this war will get. People—innocent people—will be dying in the streets. It'll be the most vicious thing either of us has ever seen in this country. It'll be a terrifying few years."

"And how is that different from not prosecuting the bastards?" Kennedy asked. "They shot Jack. They shot Hoover. What's to stop them from shooting you?"

LBJ shook his head. "I hate being fucked in the ass. You'd think Edgar would've known this agent was dirty."

Kennedy shrugged. "Hoover didn't know everything."

"I used to think he did." LBJ's smile was rueful. "That's the hell of it. If these fuckers can get Edgar, they can get anyone."

Kennedy nodded.

"You're right," LBJ said and stood up. "I don't see a goddamn choice."

He swept his hand toward the door, indicating that the meeting was over.

"Let's do this thing."

LBJ headed out of the Oval Office, and Kennedy followed, trying hard not to smile.

30

WALTER CAIN STOOD in the manager's apartment of the Sleeping Giant Motel. The apartment had a door with a bell, a small counter for sign-ins, and a sitting area to the right. Behind the counter, a door opened into a kitchen, and to the side of that kitchen, he could see the beginnings of a living room. There was probably a bedroom or two back there as well.

A hotel manager could raise a family here. It was a nice little place, not far from Quinnipiac College, a place where people came and went, and where people often remained.

His plan was simple: He'd get a room for the week under his new name and, during that week, he would get the rest of his identification. Once he had that, he could pick wherever he wanted to go.

He'd been waiting just a few minutes, while the manager checked in the back to see which room he wanted to lose for the entire week. What the manager had actually said was that he'd find the room where Cain would be the most comfortable. But Cain knew how these things worked. He no longer looked like a well-off New York business man. With his dungarees—which he rubbed in dirt before he put them on, just so that they wouldn't look so new—his flannel shirt and his dark blue wool peacoat, he looked like a working man down on his luck.

Not someone a motel manager wanted near the parents of college students, should they arrive for a big game or something.

The manager came out of the kitchen. He was a short man with very pale skin. He wore a plain gold wedding band on his left hand. Cain studied that band. Maybe he should get one, just so that he wouldn't seem quite so threatening—a guy who was getting ready to move his family to New Haven, a guy who knew nothing about the town or the new job he'd found.

"Sorry that took so long," the manager said as he approached the desk. "I got the TV on back there. This Hoover thing has got me. I can't seem to stop watching it. Like Kennedy, you know. You think some people are indestructible. Presidents. Hoover. You know."

Cain nodded. The manager handed him an index card with the number 27 stamped on the top.

"Just fill it out. I know you're moving, so put down last known address, okay? And since you're moving, I'll need the entire amount up front."

Cain filled out his new name, Arthur Phelan, while trying to come up with a past address. Finally, he took the street address from the house he grew up in and set it in Columbus, Ohio. He figured his accent was generic enough to make him seem like he was from the Midwest.

He slipped the card back to the manager and reached for his wallet. Some of his cash was in a locker at the train station, but he'd put enough to cover the room here. The motel was pretty far away—he'd had to take a cab to get here. He told the manager he'd come in by train, and had already asked where a cheap car rental place was. The manager had loaded him up with brochures about the city and told him about the bus routes.

"So," Cain said as he counted out the seventy dollars that the manager had asked for. "What is the latest news on the Hoover shooting?"

The manager looked at him quizzically, and he realized he'd made a mistake. That early announcement never said Hoover had been shot.

"You must have heard it," the manager said. "Because they said he'd died of a gunshot wound."

Cain nodded, trying to craft a plausible lie. "I heard that part through the door. But what else? It seemed like you were gone a while."

The manager nodded. "They said four other guys had been killed. It was some big shoot-out or something. An FBI agent was supposed to meet Hoover to hand over one of those organized crime guys, and instead, the agent set him up, maybe even killed him on his own or just abandoned him to the Mafia. Ain't that something? What's the world coming to now?"

Cain gripped the money so hard that it folded. He made himself set it down and slide it toward the manager.

"Is there a television in my room?" Cain asked, trying to keep his voice calm.

"Yeah." The manager wrote a receipt. "Cronkite's doing the best job on this. But right now, he's not on. Right now, they're doing some live thing—asking that press secretary questions."

"The White House's press secretary?" Cain's heart started pounding harder.

"Yeah. The White House is issuing all this stuff. Johnson's going to make some kind of speech tonight. They've already announced. What a mess, eh?"

"Yeah," Cain said. "It is a mess."

The White House was going to cover this up. They didn't want anyone to know where Hoover died or who he died with.

Cain's left hand had formed a fist. His fingernails were digging into his palm.

He had to stay calm.

"You okay?" the manager asked as he handed Cain his key.

"This thing," Cain said. "It's got me upset, you know?"

"Oh, man, do I know. This country, it's gone to the dogs, but what are we gonna do?"

"Everything we can," Cain said, "to get the country back on track."

31

O'REILLY STOOD IN THE MIDDLE of the squad room, his hands in his pockets. He was looking up at the television someone had mounted on top of a shelf. The White House press secretary, Pierre Salinger, looked harried and tired. Even his bushy eyebrows looked like they could use a good combing.

O'Reilly felt just as dirty and grimy. He had been about to go home, take a shower, and catch a short nap. He figured by the time he got back someone would have decided what, if anything, he could do about the Hoover case.

McKinnon had already left, figuring shut-eye was more important than waiting. He was disgusted with the stall in the investigation, not realizing that this was just the beginning of the bureaucratic hell.

O'Reilly listened to Salinger talk about Walter Cain, the FBI agent whom O'Reilly had first heard about last night. That part of Salinger's story made sense, but the rest of it? The part about Hoover and his bodyguards going to that side of town to make a high-level organized crime arrest made no sense at all. Just the position of the bodies contradicted that statement.

The door to the Chief of Ds' office banged open. The man himself leaned out and shouted, "O'Reilly," then waved his hand as if he were issuing an invitation to a carnival ride.

O'Reilly grabbed the meager file he'd already created on the case off his desk, then hurried toward the office.

The Chief of Ds waited at the door. He was a tall man who was just starting to go to fat. A desk job really didn't agree with him, but he was making the best of it.

"You seen that?" the Chief of Ds asked, nodding toward the television in the squad. Apparently he hadn't looked very hard, since that was what O'Reilly had been staring at when he was summoned.

"Yeah," O'Reilly said.

"Obviously, there's a lot of crap in that statement. No one wants to smudge Hoover's reputation. They want the man to go out a hero, not some kind of pervert. They say they want to protect the integrity of the FBI."

"I figured as much," O'Reilly said.

"You go along with the hero story. If you can't, then just leave out the incriminating sex stuff, okay?"

"What if it turns out that Hoover was killed by someone he met at that incriminating sex party?" O'Reilly asked, knowing that wasn't really possible.

"That someone becomes a mob informant, someone who was trying to pass information to Hoover in a place where no one would mention that they had met."

"Anyone connected to the mob shows up at that party, they've signed their death sentence," O'Reilly said. "The mob doesn't tolerate homosexuality. People'll know that's a bogus story."

"Most people won't. You gotta remember, we're not dealing with a handful of New Yorkers and reporters who know how the City works. We're dealing with the entire world now, and the world'll have no clue."

"That this is some kind of cover-up?" O'Reilly said.

"Harmless as it goes," the Chief of Ds said. "It's how the game is played. If you can't play by the government's rules, then we'll get someone else to head the investigation."

"I can do it," O'Reilly said. "I'm just going to moan a little. You know that."

"I know," the Chief of Ds said. "You gotta tell your partner, too."

"I'm a little worried about him," O'Reilly said. "He seems really disconnected from this investigation. He doesn't want to be part of it."

"He's not used to homicide," the Chief of Ds said.

O'Reilly shook his head. "There's something more."

"You tell me what it is, I'll do something about it. Until then, I expect you two to work together."

O'Reilly nodded. He hadn't really expected the Chief of Ds to assign him a new partner in the middle of such an important investigation, but O'Reilly was already laying the groundwork. When this investigation ended, he was going to ask for someone new, someone who cared about the people he was investigating, instead of about getting through his shift with minimal effort.

"You realize," O'Reilly said, "that half the night shift was down there canvassing for that Cain guy. Bryce, the FBI agent on scene, knew something hinky had gone down, but he lied about what it was."

The Chief of Ds shrugged. "Would you admit to the FBI that someone in the NYPD shot the mayor? Not without proof you wouldn't. Sounds like this Bryce did what he could to catch the bastard."

"With our men," O'Reilly said.

"Ah," the Chief of Ds said. "The shooter was long gone anyway. Probably picked up by some of his buddies after he did the deed."

"This isn't a mob hit," O'Reilly said. "I'd stake my reputation on it."

"Don't," the Chief of Ds said. "It's not an official hit, anyway. They were blackmailing this agent. They had his fiancée. They made him act."

"Oh," O'Reilly said. "And how do we know this? It wasn't in the press conference."

"I've been getting phone calls all day. I've been briefed on the whole case."

O'Reilly felt his breath catch. *Briefed* was a good thing. *Briefed* meant that the Chief of Ds needed to know.

"So we're back on the investigation?"

"Looks like it," the Chief of Ds said.

"I thought the FBI was hot to handle this themselves," O'Reilly said. "I figured they'd find a way around the jurisdictional issues."

"They might've, if it hadn't turned out to be the mob. Hoover never paid much attention to them, so the FBI is now having to switch its focus. It needs us."

"For the footwork again," O'Reilly said. "Just like last night."

"Exactly. We're going to use all our resources. As many men as we need. You'll coordinate. They want this thing solved yesterday." Then the Chief of Ds smiled. "There's one thing the FBI doesn't understand. By keeping us on this, the collar's ours. We keep jurisdiction, we keep everything. We find Cain, we get the press victory forever."

"And the mob ends up hating us, not the FBI."

The Chief froze. "Are you worried about that? Is there something I should know?"

O'Reilly frowned. He was tired, so it took him a moment to understand that the chief just thought O'Reilly had hinted at his own mob connections.

"No, I'm clean. You know that," O'Reilly said. "You can check me out if you want."

The Chief of Ds smiled. The smile had too much relief in it for O'Reilly's taste. "I know that. I wouldn't be bringing you in otherwise."

"Thanks," O'Reilly said. "So I'm free to pursue this case."

"Yes," the Chief of Ds said.

"Wherever it leads me," O'Reilly said.

"So long as you don't mention Hoover's proclivities."

"As long as I keep the man's private life private."

The Chief of Ds nodded.

"Then I'm issuing an all-points bulletin for Cain. And I'm gong to make sure that Brunner goes over the bodies very carefully. I'm not just going to go after Cain. I'm going to pursue all leads."

"Good," the Chief of Ds said. "Sometimes investigations can get a little too focused."

O'Reilly smiled as he slowly understood. "You don't like how this is going either, do you? You think the FBI has already closed off too many channels."

"I think you're a great cop," the Chief of Ds said, "and you're gonna find everything we need to make a case."

"Against whoever," O'Reilly said.

"Against the real killer," the Chief of Ds said, "whoever that may be."

32

BRYCE HAD RETURNED TO HIS OFFICE. He'd shut off the radio while he made phone calls, coordinating his men. He needed more manpower than he'd ever commandeered before.

He sat behind his desk, phone cord wrapped around his hand, as he repeated instructions for what seemed like the thousandth time. He was calling every agent he could think of, from managers in nearby townships to off-duty agents to agents on vacation or extended leave.

He needed bodies in the field and he needed them now.

Whitson had a map and was assigning agents to various parts of the subway system, the bus system, and the train system. Bryce wasn't just having men talk to people in the ticket counter. He wanted them to talk with bus drivers and newspaper vendors, to the beggars at the Port Authority Terminal as well as the security officers near the subway entrances.

He wanted to hear about any possible sighting.

Because the evidence he had gathered so far had convinced him that Cain was being smart. Cain had cashed checks and closed accounts. He had taken only the things he needed and, until about 9 a.m., hadn't been afraid to use his FBI identification.

By identifying himself all over town through cashing checks and removing money from his account, Cain had made himself noticeable. Then he had vanished off the grid.

Which meant that he had initially been visible on purpose. He wanted investigators to think he was staying in Manhattan, which meant he wasn't.

Outside of New York, Boston, and Philadelphia, surviving without a car would be difficult. Cain didn't own a car. He would need to buy one, and to do that would take a driver's license.

He had to know that he wouldn't be able to use his own license for very long, if at all. He would need a new identity, and he would need it quickly.

Small towns made getting identification easy if someone knew how to do it. And every investigator in the FBI knew how.

But doing that would take time. And Cain had to know that his name and his image would be publicized relatively soon.

Right now, no one had pictures of Cain. He wasn't on the national news broadcasts because the FBI had the only known photographs of him.

When Bryce had returned from the bank, he had handed a junior agent one of the identification photographs of Cain and ordered dozens of copies made. But even with the FBI photo lab handling the request, it would take hours.

Cain had to know that.

But he also had to know his time was limited and his anonymity would be hard to maintain.

He would have traveled out of the city, maybe outside of the state of New York, but he wouldn't have gone too much farther. There were a lot of small towns within three hours of New York. Three hours would get Cain into a new community by noon. He would have time to go to the cemetery and to visit the county clerk before everyone had heard the news.

Bryce checked his watch. It was midafternoon. By now, if Cain had been efficient, he would have a new birth certificate and a place to stay. He might even have applied for his new driver's license.

Then Bryce checked that thought. He wouldn't have the license yet. To get a driver's license in almost any state, a man would need a verifiable address as well as his birth certificate. He would also have to take a driving test, since no previous license had been issued in that name.

Cain couldn't push that. It would seem odd. He would probably get a new home address—using public transportation in the meantime—then he'd schedule an appointment with the local Department of Motor Vehicles.

After he got the license, he would buy a car, probably a used one.

Bryce let out a deep breath. He finished the last call, hung up, and rubbed his right hand. He'd been holding that cord so hard that it had made an impression in his skin.

What he needed was a map of New York and the surrounding area. He needed to know what towns were nearby—the kinds of towns that wouldn't notice newcomers very much. Towns like seaports that had a lot of incoming sailors or towns that had a wide tourist base, although there weren't many of those this far north in February.

College towns would work as well because no one noticed strangers in a college town, not even strangers in their thirties because they might be doctoral students or visiting professors.

Bryce opened his office door to see if he could find that map and nearly walked into Whitson.

"You see this?" Whitson asked, as he thrust a piece of paper at Bryce.

Bryce looked at it. It had just come across the teletype. It was an APB for Walter Cain. It had been issued by the New York Police Department, but at the bottom was the phone number for the New York Regional Office of the FBI. The NYPD had also listed several of its own tip lines.

"It's going to every law enforcement agency in the country," Whitson said.

Bryce's sour stomach flared. "When did you get it?"

"About five minutes ago. I'm not sure when it came in."

Bryce cursed. "Who gave them permission for this? And how did they get Cain's name?"

"Haven't you been listening to the radio? The White House put it out. They say he's working for the mob."

"What?" Bryce hurried into the nearby lounge. The television was tuned to CBS. Walter Cronkite was watching as some reporter used a pointer on a large map of New York City to show the neighborhood where Hoover had been found. "Who told them that?"

"I understand that the SAC briefed the Attorney General a few hours ago," Whitson said.

Bryce remembered that. Hart had asked him some questions before calling into the main headquarters.

"And he told them that Cain was working for the mob?"

Whitson shrugged.

"This is a goddamn mess." Bryce crumpled the APB in his hand. "Has anyone told the NYPD that we don't have the staff to handle a tip line? Our phones are going to be jammed."

"I don't think anyone's told the NYPD much," Whitson said. "You want me to bring some guys off the street?"

"No," Bryce said. "What I do want is every secretary and typist and clerk up here taking phone calls. I want each tip written down and I want someone to vet them."

"Who?" Whitson asked.

"I don't give a damn who," Bryce said. "Someone besides you and me, someone who is not currently on the street searching for this man. And I want all the tips from areas within a three- to four-hour driving radius to be looked over the most carefully, is that clear?"

"Why—"

"Don't ask," Bryce said. "Just do."

Whitson nodded, his face flushed. He hurried out of the lounge. It was just Bryce and the television, which droned on about the location of Hoover's death.

Bryce had no idea why anyone would release that information. It made no sense to him, but then none of it did. He wondered if someone—Kennedy, maybe—had decided to forgo the cover story. He'd always heard that Bobby Kennedy hated Hoover. Maybe Kennedy was getting his revenge on Hoover by letting the American public know Hoover's predilections.

Bryce made himself leave the television before he got caught up in the coverage. He had more important things to do. Like find the possible towns close to New York where a capable man could disappear.

Of course, Bryce still had to cover the trains and buses that traveled a longer distance, and he needed people at the airports as well. But he wasn't going to focus on that. He would let the NYPD do that—and eventually, once the photo got released to the media, the American public would help as well.

That also meant, though, that the tip lines would grow even more crammed.

Bryce only had a short period of time before he got overwhelmed with useless information.

He needed to act quickly or Cain might slip through his grasp forever.

33

CAIN UNLOCKED THE DOOR to number twenty-seven. It was at the end of the U-shaped building, as far from the main entrance as possible. Trees grew over the parking lot here. Someone would really have to search to see if twenty-seven was occupied.

Normally that would have made him feel good, but at the moment, he just wanted to get inside and turn on the television set. That manager had to have gotten the details wrong. There was no way that the White House could cover up something this big.

When Cain had left the scene, the NYPD had been there. The NYPD wouldn't go along with this—would they?

He stepped inside. The room smelled of perfumed deodorizer and recently smoked cigarettes. A double bed sat below an air conditioner. Beneath the window were two chairs and a cheap round table with a seashell ashtray as its only decoration. Ashtrays sat on the nightstands and bureau as well.

The television was tucked into a corner. He closed the door with his foot, put the key on the bureau, and turned on the set.

The TV had been left on NBC. Chet Huntley sat at his desk, a cigarette in his hand. He was pointing at a hand-drawn map of the Upper West Side, drawing a circle near the alley where the body had been found.

Cain turned up the sound. Huntley was talking about the horrible betrayal of Hoover and the FBI agent turned mob stooge.

"We hope to have some kind of photograph of this man, Walter Cain, shortly," Huntley said. "So far he's on the loose, armed, and dangerous. The New York Police Department has issued an all-points bulletin. Anyone who sees this man should call the number on your screen."

Huntley's face disappeared and a hand-written phone number appeared in its place.

Cain's heart was pounding so hard that it hurt. They weren't supposed to have his picture—not yet. Or his name.

He made himself take a deep breath. Hardly anyone had seen him today. Those that had seen him hadn't really looked at him. The county clerk hadn't even looked up when he'd written down his request for that birth certificate, and the manager was preoccupied with the Hoover case.

Which made Cain nervous. Maybe the manager was the kind of guy who saw criminals in every sensational story.

Cain changed channels to CBS. Cronkite was sitting at his desk, with other reporters at desks behind his. A giant clock on the wall gave the time.

"...tell us that Agent Cain was blackmailed by the mob to do its dirty work. His girlfriend, Essie Seward, was a sometimes prostitute who had worked for the mob in the past."

"What?" Cain's knees gave way. They were mentioning Essie. As if she were still prostituting. As if she hadn't been redeemed at all.

"...had held her hostage while they sent Cain to meet with Hoover. They had told Cain that she would go free when the job was over. Instead, they killed her long before they contacted Cain..."

"No," Cain said. "No."

They had it all wrong. He slammed the TV off and paced the room. They were lying about everything, not just him, but Essie, too. They were destroying Essie all over again.

He had to think. He couldn't go after all the hypocrites—no one would let him near the people putting out this false story, not now.

But no one was contradicting the story, either. The NYPD probably didn't have all the facts, and the FBI was clearly making this up. The FBI were the only people who knew the truth about Essie.

The reporters were only reading the information the FBI sent them. No one had time to check the facts yet.

No one had time to know the facts.

He had to get the facts to someone else. Someone who would pursue them.

Cain had to stay away from the FBI. And the NYPD was mobbed up. There had always been guys on the take in the NYPD. They would try to change this story.

And the mob itself would try to take control of it. Cain knew enough about the mob to know they wouldn't like the lies.

So the NYPD would clarify some of this stuff if they could.

Hell, the mob would clarify some of it.

But no one would believe them, not with all this other information coming out of the White House.

Why would they lie about the mob anyway? That part made no sense.

A headache was building between his eyes. But he couldn't let it take him over. He had to think. He had to remain clear.

In the past few years, he'd cultivated a few reporters, been their anonymous source on harmless FBI matters. Those reporters would take his call and listen to him. They'd investigate anything that he told them, even if they did believe the crap the government was putting out.

They'd want the secondary story. They'd sniff out the details.

And they'd love the dirt on Hoover.

That was the important thing.

Destroying Hoover and clearing Essie's name.

He reached for the phone on the nightstand next to the bed, then stopped. He knew better. He doubted anyone would have put a trace on the phones of the people he knew in New York—at least this quickly—but he wasn't going to take any chances.

Besides, newspaper reporters often recorded their telephone calls, just for accuracy's sake.

Cain grabbed the key off the bureau and headed out of the room.

There had to be a pay phone near the college. He would call from there. He would make sure everyone knew the government was lying. And he would do it now.

34

THE PHONES KEPT RINGING all around him. O'Reilly took no comfort in the fact that they were ringing with leads for his case. The department had a room with dedicated phone lines where dozens of women answered and wrote down tips. The tip line had been in place for nearly a decade now.

But apparently this case had overwhelmed it, and people were calling on the emergency and non-emergency phone numbers. God knew what would happen if there was a real emergency in the precinct. It might take that person hours to get through.

O'Reilly had taken his own phone off the hook. If anyone wanted him, they'd have to come to his desk. He was reading the redacted files the FBI had "shared" with the NYPD. Some of the files were on Cain and many were on the various mob families. So far, none of them, not even the file on Cain, had information that O'Reilly couldn't have gotten himself.

"Hey, Seamus."

O'Reilly looked up. His partner, Joseph McKinnon, was standing in front of him looking freshly showered and somewhat rested.

"They stopped me on the way in and said that someone in the press office needs to talk to you ASAP."

"Have him come up here," O'Reilly said.

"I did." McKinnon looked over his shoulder at the tall red-headed man with the wide chin and bright green eyes. The man looked like he could head in front of the cameras at any moment.

Even his suit seemed freshly pressed.

The man saw McKinnon's look and came over with his hand out. "Garvan Cavanaugh. I'm with the NYPD press office."

O'Reilly just looked at his hand. "I'm buried here. I hope this is important."

Cavanaugh pulled a chair over and sat down. "I think it might be. A reporter for the *Post* just called me. He says he got a call from a man named Walter Cain."

"Yeah," O'Reilly said. "I'm sure if you ask anyone in this room if they've spoken to Walter Cain or a relative of Walter Cain in the past five minutes, they will have. Every nut and his dog has called already and I'm expecting the cats on the line soon."

Cavanaugh smiled even though O'Reilly really hadn't meant the comment as funny.

"The reporter believes that this actually was Cain."

"Because the moon is full or because this reporter believes everything he hears?"

"Because Cain's been planting information with him anonymously since Cain joined the FBI."

That got O'Reilly's attention. "You're kidding."

Cavanaugh shook his head. "He knows Cain's voice. He thinks it really was Cain."

"And you're here for him as a good citizen, to turn Cain in."

"I'm here because Cain told him some stuff that the reporter wanted verified. Stuff about the investigation that sounds pretty strange. Stuff about Hoover's sexual persuasion, some kind of party last night, and the way the murders were committed. Cain wants a promise that this stuff'll run in tomorrow's *Post*, but the reporter's not running any of it without verification."

"You want me to verify?" O'Reilly said. "As the guy from the press office, you should know we don't talk about ongoing investigations."

"As the guy from the press office with dreams of someday doing detective work, I'm thinking maybe this reporter'll give up some information if we approach him right. Maybe tit for tat. He's pretty shocked at the whole shooting, and really doubts this mob double-agent thing."

Him and everyone else with a brain, O'Reilly thought. But he didn't say.

"How about I talk to him?" O'Reilly asked. "Can you get him in here?"

"He's more likely to talk out of the precinct," Cavanaugh said. "He likes the Hull Bar near the *Post*'s offices. Meet him there, and he'll talk."

"Like I have nothing better to do," O'Reilly said.

"I'll go," McKinnon said.

And he would too. He might even do a good job of it. But McKinnon still lacked finesse. And reporters usually required finesse.

"You think this is for real?" O'Reilly asked Cavanaugh.

"I do. You know everyone has a pet reporter that they dump information on. It sounds like this one was Cain's. The guy really sounded shook."

"The guy needs a name," O'Reilly said. "I'm already going to waste an hour I don't have to run to the Hull. I need to know who I'm looking for."

"His name is Albert Frear."

"*The* Albert Frear?" O'Reilly asked. Frear had been a pain in the ass to law enforcement for years. He broke stories about ongoing investigations without thinking about the consequences. O'Reilly's old partner said it was hard to blame him when the guy kept winning journalism awards for his in-depth pieces. As long as he got rewarded, he would keep sinning.

If he had a source in the local FBI, that explained how he got some of his stories. Maybe even explained how he got a lot of his stories.

"Yep, that Frear," Cavanaugh said. "See why I'm inclined to believe him?"

O'Reilly nodded. "Tell him he's got twenty minutes of my time, and that includes me eating a burger while I'm talking to him. Tell him I might not be inclined to talk at all if he's rude. And tell him he's buying."

Cavanaugh blanched. "Reporters don't buy."

"This one will," O'Reilly said as he stood. "And if he's not there when I'm done with my burger, I'm leaving. Got that?"

"Got it," Cavanaugh said. He reached for O'Reilly's phone. The moment he hung up the receiver, the phone rang.

"See what we're facing here?" O'Reilly asked.

McKinnon grinned. "Want company?'

"I want Cain. Figure out how to find him."

And with that, O'Reilly left.

35

WHAT BRYCE NEEDED was a way to overlay the transit map on top of the large map he'd found of the Northeast. He supposed he could go into the equipment closet, get the overhead projector and actually draw a couple of overlays but that would take too much time.

All he could do was guesstimate, and what he'd been guesstimating was overwhelming.

There were too many cities in too many counties that were possible places Cain would have gone. Bryce could track him down, but not in a timely fashion.

And he didn't really have the manpower to help him in his search.

He had managed to get some help. He'd had agents talking to county clerks in the three-hour radius, asking for the names of men who had requested replacement birth certificates.

So far he had three possibles: Belford P. Lawson in Westchester County, New York, born 1930; Lawrence Knapp in Bergen County, New Jersey, born 1934; and Gerhard Wheeler in Orange County, New Jersey, born 1929. All three men had requested their birth certificates from the county clerk this morning.

Bryce still had dozens of phone calls to make. He'd assigned Whitson Connecticut and Pennsylvania. Bryce had New York and New

Jersey. He'd take Massachusetts when he was done with them, but he hoped it wouldn't come to that.

He had also called Border Patrol. There was a slim chance that Cain had gone all the way to Canada on his own identification. Maybe they could reel him in.

Bryce grabbed the FBI Directory from underneath his stack of papers. He needed local agents in all three of those counties to check out these men. If they had other identification, they were fine. If they had established residences or employment, they were also fine.

He just needed someone to eyeball them—from a distance—and make sure they weren't the man he was looking for.

"Agent Bryce?" Whitson was standing in the door to his office. He had a legal pad in one hand and a pile of messages in the other. "I may have something."

Bryce beckoned Whitson inside.

Whitson stopped in front of the desk. "People have been funneling potential good tips to me, and I figured when I got a birth certificate request in the right age group, I'd make sure there were no tips from the same location."

"Great idea," Bryce said. He was a bit surprised Whitson had come up with it. It might save a lot of time and leg work.

"I found five names so far, but only one with a tip. It's in Connecticut, one town over. It seems that a crowd was watching the announcement of the Director's death on one of the television screens at Edward Malley Department Store in New Haven, when a guy in a suit said 'What?' loudly like he didn't believe what he heard."

"I'm sure a lot of people hadn't believed it," Bryce said. It was like any other tip, some kind of overreaction to the news.

"But that's not all," Whitson said. "He said something like 'That's not what happened' or something like that. The point is that he contradicted the news report and did so loudly."

"Just disbelief," Bryce said. "It's probably nothing."

"Normally, I'd agree with you," Whitson said. "But we have three different tips. Three different people called it in. One man, one woman, and a sales clerk—gender not recorded. Whoever this guy was, he worried the people around him."

"But he was wearing a suit," Bryce said.

"The sales clerk said he had just bought clothes and was leaving the store."

Bryce let out a small breath. "You didn't say that. You should have said that first."

Whitson nodded, his cheeks growing red. Bryce silently cursed himself. The kid had come up with a good idea, and Bryce had reprimanded him.

"What's the name on the birth certificate?" Bryce asked.

"Arthur Phelan."

Bryce picked up the phone and dialed the operator. When the woman answered, he said, "I need directory assistance in New Haven, Connecticut."

"I'll connect you."

There were some clicks on the line and then another voice answered.

"I need the phone number for an Arthur Phelan. P-H-E—" He looked up at Whitson to make sure he was right. Whitson nodded. "—L-A-N. He might not be in New Haven proper, so please check outlying areas as well."

The operator acknowledged his request, then put him on hold. He should have done this with the other names before he contacted the local agents.

Then there was a click as the operator came back on the line. "I'm sorry, sir. We have no Arthur Phelan."

"Do you have other Phelans?"

"No, sir."

"You've checked Milford and Hamden and Meridian…?" He struggled to remember the outlying areas.

"And Fair Haven and East Haven and all the others, yes, sir."

"Thank you." He hung up and tapped his pen on the legal pad. "She didn't have him. Although that doesn't mean anything. Not everyone has a phone."

"But it's a start," Whitson said.

Bryce ripped the three names off his pad. "See if there are any tips near these men. If there are, we'll try the same thing."

"I think this is our man," Whitson said.

"Did the clerk say he was unusual?" Bryce asked.

"No," Whitson said. "He wasn't even in a hurry."

"How was he dressed?"

"Thick boots, a flannel shirt, and a Navy-style peacoat."

Standard blue-collar outfit for that part of Connecticut. Bryce frowned. Maybe Cain had bought the clothing at the department store, but hadn't had time to change before the announcement was made.

"Hand me the tip," Bryce said. "I'll call the sales clerk. You check these others out."

Whitson almost smiled. "You think Phelan's our man, too, don't you?"

"I think there's a chance," Bryce said. "But I'd hate to be wrong."

36

Angie Novello wended her way around the still-unsorted filing cabinets and handed Kennedy a slip of paper. He was sitting behind his desk studying a list of FBI agents that Jake Haskell had prepared for him.

All of the agents had close ties to Hoover. All of them would either be demoted or fired. There were fewer than Kennedy expected, but all of them had higher rank than he liked.

He took the piece of paper from Angie, opened it, and smiled grimly. The name inside belonged to a cleanup man he had used before. One who used to work for his father.

Angie had found both the name and the number, and Kennedy hadn't told her why he needed it. But he thanked her for her work.

Then he said, "Send Jake in, would you please?"

She nodded. She looked tired. She had had a short lunch break but that was about it. The long day was catching up to her.

Kennedy, on the other hand, felt invigorated. He had to go home sometime tonight, but even that felt like it was far away. The only thing he really needed was to get rid of the sweater. When he came to work tomorrow morning, he would have to dress like the Attorney General—or everyone's opinion of what the Attorney General should dress like—not like a ratty college student.

Haskell came through the door and had to turn sideways to pass some of the cabinets. He'd been working full time since he called Kennedy. Until Angie went to get him, Haskell had been working on rearranging the offices so that the files had a storage place.

Johnson hadn't liked the arrangement, but he had agreed that keeping them in a suite of offices in the Justice Department was better than storing them at Hickory Hill or some other site off premise. Johnson had wanted them in the White House, but, as Kennedy kept reminding him, the White House would be harder to clean out in a hurry than Justice would.

"Problem, sir?" Haskell asked.

Kennedy shoved the list at him. "You're positive all of these men had close ties to Hoover?'

"Yes, sir," Haskell said. "I can get their personnel files for you."

"I'd like that," Kennedy said. "I think we have to clean house quickly. Do you know agents who didn't get promoted because they wouldn't play Hoover's games? Agents who deserved those promotions?"

"Oh, sir," Haskell said. "I can think of a dozen right now, and I'm sure I could find more if I searched."

"I want a list by close of business tomorrow, along with their personnel files. There's going to be changes here. I'm going to take over the Director's duties until the President can find a suitable replacement. That'll take time. Hoover's shoes are hard to fill."

To his credit, Haskell didn't smile at that.

"I also want a list of recent applicants who were turned down because of their skin color or their gender. It's time to have a few female agents, and with all that's happening in the South right now, it would be very nice to have black agents who can coordinate with the Civil Rights groups. It's time to show the South that the FBI no longer works for the racists."

"I don't think we have had many Negro applicants, sir."

"Then we'll have to start a recruitment drive." Kennedy smiled. "But that can wait until next week. At the moment, we have enough to worry about. Which brings me to the case at hand. Is there any word on the manhunt for Agent Cain?"

"The tip lines are ringing off the hook, sir," Haskell said. "New York has been inundated with calls."

"Any fruitful ones?"

"Not yet, sir, but it's early. New York has a hunch they'll find this guy within the week. SAC Hart even says it's possible they'll find him by tomorrow."

Kennedy nodded. He didn't believe that, but he had to act on it. "I want to remain apprised of any changes in the investigation. If there's a small lead, I want to know about it."

"Yes, sir."

"Thanks, Haskell." Kennedy looked back at the pages, ostensibly dismissing Haskell. Then Kennedy looked up, as if he'd forgotten something.

He hadn't. He just wanted Haskell to think he had.

"One more thing, Jake," Kennedy said.

Haskell was already halfway to the door. He had to walk back through the thicket of cabinets.

Kennedy handed him the note. "Call this guy, will you? Give him a message. Say it's from me. Not from the Attorney General or the A.G.'s office, but me, Robert F. Kennedy, Joe's son."

Haskell frowned at the piece of paper. "What's the message, sir?"

"Tell him that when we catch Walter Cain, we're going to need some press coverage."

Haskell blinked at Kennedy. "Press coverage? Won't the major news outlets handle that?"

"They will," Kennedy said. "But we need the story to go our way. This message'll take care of that. Can you make the call for me?"

"Sure," Haskell said. "You want me to do that when we catch Cain or before?"

"Call as soon as you leave," Kennedy said. "Later you can let him know exactly where the public press briefing will be."

Haskell folded the piece of paper, but kept it in his hand. "All right, sir. Is there anything else?"

"That's more than enough," Kennedy said. "I think we're going to be busy from now until the election."

"And beyond, sir."

Kennedy nodded. He liked that. He'd need time to campaign, but not until summer. Until then, Johnson had to do the stump speeches and make the case to the voters.

Which would keep Johnson out of Washington. For the next six months at least, until the Democratic National Convention, where the Vice President was officially chosen, Kennedy would be here more than the President himself.

Someone had to run the government.

And Kennedy was more than willing to do so.

Just like he had done before.

37

THE BAR THAT ALBERT FREAR directed O'Reilly to was one of those narrow mahogany and red leather places that sank deep into the block. It had only one window next to an anonymous wooden door. The window was covered with the bar's name in gold paint. The air inside was blue from decades of cigarette smoke. Lamps hung low over the tables, but didn't give off a lot of light because of the thick yellow and tar film that coated the shades.

O'Reilly sat at the bar. He was halfway through a very good hamburger when someone sat down beside him.

"Detective O'Reilly?" The man held out his hand. "Albert Frear."

Albert Frear was both older and fatter than his photo. He also had less hair. But his fat was the beefy muscle-gone-to-seed of an ex-jock. O'Reilly figured Frear could probably hold his own in a fight.

"Didn't think you were going to show," O'Reilly said. "I only got about fifteen minutes now. I told you I'm tight for time."

"Sorry," Frear said in that perfunctory way of people who were only apologizing to be polite. "I got held up checking facts."

O'Reilly was clearly supposed to ask what kind of facts Frear was checking. "Cavanaugh should have told you that we don't discuss ongoing investigations."

"He did. He always does. But I told him I got some information that might help you if you help me."

"I'm not promising." O'Reilly washed down the last bite of burger with a clear glass stein of cola. He didn't dare drink beer when he was this tired. He had to remain as clear-headed as possible.

"Well, lemme ask you some questions, confirming what Cain told me and then you can—"

"No," O'Reilly said. "You tell me what you have to share, and I'll tell you if it's worth my time."

Frear waved down the bartender and ordered a beer. After the bartender left, Freer said, "I may know where Cain is."

"'May' isn't worth anything. I may know where he is too, but that doesn't mean that I'm right."

"When we were talking on the phone, I heard some stuff in the background. College kids, saying things. I'm not giving you more than that, but I will if you answer some of my questions."

College kids. A college town was a good place for a man to hide out. No one noticed strangers in those places.

"All right," O'Reilly said. "You've got ten minutes. And anything I say is on deep background. Use my name and no one with the NYPD will ever talk to you again."

"Okay," Frear said. "It's a deal."

O'Reilly sat back down. Frear grabbed a notebook from his pocket. The writing on it was a scrawl, probably some form of personal shorthand. This guy didn't miss a trick.

"Cain and the government agree on where Hoover was found, but not on why. Cain says there's a party for degenerates every Thursday night in the penthouse suite in one of the buildings off that alley. He says Hoover regularly attended when he was in town."

"If the party's a regular thing, a smart reporter like you could probably confirm it without my help," O'Reilly said.

Frear smiled. "Now we're getting somewhere."

"Not really," O'Reilly said. "I'm just telling you how to do your job."

"I already did. The party's real. And this girlfriend of Cain's was named Essie Seward. She committed suicide. I called the M.E. and confirmed that too. The examiner was there when an FBI agent—Bryce? Brees?—showed up. He was heading out to tell Cain *after* the woman died. There was no organized crime involvement."

"You checked that too," O'Reilly said as calmly as he could. He wanted to thunk himself on the head for failing to check into the girl-friend's death. But he didn't want Frear to know that he had more information than O'Reilly had.

However, the news about Essie Seward explained that look Bryce had on his face when he confirmed that the sedan had been taken out by Cain.

O'Reilly asked, "What haven't you checked?"

"Could this shooting have been done by one guy?" Frear asked. "I mean, five bodies, different locations, all of them FBI. That's the hardest part for me to believe."

O'Reilly thought for a moment. It would be all right to answer this one. "Yes. One man could have done it, with proper training."

Frear nodded. "My other question is just as simple. Did the FBI ask you to keep this investigation quiet?"

"To maintain the integrity of an investigation, we have to keep things quiet, whether we're FBI or NYPD." O'Reilly said.

"I know," Frear said. "But I mean more than usual. Are you supposed to keep details to yourself?"

"Not to my knowledge," O'Reilly lied. "But then, I work for the NYPD, not the FBI. They have no jurisdiction over this case. It's ours."

"You gonna let information about Hoover's predilections come out?"

"The case is the case," O'Reilly said. "I'm against releasing any information to the media, but I'm often outvoted."

"That's a no?"

"That's a you're asking the wrong person."

Frear nodded. He put the notebook away. "May I call you with more questions?"

"Depends on the kind of information you give me," O'Reilly said. "Let me put a tap on your line. If Cain calls you again, we can trace him."

"I can't do that," Frear said. "The paper would never stand for it."

"Cain have your home number?"

"No," Frear said. "He always called me at the *Post*."

"Give him your home number. Let me trace the call."

The bartender set down Frear's beer and O'Reilly's bill. Frear made no move to take it, so O'Reilly passed it to him. Frear set it next to his bar napkin.

"All right," Frear said after a moment. "I'll do that."

"Good," O'Reilly said. "Then I'll answer more questions when the trace is in place. Give me your home address and phone number."

Frear scrawled both on a piece of notepaper and slid it to O'Reilly.

"Now," O'Reilly said. "What did you overhear?"

"I went to Yale," Frear said.

Bully for you. What went wrong? O'Reilly had to bite his lower lip to keep those words from coming out. Instead, he said, "Yeah?"

"There's a lot of colleges in the New Haven area. There's Yale, there's University of New Haven, there's Southern Connecticut State College—"

"And some community colleges, yeah I know," O'Reilly said. "I've been to New Haven."

"One of the nearby schools is Quinnipiac College by Sleeping Giant Park in Hamden. The school has a reciprocal agreement with two other nearby colleges so that kids can take specialized classes. Those colleges are Albertus Magnus and UNH."

"Yeah." O'Reilly was getting impatient.

"When Cain was talking, some kids behind him were making a date to meet. One of them said he had a class at Magnus and another said that was okay since he'd be at UNH. Then someone interrupted them and asked about a Sleeping Giant. The response was, 'It's not far.'"

Frear took another sip of his beer before adding, "I didn't think much of it while Cain was talking. I was taking notes. But when I hung up, I realized what I heard. There's a lot of pay phones near colleges. He had to be at Quinnipiac."

O'Reilly's heart started pounding hard, but he didn't let Frear know that this was good information.

"You're positive you talked to Cain?"

"You guys keep asking me that. I keep saying yes. I've talked to him a dozen times in the past. I know his voice."

O'Reilly nodded. He took one last sip of the cola, then headed toward the door.

"It's good info, isn't it?" Frear yelled after him.

O'Reilly didn't answer. But as he let himself out into the February cold, he thought, *Yeah. It's good. It just might be the break we need.*

38

BRYCE'S TALK WITH THE CLERK at Malley's was productive. She had given him a fairly concise description of Walter Cain, right down to the briefcase. She probably wouldn't have remembered him except for two things: He didn't look like the kind of man who would need those clothes, and he had acted so strangely when the Hoover announcement first aired.

Bryce hung up the phone and looked up to see Whitson standing in front of him, clutching a single piece of paper.

"We have another tip from Hamden," he said. "That's right near New Haven."

Bryce knew that, but he didn't say anything. Instead, he took the piece of paper. The caller was identified as the manager of the Sleeping Giant Motel. He thought that the man who had killed Hoover had checked in just a few hours ago.

"I talked to the secretary who took the tip," Whitson said. "The caller sounded scared. He didn't want to call the local police because he thought they'd 'screw it up.' He wants someone to call him back."

It wasn't unusual for tipsters to want a return call. It made them feel important. Normally, Bryce would have shoved the call back at the secretary on the tip line.

But this one he handled himself.

He dialed the number.

A man answered, sounding somewhat cheerful. "Sleeping Giant Motel."

"I'm calling for a Douglas Tynan."

"Speaking." Now the voice sounded nervous.

Bryce identified himself. "I understand you called our tip line."

"Yes, I did. I have a man here, he looks like that picture they just put up on Channel 3. He—"

"What name did he use when he checked in?" Bryce asked.

"It's not the name you guys broadcast. I figure he's traveling incognito."

"What's the name?" Bryce asked again.

"Um, I dunno. Lemme check." Tynan set the phone down. Bryce could hear paper rustling, and then Tynan picked up the phone. "Arthur Phelan. He says—"

"That's good, Mr. Tynan. Do you have family or other guests at the motel?"

"It's slow season, so we only have a few people."

"Are they near Mr. Phelan?"

"No, he requested a week. He paid in cash. I figure guys that look like him need to be far away from the families, you know."

"How does he look?" Bryce asked.

"Kinda…mean, I don't know. He's clean enough and stuff, but he was…off, I don't know how to describe it. He made me nervous, quizzing me about the killings and stuff."

"He quizzed you?" Bryce asked.

"I told him I was watching it in the back. He seemed pretty angry when he found out what they were saying about the guy who killed Hoover. That was when he asked if there was a TV in the room."

"Is there?" Bryce asked.

"Yes."

"Is there a phone?"

"Yes."

"With a direct line?"

"No. It goes through here."

"Are you the only staff member there?"

"Yes." Tynan's voice broke.

"Okay. I'm going to send one of my men there to relieve you, and you're going to show him how to operate the phones. Do you have family at the motel?"

"Not tonight. My wife and the kids went to Boston to see her mom."

"Good," Bryce said. "You're going to join them. But not until my man gets there. If Phelan comes into the office, you act like everything's normal. If he sees your replacement, you say that's the night clerk. You got that?"

"Yes." Tynan's voice sounded a little stronger. "You're in New York, right? Won't it take a while for someone to get here? I could call the New Haven Police to send a guy over."

"Please don't," Bryce said. "Local police departments can't handle this man. We have trained agents in Connecticut. It shouldn't take more than fifteen or twenty minutes for someone to get to you. You can hold out that long, can't you?'

"Yes. I mean, I haven't seen him since he went into his room. Except that he left once and got some groceries. I saw him go back. He hasn't left since."

"Good. I need your address and his room number."

Tynan gave him those. "Should I evacuate the other guests?"

"No," Bryce said. "We'll do that. They won't be in any danger unless or until he sees law enforcement. By that time, you and your guests'll be long gone."

"Okay." Tynan didn't seem okay. His voice was shaking.

It would only be a matter of time before the man screwed up. Bryce thanked him, hung up, and immediately called the Connecticut Regional Headquarters. It was in Hartford. They had a couple of agents in New Haven. The Connecticut SAC promised to send them immediately.

"It's essential that we don't tip Cain off," Bryce said. "He was one of us until yesterday. He knows the routines and procedures."

"We can handle it," the SAC said.

"You can't," Bryce said. "He's a Green Beret. He'll pick you off before you even know that he's seen you. Do what I say, send in one man to replace the manager, then hang back. Guard all sides of the building, but don't get close. We need this man alive. I want him to stand trial."

Cain could stand in for Oswald as well, and maybe that would calm some of the panic that was starting to build.

"We'll take care of it," the SAC said.

"No police, no state troopers. This is strictly an FBI operation. You got that?" Bryce asked.

"Agent Bryce, it was an FBI operation the moment he killed our Director."

With that, Bryce knew the SAC would listen to him. The operation would go as smoothly as it possibly could.

"Thank you," Bryce said. "I'm heading out now. I'll be there as quickly as I can."

He hung up. Whitson was still standing by his desk.

"We found him," he said quietly.

Bryce nodded as he stood and reached for his coat. "Yes, we found him. But now we have to catch him. And that's the hardest part."

39

O'REILLY HURRIED OFF THE ELEVATOR into the detective squad room. The phones still rang like crazy, and people were talking on them, looking serious and taking notes. Someone had moved a television into the main room. It blared through the noise, the all-day coverage of Hoover's murder becoming a matter of guesswork for the reporters.

McKinnon sat at O'Reilly's desk. He was writing on some paper as he talked on the phone. When he saw O'Reilly, he hung up without saying goodbye.

"Looks like it went well," he said.

"It's a good lead," O'Reilly said. "Call the Connecticut State Troopers. Tell them our guy has been seen near Quinnipiac College. Tell them he may have changed his appearance or may be using a different name."

"What should they do if they find him?" McKinnon said.

O'Reilly looked at the man as if he were crazy. "Arrest him and hold him for us."

"Just asking," McKinnon said. "With today's events, you never know who might get trigger happy."

"They better not," O'Reilly said. "This guy comes to us. I want to find out what the hell he was thinking and if he really does have mob ties."

McKinnon's cheeks flushed. For a man who had worked two years undercover, he didn't handle criticism well. Nor did he handle setbacks. "What if they shoot anyway?"

O'Reilly shook his head. "Tell them to keep their guns holstered. We'll handle it. They'll get full credit for the arrest."

"Got it." McKinnon looked around, searching for an empty phone. He had to head to the back of the room.

O'Reilly grabbed his own phone. Quinnipiac College was in Hamden, but he didn't know the town well. He wasn't sure who was local law enforcement there.

So he called New Haven's police department and asked for an old friend, Norman DeFine. DeFine had been NYPD until he couldn't take the big city any longer. He applied for a detective's position with the New Haven PD and never looked back.

After a few minutes of catching up, O'Reilly told him that they believed Hoover's killer was in the area of Quinnipiac.

"Don't know if that's your jurisdiction or not. You'll need to canvas hotels and restaurants, bus and train stations. He might have been passing through or he might be staying. We're notifying the Connecticut State Police to watch for him."

"We'll take care of it," DeFine said.

"We need him alive," O'Reilly said. "We doubt he was working alone. We need names from him."

"If we find him, I promise you, you'll get him alive. I'll contact the outlying districts and we'll set up a grid search. We'll be discreet. This guy sounds dangerous."

"Ex-military and FBI," O'Reilly said. "He'll be on top of everything."

"We're not NYPD but we're good," DeFine said. "We'll find him if he's here. You coming up?"

"If you find him," O'Reilly said. "Otherwise I'm better off here."

"Roger that," DeFine said, and after a few more clarifying questions, he hung up.

O'Reilly hung up too, hand still on the receiver. He looked across the room, searching for McKinnon. He was still on the phone, but he didn't look like he was talking to someone he didn't know. He was smiling and nodding.

That was one more thing about his new partner that irritated O'Reilly. McKinnon didn't seem as driven as the other detectives O'Reilly had worked with. Maybe it was a generational difference. O'Reilly was really beginning to feel his age.

Especially this late in the afternoon. He should have been just getting up. Instead, he'd been up for twenty-four hours. He used to be able to work double- and triple-shifts without any measurable problems.

Now he felt each hour of those twenty-four. He would have to catch some shut-eye soon or he wouldn't be any good to anyone.

Maybe he had an hour with the New Haven P.D. on the case and McKinnon running the Connecticut State Troopers. One hour wouldn't be much. It would clear his head if nothing else.

He stood and headed over to McKinnon. McKinnon's smile faded as O'Reilly approached. Then McKinnon said something to the person on the other line and hurriedly hung up.

"Everything okay?" O'Reilly asked.

"They're going to sweep the whole state, focusing particularly on roadside motels and public transportation. They wanted to know if we want them to contact all the local police departments in the state and have them check as well."

"It wouldn't hurt," O'Reilly said. Then he nodded toward the break room, where the department had cots set up for just this kind of thing. "I'm going to get an hour or two of shut-eye. Wake me if anything happens, anything at all."

"I'll make sure," McKinnon said. "Sleep good."

O'Reilly wasn't sure he'd sleep at all. But he'd get some rest. And rest would help him for the next twenty-four hours.

He knew he was going to need it.

40

CAIN LAY ON TOP OF THE BED, sweating. Heat was blasting through the electric wall unit. He had cranked the thing on high because the room had been cold. Now it was too hot.

The television blared. David Brinkley sat beside Chet Huntley now, and they were discussing what would happen to the FBI without Hoover as Director.

Cain wanted to shut the television off, but he needed to know what everyone was talking about. He got off the bed, turned down the heat, and walked into the bathroom. As he splashed water on his face, he heard a car door slam.

He slipped out of the bathroom and went to the picture window, lifting up one edge of the curtain. His mouth went dry.

A Connecticut State Trooper's car had parked in front of the motel office. A trooper had gotten out and was walking toward the main door.

Cain let the curtain drop. He reached for his bag, removed his gun, and brought it back to the window with him. Then he moved the curtain just enough to see the car and the manager's door.

The trooper appeared to be alone. If they thought that Hoover's killer was here, they would have sent entire squads. No one would have come here by himself.

They were canvassing. They were searching hotels and motels. Maybe they were searching around the Northeast or maybe they were following routes to Canada.

Cain's heart was pounding. He held the gun tightly. The worst thing he could do was panic. He couldn't think everything was about him or it would become about him.

Crime happened everywhere. He wasn't the only person the police were searching for.

He made himself breathe slowly, and to try to think clearly.

He had given a false name. He had paid in cash. He was dressed like some kind of blue collar worker, not like an FBI agent. There was no reason to link Arthur Phelan to Walter Cain.

Even if the trooper was looking for Cain, he wouldn't find him here.

Cain had slowed his heart rate by the time the trooper left the office. The trooper was whistling. He looked calm. He wouldn't have looked calm if he thought Cain was in the complex.

The trooper got into his car and slowly drove off.

Cain leaned against the wall, feeling more relief than he should have. He was too emotional about all of this. He needed to separate himself like he had done before he killed Hoover. He needed to go back to his training, become the man who could hide in the open for days and not get caught.

He was about to let the curtain drop when he saw movement. A sedan out in the trees just beyond the parking lot.

A black sedan.

FBI?

It couldn't be. They wouldn't have let a Connecticut State Trooper waltz into their surveillance. They would have some kind of coordinated effort.

Cain let the curtain drop.

He was heading back to the bed when the door slammed against the wall. He whirled, shooting as he turned. Two men went down, but half a dozen more came in, guns drawn. Two more leaned in the front window.

Cain pulled the trigger, shot again just as someone tackled him from behind. He went down, hitting his head on the edge of the bed and twisting his neck. Someone put a knee on his back while several more hands held him in place.

His gun was gone, then he was handcuffed so tightly that he thought his arms would come out of their sockets.

He didn't struggle. He should have struggled, but he didn't.

Running had been the wrong thing to do.

He knew that now. He needed a trial. He needed to tell everyone what Hoover was.

Cain let the agents pull him to his feet.

He would cooperate.

He would get the best lawyer in the business and then he would talk to Frear, giving him an exclusive—even if it meant the death penalty because he admitted too much.

Blood ran down Cain's jaw, probably from the hit as he went down. As the agents led him out of the motel room, someone grabbed the back of his head and slammed his face into the door.

So that was how it was going to be.

He steeled himself.

He would survive it.

He had to.

For Essie.

41

BRYCE PULLED UP outside the Sleeping Giant Motel. The parking area and the street were littered with black FBI sedans. Some Connecticut State Trooper cars were parked near the perimeter and so were some local police vehicles.

He didn't see Cain.

The door to a motel room on the end of the U-shaped building was open. Blood spattered the concrete outside and the windows were smashed.

That had to be where Cain was arrested.

Where two agents died.

Bryce had taken a radio car from New York so that he could listen to the chatter on the FBI bands. He knew they had Cain. He also knew that Cain had killed two agents in the takedown.

The mood here would be grim.

Bryce got out of the car, holding up his badge. "I'm the agent in charge of the investigation. Where is Walter Cain?"

A young agent in an ill-fitting black suit pointed toward a modified squad car near the manager's apartment. The door to the apartment was open as well.

From what he'd heard, Bryce knew that no civilians had been shot here. At least that part of this had gone well. An FBI agent had been in place when a Connecticut State trooper had dropped by, searching for Cain. Apparently someone else had had information that Cain was in the area.

The FBI agent had handled it, but the trooper's arrival had clearly alerted Cain. The local SAC had decided to send a large team into the motel room to arrest Cain, against Bryce's orders, figuring the entire operation had been blown.

Fortunately, they hadn't killed Cain.

Bryce made his way to the squad. Cain sat inside. He was wearing a flannel shirt and dungarees. His thick workman's boots were covered in blood.

The agents had used heavy duty cuffs on him. His face was black-and-blue. It looked like he had a broken nose. Some blood had dried along his mouth and jaw.

Bryce found the local SAC. He was an older man with the grayish skin of someone who was terminally ill. His hair was thin and his eyes bloodshot.

Bryce identified himself. "I'm to take Walter Cain back to New York."

"You're not taking this man alone. He's dangerous," the SAC said.

"Yeah, I know," Bryce said. "I'd like two of your best men to accompany us."

The SAC nodded. "We get credit for the arrest?"

"But not the find," Bryce said. "I located him."

"Fair enough," the SAC said. "He's yours. You want the squad?"

It was probably safer than Bryce's radio car. The squad had the divider between the front and back seats as well as no door handles in the back.

"Yeah," he said.

Besides, he wanted to talk to Cain without anyone overhearing. He could do that in the squad. He couldn't do it in the radio car.

He figured it might be his only chance to interrogate Cain, since orders had come down all the way from the A.G.'s office that Cain was to be turned over to the NYPD. No one wanted jurisdictional issues to ruin a trial.

Which probably explained why the Connecticut State Troopers were here as well as the local police. Everything was happening by the book.

"I was told to tell you when you got here that you have to call Hart in the New York office," the SAC said.

"You have a secure phone?" Bryce asked.

"I don't think that's an issue. He has some last-minute instructions. Otherwise, we have to take you to our office, and that'll be a hell of a delay."

The SAC glanced meaningfully at Cain. Although he was conscious, Cain wasn't looking at anyone. He was staring at the back of the seat in front of him.

"Keep your best men on him," Bryce said and walked into the manager's office.

It bore the signs of a makeshift law enforcement headquarters. Chairs had been moved, the desk was covered with radios and paperwork, and coffee cups were strewn everywhere.

Bryce picked up the phone and dialed the New York office, asking for Eugene Hart.

Hart answered immediately. "Bryce, just got word that the handover is happening tonight. The White House wants this in prime time. They want the entire world to know that the FBI can still function without Hoover. They also want everyone to know that we're doing this by the book. So you have to take Cain to Foley Square. The handoff will be outside the United States Courthouse."

"In front of cameras?" Bryce asked. "Jesus, sir, don't they remember November? You're running the risk of another murder on television."

"Didn't you tell me that you don't believe the mob story? Well, I don't either. And if we're right, no one'll shoot at Cain. Besides, we'll have our people strewn throughout the crowd. The NYPD will be on fullest alert. We'll handle it."

"Can't we change the meet?" Bryce asked.

"It's not our call," Hart said. "Just get him there, make the handover, and get out. I'll take it from there."

Then he hung up.

Bryce stood with his back to the door for the longest moment. He hated it when politics trumped sense. And it didn't matter that Cain wasn't mobbed up. The United States Courthouse in Manhattan had a wide flight of stairs, a long sidewalk, and a lot of open spaces. People could hide anywhere. There wasn't enough manpower to protect Cain.

Bryce did not like how this was going. Cain was going to be the fall guy, and in some ways, he deserved it. But he deserved it for losing his mind when Essie died, not because of some made-up mob story to save Hoover's reputation.

Didn't the men in Washington understand that pissing off the mob was worse than revealing Hoover's sexual pastimes? Or did they realize it and want Cain out of the way?

Bryce picked up the phone and dialed the operator. He asked for O'Reilly's precinct in the Upper West Side. When he dialed that number, he asked for O'Reilly.

O'Reilly was a man he could trust.

Together, they would keep Cain alive.

They would have to.

42

WHEN PRISONER EXCHANGES took place near the courthouse, they usually took place in a specially designated area behind the building. It was secure, with only one exit and entrance.

This exchange, as ordered by the brass, was supposed to take place out front, near the courthouse steps. Press already lined the area. Dozens of NYPD cops in uniform kept everyone behind barricades. The Police Chief and the head of the local FBI were supposed to be near a podium so that they could make congratulatory speeches.

O'Reilly drove past it all as slowly as he could. Bryce had been right; the entire affair smelled of disaster.

"I still think we should tell the chief what we're doing," McKinnon said. He hadn't liked this idea from the start. It clearly made him nervous.

When O'Reilly asked why, he said that he was afraid his career would be over if Cain got away on his watch.

And if Cain gets shot on your watch? O'Reilly had asked.

McKinnon had no answer for that.

They drove around back. There were no barricades here, no press, no extra sharpshooters keeping an eye on the crowd. Bryce was coming back with two agents. Cain was injured and well chained.

Nothing would happen back here. Once the exchange was complete, they would put Cain in one of the courthouse's holding cells.

KRISTINE KATHRYN RUSCH

Then O'Reilly would walk through the courthouse to the front and inform the Chief of Detectives that Cain was already in custody.

They could bring some reporters to see him behind glass, but he wouldn't have to go out into that media circus.

He wouldn't have as great a chance of getting shot.

O'Reilly pulled into the exchange area. There was nothing here except concrete, high walls, and a door leading into the courthouse, a door to which he had a key.

O'Reilly got out, checked the perimeter, and then stood in the cold. McKinnon didn't check anything, which irritated O'Reilly. Instead, McKinnon stood near the back door and smoked a cigarette, his hand shaking.

The man was too worried about his career. He should have been worried about the process. Or about Cain. Or about the dead FBI agents.

But McKinnon didn't seem to worry about anyone except McKinnon.

O'Reilly figured they might be early, but they weren't that early. After about ten minutes, a remodeled New England squad car pulled in. Two men in black suits sat up front.

He couldn't see the men in the back.

McKinnon put his hand on his weapon. O'Reilly signaled him to wait. He'd never seen McKinnon that nervous.

The agents up front got out and opened the door to the back. Agent Bryce stepped out. He hadn't even changed clothes from the night before. His hair was rumpled and he looked as tired as O'Reilly felt.

Bryce leaned into the squad and helped another man out. That man was cuffed and chained. He even wore ankle bracelets around very thick boots. His face was battered and swollen, but it was clear that this was Walter Cain.

"Roughed him up a little, did you?" O'Reilly asked with a grin. "Is that why you wanted to do this back here?"

"I got him this way. The New England clowns did the damage."

Bryce had a hand on Cain's arm. Both men looked up, scouting the area much like O'Reilly had.

262

Bryce said, "Let's finish this inside, what do you say?"

"Smartest request you've made all day."

McKinnon still had his hand on his gun. O'Reilly frowned at him as he unlocked the door.

"You look like a fucking rookie," O'Reilly said to him quietly. "The man's not going to get away."

McKinnon nodded, then slipped inside first. O'Reilly followed. The holding area was large and empty. The door stood open. He debated closing it, then figured that it really didn't matter. The only important door was the one leading outside, and that one locked automatically. A secondary key—one he didn't have—opened the door to the outside.

He leaned out the back door. "All clear."

Bryce pulled Cain into the courthouse. Cain shuffled across the snow, head down. He didn't look as fierce as O'Reilly wanted him to. O'Reilly wanted him to look like some kind of gorilla—an angry, large man who seemed formidable.

Instead, he looked like an athlete who'd gotten beat up by the school bullies. He was trim except for that black-and-blue face.

For that face alone, it was good they were making the exchange back here. That kind of damage wouldn't play well at trial, and the last thing they needed was some footage of that.

The other two agents had Cain's back. They had their guns out and were looking around as if expecting trouble.

Bryce had them well prepared.

But nothing happened. Bryce got Cain inside. The door closed. The agents stood in front of it, facing the open door now. McKinnon was in the hallway, making sure no one interrupted them.

"Look," Bryce said. "I talked to him on the way back. I'll write up the report and give it to you. He claims this whole mob thing is a setup, and I believe him. I'm the one who broke the news to him that his girlfriend committed suicide. It's what set him off in the first place. He wants a trial and he wants to talk to the press. He wants to clear this up. I don't think he would have let us take him alive otherwise."

O'Reilly nodded.

Cain brought up his head. He looked at O'Reilly through eyes nearly swollen shut.

"I want to be booked," Cain said. "I want a lawyer, and I want a trial. There will be no plea. Is that clear?"

"Yeah," O'Reilly said.

"You got a place for him?" Bryce asked.

"We have a holding cell just down the hall."

"We'll help you," Bryce said.

O'Reilly shook his head. "We've got it. It's only a few yards. But this door locks. You're going to have to go out front."

"I'll tell the brass that the exchange has already taken place inside."

O'Reilly looked at him. "I was planning to do that."

Bryce shrugged. "My career's already for shit. You don't need to hurt yours. I'll do it."

"Thanks," O'Reilly said. He took Cain's arm. It was solid muscle. Bryce was right. If Cain hadn't wanted to come in, he wouldn't have.

O'Reilly led him out of the room and down the hall. McKinnon already had the door to the cell open. Bryce and the other two agents went in the opposite direction heading for the front door.

As O'Reilly brought Cain close to the cell, Cain stopped moving. O'Reilly cursed silently. The man was going to be trouble after all.

Then he saw McKinnon. McKinnon stood in front of the holding cell, his gun drawn.

"What are you doing?" O'Reilly asked.

"I have orders," McKinnon said. "You're making them really hard to fulfill."

O'Reilly felt cold. Maybe Cain had lied. Maybe there were mob ties. Which meant that McKinnon was dirty.

"We promised this man a trial," O'Reilly said. "The country needs the trial. Joseph, I won't tell anyone about this. Let's just go with my plan."

"I wish we'd never gone with your plan," McKinnon said. "Because I'm not looking forward to this."

O'Reilly started to pull Cain out of the line of fire when he realized the gun wasn't pointed at Cain. It was pointed at him. He moved, but not fast enough.

He thought he saw a flash, but he wasn't sure. His legs went out from underneath him and he landed on his back. He tried to ask what the hell was happening, but he couldn't.

He couldn't say anything.

Then he couldn't see anything.

And then he slipped away, into nothing at all.

43

BRYCE HEARD THE REPORT. It echoed off the marble floors, sounding like an explosion. He ran back to the holding cell, the other two agents at his heels.

He expected to find Cain on the ground. It took him a moment to realize O'Reilly was lying in his own blood. It took another moment to realize that O'Reilly was dead.

"Son of bitch," Bryce said and hurried toward the holding area. It would take McKinnon a long time to get from the holding cell to the door with a prisoner in ankle chains. Bryce had time.

But he didn't take it. He pushed open the door to the holding area just in time to see the door to the outside close. He hurried to the door, grabbed it, but wasn't able to open it. He turned.

"O'Reilly has a key," he said to one of the agents.

The agent disappeared into the hall and returned just a moment later with a ring of keys. As Bryce thumbed through them, he heard an engine start.

Why would McKinnon take Cain out of here and drive off with him?

It took a moment for him to realize why. McKinnon was taking Cain to the original meeting spot. Cain was supposed to be shot, like Oswald was shot.

And stupid McKinnon, he believed if he delivered Cain, he would survive this, and probably not even get blamed for O'Reilly's death.

In fact, he could say that O'Reilly was one of the guys who had set Cain up.

Bryce tossed the keys to a nearby agent and ran back into the hallway. Maybe if he got outside before McKinnon pulled up, he could stop this thing.

He ran down wide marble halls and he had to go up two flights of stairs to get to the main level. He took the steps two at a time, pushed his way out of the back past startled security guards.

"A man's been shot back there," he said as he ran by, but he didn't stop.

He made it to the front doors when he heard gunshots outside the entire front of the building.

He pulled his own gun, then put his back against the wall, bracing himself to head outside. It was stupid, he knew, but he had to. He was the only one who—

Who what? He no longer knew who the good guys were. McKinnon was supposed to be on their side.

Still, Bryce had to get out there.

He turned toward the doors as all of them burst open. Crowds of people ran inside, screaming and crying and shouting. He had to stay against the wall to avoid being trampled.

The gunshots continued.

He tried to push his way to the door, but couldn't. He kept getting shoved backwards.

He didn't even have to see it to know what was going on. Someone had shot and killed Cain the moment he appeared. Bystanders would be shot as well, and of course, McKinnon would die too.

Son of a bitch.

Bryce had started this by being too diligent a researcher. He was here at the end, promising Cain a trial.

But someone didn't want Cain to have a trial—and he knew it wasn't the mob. Someone had set this up to look like a mob hit, but it wasn't.

Someone was hiding something else.

Someone higher up.

The order for the meet had come from the Administration.

Someone in the Administration thought Hoover's secrets were worth at least three lives, maybe more.

Bryce fought the crowd, but he got nowhere.

Then the shooting died down.

He hadn't counted on McKinnon—and neither, clearly, had O'Reilly.

They'd almost done it. They'd almost thwarted the plot to kill Cain, the plot to keep all the secrets hidden.

But *almost* didn't cut it. And a good man was dead near a holding cell because of what Bryce had started.

A lot of people were dead because of what Bryce had done.

And he wasn't sure how to make it right.

The Enemy Within

"…the torch has been passed to a new generation…."
—John F. Kennedy

44

JOHNSON SAT AT HIS DESK in the Oval Office. The clicking of the teletype machines and a fire crackling in the fireplace were the only sounds in the room, even though all three television sets were on and tuned to different channels.

Twenty-four hours later, and the networks were still replaying the carnage. The images were out of synch with each other. One showed the police car showing up to the designated exchange site. Another showed the bodies on the ground. And a third was showing Cain, in his hand-cuffs and leg irons, slamming into the car itself as shots riddled his body.

Cain, two police officers, and one civilian were dead so far. Five others had gone to nearby emergency rooms and they all were in critical condition.

One camera had caught the main shooter. It was a fake reporter who had dropped his microphone and reached for a gun. What had attracted the cameraman's attention, according to the interview he had done right after the shootings, was the dropped mike. The cameraman hadn't expected to get a clean image of the murderer of Walter Cain.

That murderer was a bag man for the Genovese crime family. Two other bag men had been shot by police and FBI sharpshooters scattered through the crowd. But the initial shooter had survived, just like Jack Ruby had.

And unlike Ruby, this guy was willing to talk.

Someone knocked on the door near Mary Margaret's office. Johnson had half a dozen meetings scheduled. He needed to make another speech. He'd made a short, sad one last night, but he had to do something to comfort the nation before Hoover's funeral in two days.

Johnson wasn't quite sure what to say, although he'd come up with something.

The door opened and Mary Margaret poked her head inside. "The Attorney General is here. I tried your intercom. It seems to be off."

He'd shut it off yesterday. It wouldn't stop making an infernal racket. He hadn't even answered the phone for a few hours which, Lady Bird had commented wryly, meant the country had gone to hell in that proverbial handbasket.

"I forgot to reattach it," he said. "We'll do it after I see Bobby. Send him in."

Mary Margaret moved and Kennedy came in. He was wearing a suit today instead of that god-awful sweater from the day before. He actually looked like a cabinet officer.

And unlike everyone else in the country, Kennedy seemed almost cheerful. This whole disaster had revived him.

Johnson pointed to the television sets. "It's a goddamn mess."

"Yes," Kennedy said. "But now the country knows what we're up against. The mob is everywhere."

"An FBI agent, a police officer? The country's not going to be able to trust anyone," Johnson said.

"I'm going to purge the FBI. We'll get rid of Hoover loyalists, but we'll also look for hints of mob connections. We'll help local police departments do it too."

"It won't be that simple, Bobby, and you know it. The mob's entrenched."

Kennedy nodded. He grabbed one of the nearby chairs and sat even though Johnson hadn't given him leave to. "We're going to dig them out. What happened yesterday was a tragedy, but it's one America can understand. And when they realize this is what happened to Jack too, no one—not anyone in a labor union or in a police department—is going to want to be even peripherally connected to the Syndicate. The Syndicate screwed up here. They just made themselves the most hated group in America."

Johnson looked at the three television sets. One now showed Walter Cronkite, glasses off as he talked to an expert. Another showed Detective McKinnon coming around that damaged police car, weapon drawn, ready to save a life and instead losing his own. And the third showed the crowd as it fled through Foley Square.

"A shootout on the streets of New York," Johnson said quietly. "What the hell was the mob thinking?"

"It was a show of force," Kennedy said. "They wanted us to know what they can do."

"We shouldn't've done this exchange in public."

"We took every precaution," Kennedy said. "We set up Agent Bryce and Detective O'Reilly to make the exchange in the back. We didn't expect McKinnon to thwart us."

Johnson peered at Kennedy. Johnson hadn't heard about Bryce or O'Reilly. He had the distinct sense Kennedy was lying, that Bryce or O'Reilly had taken it upon themselves to stay away from the front of that building.

Two men with sense. One was dead. The other had spent the last twenty-four hours debriefing.

"You know," Johnson said, "I think you're enjoying this."

"I don't enjoy the fact that people are dead," Kennedy said. "But I have a purpose now, Lyndon. I'm going to avenge all of them when I avenge Jack. The Syndicate hasn't destroyed the dog. It's coming after them, teeth bared. *We're* coming after them."

"Just so long as they don't shoot us too," Johnson said.

"It's a war, Lyndon," Kennedy said. "We'll take every precaution, listen to every warning. You might not be able to glad-hand as much in the campaign as you normally do, and people'll understand. But you know what they say about war?"

Johnson frowned. "What?"

"This country has never switched leaders in the middle of a war." Kennedy grinned at him. "And if you stay confident and we do what I plan, this is a war we're going to win."

Johnson stared at him. He understood Kennedy's need for revenge. It made sense to him, more than that moping that Kennedy had indulged in since Jack's death.

But what Kennedy, in his zeal, didn't get was that this was a goddamn civil war. Another one. Only it would get fought in the streets of the urban north and in Dallas and in Las Vegas. It would be longshoremen against Marines, not Confederates against the Union.

And while the government claimed to be fighting for the American way of life, really they'd be destroying it.

Everyone had ties to the mob. Him, Kennedy, Kennedy's father—every little guy who worked in every steel mill across America.

They were heading into something ugly and uncharted. And if Johnson had had a vote, he would have voted against this action right from the start.

But he didn't get to vote. He'd only been a few cars away when Jack Kennedy was assassinated. Johnson had been afraid for his life ever since November 22. So he would fight this war. Hell, he would lead it.

But he wouldn't enjoy it.

Not like Bobby was.

Johnson was glad Bobby was leaving Justice in less than a year. He'd be muzzled and powerless as Vice President, just like Johnson had been.

Then Johnson would run this nasty little war his way. And maybe then, he'd have an idea on how to get the country back on track.

45

BRYCE LET HIMSELF into his apartment and looked at the bed he'd abandoned a lifetime ago. It looked as uninviting now as it had then. He wandered into the kitchen and was greeted by the stench of sour milk.

He hadn't cleaned up before he left to go to the Hoover crime scene. He hadn't been home since.

He sank into one of the nearby chairs. He'd slept a little at headquarters, which had been good. It gave him a clear head.

When he'd left the courthouse, he was going to hand in his resignation and run to the press, just like Cain had wanted to do.

But that would give Bryce a cycle of news stories that would disappear as fast as they appeared. Someone would counter those stories, and Bryce would become the agent who had liked Cain so much he'd gotten the man killed.

As it stood right now, Bryce had received a promotion and a suddenly spotless reputation. He'd been the guy who had tried to stop another mob killing. He was gifted, by the media and SAC Hart, with a kind of second sight.

The story went that he had tried to prevent Cain's death and had failed. McKinnon, a guy who sold out when he was undercover at vice, had fooled both Bryce and, more importantly, his partner, O'Reilly.

The department had records of phone calls between McKinnon and the Genovese family, including two calls that McKinnon made the moment he found out where Cain was. He'd sent the Genoveses to New Haven, but Bryce had gotten Cain out before he could be killed there.

Bryce believed, just like everyone else, that there was at least one mobbed-up guy in this entire mess—and that was Joseph McKinnon. But he didn't believe Cain had mob connections. Nor did he understand how it all worked, since the initial stories had Cain tied to the southern mob—Marcello—and the Chicago mob of Giancana.

Not the Genoveses of New York.

There was some kind of mess here. A mess that went through the FBI, maybe through Hoover himself, and into the Administration.

This was still Bryce's case. And he would solve it.

He realized, after he woke from his nap on his break from all the debriefing, that he couldn't solve anything by going to the press. The information he needed was secret, held by people in the very organization he worked for.

They had to believe he was loyal. They had to believe he would help them.

And only then could he find out what went wrong.

Only then could he put right what his initial investigation had started.

He'd said that once in the debriefing, that this was all his fault. Hart had given him an odd look.

You didn't tell Walter Cain to go on a shooting rampage, Hart had said.

But I could have prevented it by handling this differently, Bryce had said.

Until later, Hart said. *When something else set him off. He was a time bomb, Frank. You just monkeyed with the fuse.*

Bryce agreed with that. The bomb had gone off earlier than expected—and caused a lot of damage. But what Hart forgot about bombs was that often they got discovered before they exploded, and then they were neutralized.

There'd never been any time to neutralize Cain. Maybe that was what Vance Nolan had been working on, figuring out how to calm Cain down or get him out of the FBI.

They'd never know.

And if Bryce didn't stay in the organization, no one would ever know why Cain's solo vendetta had become a government-sanctioned story of a mob hit.

But Bryce was going to find out.

He'd learned a lot in the last few days. He could be a guy pissing in the wind, like Cain had been, a guy who lost control of his agenda and became something else—maybe even something he didn't believe in.

Or he could work from the inside. He could bring down the people in the Administration who had unthinkingly set up a shootout in the streets.

He had no idea how he was going to achieve this. He just knew he had to try.

He got up and grabbed the dirty dishes from the countertop. Then he ran some water in the sink. He found some dish soap and poured it into the scalding water.

It was time. Time to clean house.

And he was the only man who could do it.

ABOUT THE AUTHOR

USA Today bestselling author KRISTINE KATHRYN RUSCH writes in almost every genre. Generally, she uses her real name (Rusch) for most of her writing. Under that name, she publishes bestselling science fiction and fantasy, award-winning mysteries, acclaimed mainstream fiction, controversial nonfiction, and the occasional romance. Her novels have made bestseller lists around the world and her short fiction has appeared in eighteen best of the year collections. She has won more than twenty-five awards for her fiction, including the Hugo, *Le Prix Imaginales,* the *Asimov's* Readers Choice award, and the *Ellery Queen Mystery Magazine* Readers Choice Award.

To keep up with everything she does, go to kriswrites.com. To track her many pen names and series, see their individual websites (krisnelscott.com, kristinegrayson.com, krisdelake.com, retrievalartist.com, divingintothewreck.com, fictionriver.com). She lives and occasionally sleeps in Oregon.

"TOLD IN ROUGHLY ALTERNATING CHAPTERS SET IN 1913
AND 2005, [SNIPERS] IS A DEFT MIXTURE OF SF AND
MYSTERY WITH SOME VERY SHARP PLOTTING, SOME NICE
TWISTS, AND A TRIO OF COMPELLING CHARACTERS."

—BOOKLIST, STARRED REVIEW